Before It Stains

OTHER R. E. BRADSHAW TITLES:

OUT ON THE SOUND
(ADVENTURES OF DECKY AND CHARLIE, # 1)

SWEET CAROLINA GIRLS

THE GIRL BACK HOME

WAKING UP GRAY

RAINEY BELL THRILLERS:
RAINEY DAYS
RAINEY NIGHTS

Before It Stains

R. E. BRADSHAW

Published by
R. E. BRADSHAW BOOKS, LLC

USA

• R.E.B.BOOKS •

Before it Stains

R. E. Bradshaw
© 2011 by R. E. Bradshaw. All Rights Reserved.
R. E. Bradshaw Books/DEC2011
ISBN: 978-0-9835720-4-6
LCCN: 2011961921

http://www.rebradshawbooks.com
Rebecca Elizabeth Bradshaw on Facebook
Twitter @rebradshawbooks

For information contact rebradshawbooks@gmail.com

No part of this book may be reproduced or transmitted in any form or by any means, electronic or mechanical, including photocopying, recording, or by any information storage and retrieval system, without permission in writing from the author and publisher.

Warning: The unauthorized reproduction or distribution of this copyrighted work is illegal. Criminal copyright infringement, including infringement without monetary gain, is investigated by the FBI and is punishable by up to 5 years in federal prison and a fine of $250,000.

This novel is entirely a work of fiction. The names, characters, and events portrayed in it are the work of the author's imagination. Any resemblances to actual persons living or dead or events are entirely unintentional.

Acknowledgments

There are always people to thank when a book is ready to publish. I am very appreciative of the many who helped me get through this one.

To the readers, thank you for your constant support and pushing me to write more. I hope I can keep you entertained for years to come.

To the beta readers, thank you for your insights and encouragement. It really does make a difference to have you there to bounce ideas with.

To my editor, once again, thanks for keeping me focused.

To my friends who let me ask questions about their relationships and shared their heartwarming and heartbreaking moments, I am forever in your debt. Thank you for trusting me with your most private emotions.

To my family, Deb and Jon, the years we've spent together have meant so much. You make writing about true love and family commitment easy. Through laughter and tears we made it work and I will always be grateful to have both of you in my life.

I am truly blessed and thankful to have all of you on this ride with me.

REB

About the book…

Falling in love is easy. Staying in love is work.

Stephanie Austin has it all - a loving wife of 17 years, a handsome teenage son, a comfortable home in the suburbs, professional success, and a bright future. At forty, Stephanie's life is all she'd ever dreamed of, but like the old blues song says, "What a difference a day makes."

Betrayal by the woman she loves, thought she knew, and always trusted, cuts deep. Forgiveness is a simple word, but is it possible?

This is a story about love and family, with all the joys and pains of a lifetime commitment. When Stephanie's perfect world starts spiraling out of control, the fate of her family rests in her hands. With the help of her mother, friends, an old flame, and a healthy dose of humor, Stephanie must decide if she can put aside the hurt and figure out how to clean up the mess, before it stains their lives forever.

From the Author…

I am often asked to write stories about women in long-term relationships, a story that does not involve new love, but an established committed romance. I thought about it for a long time. In any good story there is a complication, something standing between the protagonist and a happy ending. I wasn't interested in a story of illness or death. So what could complicate an otherwise happy union? Ah, a betrayal of trust would definitely muddy the water.

Cheating is a hot button issue. There isn't much gray area in most people's minds. Not too many people would take the time to figure out what went wrong. It's hit the door and don't look back. I was one of those people, but then I wrote this novel. I began to question that stance as the words formed on the page. Would the circumstances of the broken vows make any difference? What if there was a child involved? Does that slow a person down long enough to reflect on the real issues, not just the pain and pride? When faced with dissolving a family unit, would it then be a harder decision to make?

A family court judge told me that sex outside of marriage is rarely about love, but a symptom of a deeper problem within the marriage. I believe that. I also believe that a marriage can survive, if both people involved are truly committed to making it work. Think about it. With all the adultery going on, some couples must repair the damage and move on. How do they do it? How do they clean up the mess, before it stains everyone involved forever?

Sometimes it takes more strength to stay and work it out, than to walk out the door. That's what this novel is about. If it has a message it is two-fold; communication is the key to a good marriage and never take your happy life for granted. Writing this novel reminded me to notice the little things and count my blessings.

REB

Before It Stains

Forgiveness is the answer to the child's dream of a miracle by which what is broken is made whole again, what is soiled is made clean again. ~ Dag Hammarskjold

CHAPTER ONE

"Stand still. I need to fix your tie."

"Mom, stop fussing over me. I'm fine."

Stephanie Austin fingered one of the blond curls framing her son's face. "Have I told you how much I love you, today?"

"Yes, about a dozen times. Is she ever coming out of there? I need to go."

"She's on the phone with her agent. You have plenty of time. Do you want a snack before we leave?"

"No, I just want to get out of here before you make me change my shirt again."

Stephanie chuckled at the six-foot-two man-child she now had to look up to. "This is your first formal dance. I want you to look nice in your pictures. What color did you say Jordan's dress was?"

"It's blue," the fifteen-year-old answered.

"What color blue?"

Before It Stains

"Come on, Mom. It's blue. I'm not changing again. Could you please tell Mo it's time to leave? Jordan will be pissed, if I'm late."

"Give her a few minutes. If she's not out by then, I'll knock on the door, and 'pissed' is inappropriate language in front of your mother. Try angry, or upset next time."

Colt mocked her, using perfect pronunciation with a bit of British accent thrown in, "My girlfriend may be annoyed if I am not punctual."

Stephanie playfully tussled his hair. "You *are* annoying."

She stepped back and took in the lanky, blue-eyed teenager. Colton Hunt Austin, shortened to Colt, was growing up. He was no longer the boy who crawled into her lap, just to get a hug. He was on the cusp of becoming the man he would be and she wasn't the most important woman in his life anymore. It was at once a moment of joy and sadness. Stephanie couldn't help it when she grabbed him, pulling him into a bear hug.

"Mom, I'm just going to a dance. I'm not getting married."

Stephanie clung to him. "I know, honey. I just want to hold you one more minute, before you're no longer my baby boy."

Colt smiled down at his mother and hugged her tighter. "I'll always be your baby. I'm the only one you have."

Stephanie released her hold on him and gestured toward the office door. "Go on, knock on the door. She may have lost track of time."

Colt hesitated. "Are you sure? She's been so uptight. I don't want to make her mad."

"She's got a lot on her mind, right now. You know how important this is to her, to us."

"Yeah, but she's been a real bitch, lately."

The smile left Stephanie's face. "Colt, watch your language. I will not allow you to speak of Mo that way. Got it?"

Colt ducked his head and pawed at the floor with the toe of his shiny, new, size thirteen, shoe. He was growing so fast, new shoes and clothes were a common occurrence.

Colt answered, "I'm sorry, but you heard how she went off on me for leaving my bike in front of the house."

"That's because that's an extremely expensive bike you just 'had to have' and then you leave it where it could be stolen."

"I'm never going to stand a chance against you two, am I? You always take up for each other."

"Honey, we love you and want you to show some respect for the privileges you have. That's not taking up for each other. That's working together as a team."

Colt grinned. "Yeah, your team against me. I guess it's okay, since most of my friends wish you were their parents."

"So, count your blessings and go knock on the door. Be polite and ask her if she's ready to go."

Before Colt could move, the door to the study opened. Dr. Maureen Hunt, or "Mo" as she was affectionately known, stepped into the den. At five-feet-seven inches tall, she was thin, but tautly muscled, in contrast to Stephanie's more softly curved five-eight. Mo's coloring differed with the rest of her blond, blue-eyed family. Her black hair, cut in the latest short bob, accentuated her exquisite hazel eyes. They met when they were both twenty-three and even after seventeen years, Stephanie's heart skipped a beat every time Mo walked into the room.

Before It Stains

Mo took in the dapper young man in front of her. "You clean up *real* good," she said, in an exaggerated drawl.

"You don't look so bad yourself," Colt said, obviously relieved his MoMo was in a good mood. He called her that from the time he could talk. He dropped the second Mo when he entered middle school. It was a mutual decision between the two of them.

Stephanie smiled at her family. "See, you've taught him well, Mo. He already knows how to schmooze a woman."

Dressed in black slacks, white shirt, black silk vest, and thin black tie, Mo was dazzling. The androgynous outfit balanced well with her feminine features. Her eyes sparkled. Worry lines, recently deeply creased, softened on her brow. Mo looked over at Stephanie, smiling broadly.

"Your mom looks pretty good, too, don't you think?"

Colt turned back to Stephanie. She was wearing her favorite red dress and heels, her special occasion ensemble. It was going to be an extraordinary, event-filled evening for them all. Stephanie had taken care to make herself as attractive as possible. The twinkle in her family's eyes told her she had done well.

"Mo, you better hang on to her tonight. One of those Hollywood types might think she's too pretty to leave in Durham."

Mo put her hand on Colt's shoulder, admiring Stephanie, and said, "Believe me, Pony Boy -" her nickname for Colt, "- I won't let her out of my sight."

Stephanie blushed under the attention. "Oh hush, you two." She reached for her digital camera on the coffee table. "Stand there and let me take your picture."

Colt looped his long arm over Mo's shoulders. Mo smiled up at him, wrapping an arm around his waist. Stephanie snapped the picture of her happy family. She loved them both more than life itself. Colt stepped over and took the camera from her hand.

"Now, let me take a picture of you guys."

Mo moved in and took the camera from Colt. "Let's do a family shot, okay? I'll set this on the bookshelf."

Mo fiddled with the camera and then ran back to take her place in the picture. She stood in front of Stephanie, who wrapped her arms around Mo's waist. Colt stood behind Stephanie, a hand resting on her elbow. Colt was becoming a man, Mo's dreams were coming true, and Stephanie had the life she always wanted. They smiled at exactly the right moment and the image of the perfect family was frozen in time. Stephanie would add this photo to all the others in the house, proof of their happy lives together.

Stephanie forgot one important thing about photographs. The real story is most often in what is not seen.

#

"You call us, if you need anything," Stephanie said to Colt, adjusting his tie one more time.

"Leave him alone, Steph. He's just going to a dance." Mo waved at Colt. "Have a good time, Pony," she said, as she sat down behind the steering wheel.

They were dropping Colt off at his girlfriend's house, where a group had gathered to ride to the dance in a stretch limo Hummer, provided by Jordan's extremely rich, but mostly absent father. Stephanie, along with the other mothers, had taken pictures of the group, until it became evident the children were about to revolt. Fathers talked softly, a gentle hand placed on a teenage shoulder. Mothers made final primping preparations to their son or daughter's attire. Stephanie had to let her young man go.

Before It Stains

A foreboding uneasiness seized her breast. She felt the beginning of the end of life as she had known it. These were the first steps toward her tight knit family divesting itself of the bonds that held them together. She wondered if all the other mothers were experiencing the same sense of loss. Stephanie had been feeling it for months. Colt was no longer dependent on her. Sure, he still wanted her to clean up after him, cook his meals, give him rides to practice, but left on his own he could manage those things. She and Mo had taught him well. Soon, he would be driving and that would be the end of innocence.

Stephanie was looking forward to having time alone with Mo, once Colt was in college. It was three years down the road - he was about to start his sophomore year - but it loomed large in Stephanie's future. She warmed when she remembered how she and Mo never slept with clothes on and ran around the house buck-naked the first two years they were together. During those days, sex had been as close as a passing glance. They always enjoyed a healthy sex life, but it was nothing like it had been before their son was born. He seemed to have a sixth sense that they were up to something and interrupted them on many occasions. As much as it pained her to see Colt growing away from them, after years of always putting his needs first, Stephanie was ready to put her relationship with Mo back on the front burner.

"I love you, honey. Text me when you get back to Trevor's house tonight. I trust you to make good decisions."

Mo leaned over and looked out the open passenger door. "Yeah, peer pressure sucks. Get in the car Steph. You're torturing the boy."

Colt smiled at Mo. "Thanks. I love you guys. Now, go have fun. See you tomorrow."

Before It Stains

He pecked Stephanie on the cheek and jogged back to Jordan's side. Stephanie sat down on the passenger seat and closed the door. Mo reached over and patted her leg.

"Honey, he's a momma's boy. He's never going too far away."

While Stephanie searched in her purse for a tissue, before the tears welling in her eyes ruined her makeup, she said, "I don't know why this is hitting me so hard. I've just felt off-balance lately, overly emotional. I feel like the other shoe is about to drop. Maybe my hormones are out of whack."

Mo removed her hand and cranked the car, backing out of the driveway. She aimed the car toward downtown Durham, before saying, "I know you've been alone a lot lately, with me traveling so much, and Colt off with his friends. I promise, after this next week, I'll set aside some time for us. Just hang in there."

Stephanie placed her hand over Mo's on the gearshift. "Baby, you've been working toward this moment all of your life. My spending a few nights alone is worth seeing you sparkle. This is your moment. I'm very proud of you."

Mo glanced from the road to Stephanie. "I couldn't have done it without you. You know that, don't you?"

Stephanie leaned over and gave Mo a peck on the cheek. "You're the one with the talent. I'm the one who's going to spend all your money when you're a famous director."

Mo laughed. "We're not there, yet. Michaela did say the prospects were good that we'll be picked up by a distributor, but I'm not going to breathe until I see somebody's signature on paper."

"I'm glad you found her. I was worried, at first, because she's so young, but she turned out to be a good agent."

"Michaela isn't that young," Mo contradicted.

Before It Stains

"Thirty is young. When you said you were getting an agent last spring, I expected a gray-haired woman with a cigarette stub hanging out of her mouth. Not a black-haired bombshell with superior assets."

Mo's tone turned serious. "Sometimes I wonder if her assets are what the studios are attracted to and not my work."

"Whatever it takes to get you where you want to be, Mo. Her looks might get you in the door, but your talent will keep you there."

"You've always believed in me," Mo said, her voice cracking a little. "I don't know how to make it up to you."

Stephanie ran a fingertip along Mo's jawline. "Oh, I can think of a few things. Remember we are kid-less until tomorrow evening."

Mo grinned over at her. "You want to skip the party?"

"No, this is your night. People are expecting you. I get to stand by and watch all those women gush over you."

Mo's brow furrowed. "That doesn't bother you, does it? I don't encourage them."

Stephanie replied, sarcastically, "No, honey, it doesn't bother me. It makes me all warm and fuzzy inside."

Mo shot her a pained look.

Stephanie grinned. She leaned over and squeezed Mo's arm. "It's okay, really. I know you're coming home with me."

Mo seemed relieved. She squeezed Stephanie's hand and winked. "We'll hang at the party for a couple of hours. Then it's you and me, a bottle of champagne or two, and some long overdue sheet time."

Stephanie returned Mo's seductive grin. "You know what happens when I drink champagne."

Before It Stains

"Yes, I do. Why do you think I brought home three bottles?"

#

The North Carolina Gay and Lesbian Film Festival's Plaza Party was in full swing when Stephanie and Mo arrived. Held at the historic Carolina Theatre in downtown Durham, the Plaza Party was the premiere event to see and be seen at the festival. Mo led Stephanie by the hand toward the entrance of the theatre and deposited her next to some of the crew from the documentary Mo wrote and directed.

Shouting over the Lady Gaga tune thumping through the plaza, Mo said, "Stay right here. I'll go find us something to drink." She leaned in, kissed Stephanie on the lips, and whispered in her ear, "You're the prettiest girl here."

"Thank you," Stephanie said, smiling and adding, "Just water for me, honey. I'll drive home. Enjoy your night."

Stephanie watched Mo walk into the crowd. Congratulating hands reached out to her. People hugged and grabbed at her, wanting to be close to the Belle of the Ball. The hometown girl had done them proud. One woman after another kissed her on the cheek. Mo only made it a few yards before the crowd swallowed her.

A familiar voice cut through the music. "She's the star of the show."

Stephanie looked down to see Patrice Jennings, or PJ, Mo's Director of Photography, standing beside her. PJ liked to tell people she was five-feet-three inches tall, but Stephanie doubted she was even five-two. She kept her hair closely cropped on the sides, but let the top grow into a tight rectangle a few inches tall. It helped PJ pretend she wasn't the shortest person in the room.

Before It Stains

"Hey, PJ," Stephanie said. "Everybody sure wants a piece of her these days. There's hardly any left for Colt and me."

"I know what you mean. I had to make an appointment with her, just to talk about what she wants me to do with the project we planned for the fall semester. Now that she's taking a leave of absence, I don't know where that stands."

Stephanie had become well versed in apologizing for Mo. She was absent from all of their lives so much lately. "She isn't avoiding you, PJ. I'm sure she'll catch up with you when the excitement settles down. I'm happy for her, for all of you. It must be exhilarating to finally be recognized for your hard work."

PJ took a sip of wine. She raised her glass and said, "Here's to her not forgetting the little people."

Stephanie put her arm around PJ's shoulder. "You two have been together since your first year in college. She'll take you with her. You wait and see."

"She already asked. I'm not interested. I like teaching. I'm not willing to play the game she's playing."

The disgust in PJ's tone led Stephanie to ask, "What do you mean? What game is she playing?"

PJ did not have the opportunity to answer. Mo burst out of the crowd with the drinks, then led Stephanie, PJ, and the rest of the crew to a large reserved table in a private part of the plaza. The table was set up with appetizers and bottles of wine. Stephanie knew the people joining them. This was a privately funded project, with no ties to the university, but most of the crewmembers were Mo's students. Stephanie spent weeks providing craft services while they were shooting the film. This project had truly been a group effort.

A young man said, "Wow! We've moved up. How'd you swing this, Dr. H?"

Before It Stains

Hardly anyone called Mo by her official title of Dr. Hunt. It was Dr. H, Dr. Mo, or simply Mo to the older graduate students when they were off campus.

Mo pulled out a chair for Stephanie, answering, "Michaela set it up."

"I'll bet she did," PJ mumbled, but not low enough. Stephanie heard her words clearly.

Once seated, the talk turned to the excitement of having the hit of the festival on their hands. After a few minutes, Mo stood up. The table quieted as she began to speak.

"I really want to make sure you all know how much I appreciate the hard work you put into making this film a reality. It would have never happened without the efforts of each and every one of you," she paused, grinning, "and a sizable donation from the Smith Foundation."

A voice from the back sounded. "Thank God for rich people."

The table laughed and settled back down when Mo moved over to stand by PJ.

"When this project was just scribbles on a note pad, PJ saw clearly what it could be. This is her moment, too. None of us would be enjoying this evening quite as much, if not for her vision."

Spontaneous clapping erupted. If PJ's skin weren't chocolate brown, she would have been blush-red from the neck up. She exchanged looks with Mo and even though they were both smiling, Stephanie read something in PJ's eyes. Was it disappointment? PJ was Mo's oldest friend. They met as freshmen film students, went through a very brief affair, and had remained best friends through graduate school. PJ went off to the professional film world, learning her trade, while Mo stayed behind to get her doctorate. Gradually, Mo worked herself into a tenured position. At the first opportunity, she secured a faculty position for PJ in the program. They were a team. Stephanie had no idea what happened between them in the last few days, but something was wrong. She would ask Mo about it once they were alone.

Mo continued around the table, telling amusing stories, and thanking each person individually. She finally returned to Stephanie's side.

"One night, several years ago, Stephanie read an article she found online. It was about an upcoming movie. After reading the article, Stephanie turned to me and said, 'Why do they insist a lesbian family can't be happy without a man coming in to the picture? Can't they tell a story about happy kids and their happy gay parents? Our kid is just fine, thank you.' The film we made, 'Just Fine,' grew out of that conversation. Stephanie is and has been, for the last seventeen years, my inspiration."

Mo leaned down and kissed Stephanie sweetly.

"I love you. Thank you for everything."

Stephanie stood to hug Mo, as clapping and shouts began around the table. A loud voice interrupted.

"Hello, everyone," Michaela said, drawing the group's attention. She ignored the obvious special moment taking place, rushing straight to Mo. "I have terrific news. I had to come find you right away. I just found out," she paused for effect, "we're being picked up for distribution!"

The table erupted in cheers and cries of joy.

Michaela added, "It won't be official until the paperwork is signed, but it's a deal."

Michaela wrapped her arms around Mo's neck and hugged her tightly. Too tightly for Stephanie's comfort level. What happened next nearly knocked her off her heels. Michaela's hand slid to the small of Mo's back and

Before It Stains

Stephanie was struck by the impression that it had been there before. A thought tried to cross her mind, but she held it off. It was unimaginable. In the briefest of seconds, Mo was by her side, enfolding Stephanie in her arms. She wasn't aware of how Mo came to be holding her. Stephanie had gone away for a moment and when she came back, everything was just fine.

"Congratulations, sweetheart," Stephanie said.

Mo pulled back to look in Stephanie's eyes. "People are going to see this movie. We did it, Steph."

Mo kissed away the anxiousness in Stephanie's chest. She calmed under Mo's touch. More cheers and hoots filled the air around them. When Mo let Stephanie go, Michaela was there to hug her, kissing Stephanie on both cheeks. Stephanie noticed the film industry people used this form of greeting regularly. It was as fake a gesture as the feeling behind Michaela's words.

"I'm so happy for you both."

Stephanie, full of the grace honed in cotillion classes, said, "We really can't thank you enough for all your efforts on behalf of Mo and the film."

"It's my pleasure," Michaela replied, looping an arm through Mo's. "With talent like hers, it's very easy to open doors." She turned to Mo, "Now, if I can tear you away from your lovely wife, I have some people who want to meet you. You don't mind, do you Stephanie?"

Stephanie kissed Mo on the cheek. "Go on, honey. Don't keep your adoring fans waiting."

Mo smiled. "I'll be right back and then we'll go home. There's a champagne bottle with your name on it."

Stephanie knew Mo wasn't coming "right back." There had been too many parties just like this, where PJ ended up being Stephanie's table partner, while Mo worked the room.

Before It Stains

It was the nature of Mo's business. She was always pushing a project or hunting backing for the next one. Mo's passions drove Stephanie to her from the beginning. Mo pursued Stephanie with the same intensity. Stephanie actually enjoyed watching Mo from a distance, her heart swelling with pride, but Michaela had whisked Mo out of sight. Stephanie sighed and took her familiar place next to PJ.

"Hi, my name is Kayla."

A young woman Stephanie didn't recognize, with large brown eyes and hair to match, leaned across the table, extending her hand. Stephanie took it and was greeted with a healthy handshake.

"Nice to meet you, Kayla. I'm Stephanie. Are you here with one of the crew members?"

PJ jumped into the introductions. "I brought Kayla to the party. She'll be in the graduate program this year. Thought she might enjoy meeting everyone, before she started."

"Yep, I'm finally going to finish this degree. I've been working and saving money for two years, but now it's time to get that piece of paper that says I know what I'm doing," Kayla said.

"Well, congratulations, Kayla. I'm sure you'll be pleased with the university."

"I'm disappointed that Dr. Hunt won't be there this semester. I've heard she really knows her stuff."

Stephanie smiled. "She'll be back before you're finished."

"I'm sure the university will find a suitable replacement for her," PJ said.

The tone in PJ's voice was telling. She was angry with Mo and Stephanie couldn't understand why.

"PJ, you know she's coming back, don't you?"

Before It Stains

"No, I don't know that. She's gone, Stephanie. They have their hooks in her now. Mo's already one of them. She isn't coming back."

Stephanie's face flushed hot. She shouldn't be discussing Mo's career like this in front of a student, but that didn't stop her. "I think I would know if Mo was planning to stay in LA. She isn't. Even if she gets another contract after this one, she'll always return to teaching. It's her first love."

"Yeah, you'd think you'd know," PJ scoffed.

Before Stephanie could react, Kayla said, "You make a beautiful couple. I asked who you were and someone told me you two were married and had a kid. That's just so cool."

Stephanie forced a smile. "Yes, it is very cool."

"I only met Dr. Hunt the other night at the filmmakers' party. I didn't see you there. I thought she was with that other woman, but then someone explained that was her agent."

PJ stood up suddenly. "Kayla, would you come with me to find Chase? I think he must be lost out there in the crowd." She turned to Stephanie. "Chase is another new grad student. He probably didn't see where we went."

"Oh, okay." Stephanie said. "It was nice to meet you, Kayla."

Stephanie was left alone for only a moment, before friends and crewmembers surrounded her, talking excitedly about the great news. She had no time to process PJ's mood or Kayla's comment about Mo and Michaela. Besides, Stephanie had been handling young women with crushes on Mo for years. It was harmless. Mo always came home to her.

Before It Stains

An hour passed before Mo returned without Michaela, to Stephanie's great relief. She was happy that Mo had an agent so invested in her career, but the overly affectionate way Michaela handled Mo was starting to grate on her nerves. There was too much hugging and cheek kissing to Stephanie's way of thinking. The entertainment crowd didn't appeal to Stephanie in the least. Stephanie saw very clearly what most of them were, people willing to do anything to get what they wanted.

Working among them had never changed Mo, but Stephanie was worried that it might. Mo showed signs of letting the newfound success go to her head. Michaela was obviously interested in more than a professional relationship. Stephanie remained quiet about her reservations. This was Mo's moment. This was the payoff for all their hard work together. Stephanie couldn't let a little streak of jealousy ruin what was turning out to be a profitable business tie. She reminded herself that Mo had never once given her a reason to be worried.

"Come on, let's go," Mo said, pulling Stephanie up from the chair.

Stephanie stood, looking at Mo's cheeks covered in faint brushes of lipstick. She rubbed one particularly bright red spot with her thumb.

"My, weren't we the popular girl tonight. If I was prone to jealousy, we might have a problem."

Mo smiled at her. "I came back for you, didn't I?"

Stephanie pulled Mo into her arms and whispered close to her ear, "Yes, you did. Now, take me home, get me drunk on champagne, and reap the benefits."

Mo pulled back and looked into Stephanie's eyes. "Did I tell you how much I love you, today?"

Stephanie grinned. "Don't tell me, show me."

Before It Stains

#

They finished the first bottle of champagne in bed, after barely making it in the house before the clothes started flying in every direction. They were well into the second bottle, now. It had been weeks since Stephanie had all of Mo's attention. She delighted in it, nuzzling into Mo's neck, careful not to spill the flute of champagne clutched in her hand.

"Umm, you smell so good," Stephanie said. "Is that new perfume?"

"It has to be yours on me, because I'm not wearing any," Mo responded, while refilling their half-empty glasses.

"No, it's not my perfume," Stephanie said, sitting up to take another sip. "Must be one those women who left their lipstick on your cheeks. They don't seem to be able to keep their hands off you."

Mo put her glass down on the bedside table and took Stephanie's, placing it beside the other. She rolled over, hovering above Stephanie.

"And I can't keep my hands off you. No more talking."

Mo started kissing Stephanie's neck and moved down her body slowly.

Stephanie grabbed the sheets on either side of her and arched off the bed, whispering, "Yeah, no more talking."

CHAPTER TWO

The phone started ringing at eight a.m. Stephanie saw the numbers on the digital clock and groaned, but knew she had to answer it for two reasons; she was the mother of a teenage boy and she was the managing partner of a property management business. Either one calling this early on a Sunday morning would not be good news.

"Hel…" The word caught. She cleared her throat and tried again. "Hello."

"Stephanie, I hate to call so early, but it's imperative that I speak with Mo right away," Michaela said, quickly.

Stephanie immediately closed her eyes. Glad the call had nothing to do with her, she dropped the phone on Mo's side of the bed.

"It's for you."

She felt Mo sit up and tried to drift back off. Sleeping-in was a luxury Stephanie could not afford often. She was always the first one up, ministering to her family's needs. Mo graciously got out of bed and left the room to have her conversation. Stephanie snuggled into the down pillows and slipped back into dreamland. She was sitting on the beach, listening to the waves, when she felt Mo kiss her on the cheek.

"Honey, wake up."

"I don't want to. We're on the beach and it's just us," Stephanie said, without opening her eyes.

"Okay, don't wake up. I'll leave you a note."

Stephanie opened her eyes. Mo was sitting on the edge of the bed with the phone in her hand.

"Is everything all right?" Stephanie asked, sitting up.

"No. I'm hung-over and don't feel like having brunch with a producer, but apparently I *simply must* attend." Mo put the phone down on the table beside the bed and rubbed her hands through her hair.

"Do you want me to come with you?"

"No need for both of us to suffer. You go back to sleep. I'm going to take a shower."

"I'll make you some coffee and toast. You need something in your stomach."

Mo stood up and Stephanie climbed out of the covers. She was still naked, which was a rarity in their house with a teenage boy about. Mo, now wearing a tee shirt and shorts, grinned and slipped her arms around Stephanie's waist.

"Well, that's one way to wake me up."

"Trust me, the coffee will be more effective." Stephanie said, slipping away from Mo. "Somebody fed me champagne until the wee hours of the morning. I'm not up to physical activity, yet."

Stephanie ran by Mo into the master bathroom. Mo moved to lean on the doorjamb. After seventeen years, they were way beyond personal boundaries. Stephanie sat on the toilet while Mo talked.

Before It Stains

"My flight leaves at six in the morning. Are you sure you don't want me to take a taxi, so you can sleep-in?"

"Mo, do you honestly think I'm going to stay in bed when I know you'll be in LA for a week? I doubt I'll sleep at all while you're gone."

Stephanie, finished at the toilet, moved to the sink and began brushing her teeth.

Mo continued, "I hate to be gone during Colt's tournament."

With the toothbrush still in her mouth, Stephanie said, "There will be other tournaments. He understands this is important."

Stephanie turned back to the sink and rinsed her mouth out. She washed her face and dried off with the hand towel Mo held out to her.

"He's going to pitch two games this week," Mo said. "Remind him not to overuse his curveball, and make sure he ices his arm down long enough afterwards."

"We can handle it, honey. He's only been pitching since he was eight. I think we have the routine down."

"Well, routines get old and people's minds wander." Mo said.

Kissing Mo on the way out of the bathroom, Stephanie stopped to take her robe from the back of the bedroom door and called over her shoulder, "Yes, but you're married to the queen of routines. If I didn't plan out our lives to the second, we'd be going around in circles and never see each other."

Stephanie thought she heard Mo mumble something. She stopped at the doorway and asked, "What, honey?"

The water turned on in the shower and Stephanie knew Mo had not heard her. She trotted down the stairs, each step sending a sharp pain through her head, but she figured she'd

Before It Stains

rush and get it over with. Rehydration was the remedy Stephanie chose for the champagne fog that enveloped her brain. Opening the refrigerator, she grabbed a bottle of water and chugged it down before approaching the coffee grinder.

Stephanie planned to cook them breakfast and serve it in bed, with the knowledge their son would be gone until four or five this evening. Scratch one romantic morning. Stephanie wanted to spend time with Mo before her trip tomorrow. She intended on snuggling in bed all day, followed by family dinner in the evening.

"Best laid plans," she said, pouring the coffee beans in the grinder.

#

Stephanie kissed Mo at the front door. "Just promise me you'll be home by six, so we can eat dinner as a family."

"I have to go over the distribution package with Michaela before tomorrow, but I hope I'm back a lot sooner than that."

"Lately, you haven't been too good at keeping dates. This is important, Mo. We won't be together again until next Sunday."

Mo looked hurt. "I'll be here. I promise."

"I'm not complaining, Mo, but I'm not a fifteen-year-old who misses his MoMo." Stephanie smiled to soften the blow of truth.

"I know, I know," Mo said, adding, "I'll spend some time with him tonight."

Stephanie kissed Mo again. "I love you. Hurry home."

The rest of the morning was spent doing laundry and getting Mo's clothes ready for her trip. Stephanie didn't pack the bag, but she made sure the things Mo would need were cleaned and pressed. She never minded taking care of Colt and Mo. Stephanie only hoped she could live up to the happy homemaker her mother was. What some women looked at as chores and drudgery, she saw as acts of love and commitment. Mo and Colt did their fair share of the work around the house, but Stephanie was the glue that held it all together.

It was Sunday, so Stephanie's office was closed. A service would dispense any emergencies to proper contacts. They would call her only if it were catastrophic. Stephanie started working at the property management office when she was in college. She remained with the company, even after she graduated with an MBA. She moved up through the ranks, eventually becoming the managing partner of the largest property management business in the Raleigh-Durham-Chapel Hill area of North Carolina known as Research Triangle Park, or simply the Triangle. Stephanie supported her family until Mo finished her doctorate, and even now she made more than the tenured professor. It afforded them the nice two-story house in the family neighborhood of doctors, lawyers, and faculty from the University.

Stephanie's cellphone rang about one o'clock.

"Hi, Mom. How was the party?"

"It was great," Stephanie said, grinning with the memories of the after-party in the bedroom. "How was your first formal dance?"

"It was all right, just a dance with fancy clothes. Hey, can I stay the night with Trevor, again?"

"No, honey. This is the last night Mo will be here for a week. We need to have family dinner."

Undeterred, Colt asked, "Can I come back after we eat?"

"I think Mo wants to spend some time with you. She mentioned it before she left."

"Where did she go? I thought she was supposed to be at home, for once." Mo's frequent absences were beginning to affect Colt's usually sunny disposition.

"She got a call this morning to meet with a producer. Her schedule is rather crazy these days. People are pulling her in all directions, including us. That's another reason you should spend time with her while she's here."

Colt wasn't buying it. "What makes you so sure she'll even be home for dinner?"

"She promised."

"Yeah, right," Colt spat out.

Stephanie wasn't up for Colt's surly mood. "She'll be here and so will you. I expect you by 4:30 at the latest. Got it?"

"Yeah, I got it. See you at 4:30."

He hung up. Stephanie stared at the phone. No, "Goodbye." Colt was growing up, but that didn't mean he could be rude. She was going to talk to him soon about his boundary pushing. It had to be done. She and Mo should have done it together, but waiting until they were all in the same room had been a failed strategy. Tonight wasn't the time to have the discussion. They needed some fun family time, not a lecture.

The cellphone rang in her hand. A picture of Stephanie's mother flashed on the screen.

"Hi, Mom. How was church?"

"Hey, sweetie. Church was wonderful. They left the flowers up from Gwen Barrett's wedding, yesterday. I wish you could have seen them."

"I can't believe someone I graduated from high school with has a daughter that's married. Makes me feel old."

Before It Stains

"Forty is not old and she had that baby six months after you graduated. I think it's a case of like mother like daughter."

Stephanie laughed. "It won't be too much longer before Colt is grown and married."

"I think we have a few more years, as long as he keeps his pecker in his pants."

Debra Austin was known for speaking her mind, at least to those she loved. The picture of southern grace and hospitality in public, she would often drop the façade behind closed doors. Stephanie loved that about her mother.

"He's growing up so fast. He's starting to pull away from us. I'm not prepared for all this angst," Stephanie said.

"Oh, what a surprise. My grandson is a typical teenager," her mother said, laughing.

"I always thought he'd be my baby forever. I guess I was wrong."

Debra's voice turned serious. "Steph, he'll always be your baby, but you're going to have to let him push and pull against you. It's the nature of the beast."

"With Mo gone all the time, he's struggling. I can't figure out if he's mad because he misses her, or if it's because he doesn't want to admit he does."

"He's fifteen. His reasons change with the wind. How are you doing? I know Mo's going to be gone a lot. Are you okay with that?"

"I have to be, Mom. This is everything she ever wanted. I can't let how I feel about her being away show. I don't want her worried about us. She needs to enjoy this. We'll be here when the fervor dies down."

"I saw her on the news last night. Some black haired girl draped all over her. Where were you?"

Before It Stains

"I was there, but I wasn't with Mo all night. She didn't mention she was going to be on the news."

"Maybe she didn't know. It was a story about the festival. I saw Mo in the background, behind the reporter. Who was that woman pawing at her?"

"If I had to guess, I say it was her agent, Michaela."

"Well, I'm not going to get in your business, but if one of your father's associates hung around his neck like that, I would have nipped that in the bud. Get my drift."

Stephanie chuckled. "Yes, I get your drift. It's harmless, Mom. Mo knows where home is."

"Okay, but mark my words, that little thing on her arm is going to be a problem. You nip it now, before it grows."

"Thank you, mother, but I think I can handle another young thing infatuated with Mo. It happens every semester."

"That's not a little girl you're dealing with. I've never met her, but I could tell she's a home-wrecker. It was written all over her face. After watching women throw themselves at your father for years, I can spot 'em."

"Yes, and where is Dad? He's right there with you, well, he's on his fishing trip, but you've been married, what, forty-four years. He never strayed and Mo won't either."

The silence from her mother spoke volumes.

"He never cheated on you, right Mom?"

"Honey, I've got to get my casserole out of the oven. We'll talk later. I love you."

And with that, the phone went dead. Stephanie was stunned. It was obvious she didn't know everything about her parents' relationship. She thought not knowing was the way she'd like to keep it. Just as she never wanted to imagine her parents in bed, she wanted to keep their long, happy marriage on the pedestal where it belonged, a shining beacon to her that love could last forever.

Stephanie shook off the doubts and went to the back deck to start the gas grill. She was going to slow cook a prime rib, Mo's favorite. Standing on the deck, Stephanie looked out at the backyard. The table and chairs, where they spent many evenings, had not been used since May. Summer had always been Stephanie's favorite time of year. Mo was home most of the time and they had dinners and parties, but not this year. Mo had been traveling the country from one film festival to another, promoting the movie.

Soon, Stephanie thought, soon Mo would be done with this project. The next one meant Mo would be gone for weeks at a time, but she promised to come home when she could. They couldn't uproot Colt for four months, so Stephanie would stay with him while Mo shot a pilot in the LA studio. If things worked out, maybe they would move to California, but until then, Stephanie had job security, and Colt needed structure. They made the decision as a family. With her mother's words echoing in her ear, Stephanie hoped it had not been the wrong one.

#

Stephanie finished the preparations for dinner around four o'clock. She had the rib timed to be ready at five-thirty. She sent Mo a text message, since she had not heard from her, reminding her of dinnertime. She checked the thermostat on the grill once again, and then went upstairs to take a shower. Earlier in the morning, Stephanie picked up the clothes strewn over the floor by the front door. They were now piled on the bed. Her dress would need to go to the cleaners. She picked up Mo's shirt and saw a lipstick

Before It Stains

stain on the collar. It would have to go to the cleaners, as well.

She checked the pockets, before tossing Mo's pants in the hamper. In the right-hand pocket, Stephanie found a balled up napkin. She started to throw it in the wastebasket, but something caught her eye. She carefully peeled the ball open, revealing what was written in the wrinkles. Her heart stopped. In an instant, her knees buckled and Stephanie hit the floor.

She heard the front door come open downstairs. Heavy footfalls made their way up the stairs, stopping outside her bedroom door.

A soft knocking preceded Colt calling out, "Hey, Mom, are you in there?"

Stephanie couldn't answer. She had no breath. She was frozen in place by the napkin in her hand.

He knocked again, louder. "Mom?"

Stephanie had to pull it together. He couldn't know. She couldn't tell him life, as they knew it, had just come to a screeching halt. She fought back the tears and answered him.

"Don't come in, honey. I'm going to take a shower. Get cleaned up for dinner. I'll be down in a minute."

"Are you okay?" Colt asked, concern in his voice.

Stephanie called through the door. "I'm just tired." She had to distract him. "Hey, watch the thermometer on the grill. Make sure it doesn't get over a hundred and thirty degrees."

"Sure, okay."

She heard Colt bound down the stairs. Stephanie looked at the note again, making sure she wasn't jumping to conclusions. She read it once more and knew there was no doubt what it meant. The bright red kissing lip impression was an easily recognizable color. Michaela had put them there along with the big sweeping "M" in bright blue ink, if there was any doubt. Stephanie's heart was breaking, but she couldn't fall apart now. Colt was downstairs and he didn't deserve to find out this way. Stephanie didn't deserve to find out this way either, but she had. Now, she pulled herself up from the floor and moved zombie-like toward the bathroom.

Stephanie slumped on the shower floor, sobbing uncontrollably. She lost track of time, unable to quell the rising pain that seized her chest. The shower turned cold, as her tears mingled with the water. It swirled around the drain and Stephanie watched seventeen years flow swiftly away. After a few more minutes, the pain ebbed and anger rushed forward to take its place.

"Goddamn her," she gasped. "Goddamn her."

#

Stephanie wasn't naïve. She simply chose to believe in happily ever after. Through all that she and Mo had experienced, the good and the bad, the one thing she held onto was Mo would always be with her. That was no longer true. The woman who stepped out of the bedroom and made her way down the stairs was no longer "the glass is half full" girl Stephanie had been. Mo killed that girl, the one who imagined life would always be good.

Stephanie had no idea where life would take her now. The path had been clearly laid out and Stephanie happily followed along, as her dreams came true, one by one. The storybook romance Stephanie lived did not prepare her for an unhappy ending. The hopes of one day rocking on the porch with Mo, playing with their grandchildren, living to be old and gray together had been destroyed. Up to this moment, her world was just as she planned it. She considered herself blessed to have had this life. What was she going to do now?

Stephanie's only focus was holding it together long enough to keep Colt from knowing what was happening. She found him on the back deck, dutifully watching the grill. He smiled and his dimples showed. He sensed something was wrong and came to give her a hug.

"I know you're sad because Mo's going away for a week. You never like it when she's gone."

Stephanie clung to him. "Yeah, that's it," she whispered against his chest.

"I'll keep you company, Mom. I'm sorry I was a jerk on the phone. I should have known you needed me to come home."

She looked up at her big handsome boy and said, "You're fifteen. You're supposed to want to be away from home. Call Trevor and let me talk to his mom. You can spend the night if you want."

"I thought you wanted me to spend time with Mo."

"I did, but I need to talk to her about this trip and I'm not going to make you sit through a boring evening with us, when you could be with your friends. School will be starting soon. You go on and have a good time. She'll be back next week and you can talk to her then."

Colt brightened. "I'll call him now."

He dialed the number on his cell and soon Stephanie was attempting to sound normal while making arrangements with Trevor's mom. She would be by to pick Colt up in a bit and take the boys to the movies, which was code for dropping them at the mall, so they could swagger around with all the other teenagers without a license. It was the equivalent of cruising from Stephanie's high school days.

Before It Stains

While Colt packed a bag, Stephanie pulled the rib off the grill and prepared a plate for him. She sat and watched him eat, keeping her feelings at bay for the duration. When Trevor's mom blew the horn outside, Stephanie put some money in his hand and kissed him on the cheek.

He hesitated at the door. "Mom, are you okay? I could stay home, if you want."

"No, honey. Go. Have a good time. I'll see you tomorrow."

Colt hugged her tightly and then left. Stephanie waved to Trevor's mom from the porch and went back in the house. She had not heard from Mo since this morning. Stephanie hoped she'd stay gone long enough to do what needed to be done. She climbed the stairs, heavy with the burden of knowing what was about to happen.

CHAPTER THREE

Stephanie finished her tasks and waited in the bedroom. She left the bedroom door open so she could hear Mo when she came in. She didn't have to wait long. At six o'clock, the front door opened and closed. A few seconds passed, then she heard Mo's voice.

"What the fuck," was followed quickly by, "Oh, my God!"

Stephanie heard Mo run up the stairs, before she appeared in the doorway, the wadded up napkin in her hand. She looked scared and confused, but it didn't matter to Stephanie. She had packed Mo's suitcases and left them by the door, with a note and the napkin. The note was a simple and straightforward message. It said, "You don't live here anymore."

Mo struggled for words. Stephanie waited, seated on the bed. She wasn't crying. She was resolute in her decision.

She saved Mo from her loss of words, by saying, "I'll send the rest of your stuff to LA next week. I assume that's where you'll be living."

Before It Stains

Mo regained the ability to speak. "It's not what you think, Steph."

"Oh, I think, 'I can't wait to get you alone again,' pretty much says it all."

Mo didn't respond.

"What I want to know is did you think about me and Colt, before you slept with her?"

Mo slid down the doorway and started to weep. Stephanie just stared, unmoved by Mo's tears.

"Was it worth it, Mo? Was it everything you wanted? You threw us away and for what, a piece of ass, your career? I hope you know I'm not going to be the one who tells our son what you've done. You're not getting off that easy."

Stephanie stood up and walked across the room. She stepped over Mo and said, "I sent him to Trevor's, so you have a week to figure out what to say to him."

Mo grabbed Stephanie's leg, stopping her from leaving. "Don't do this."

Stephanie jerked away. "Don't do what, throw you out on your ass? I didn't cause this. You did. I loved you more than life itself, but that wasn't enough for you. So, go to her. You're done here."

"Steph, you have no idea how sorry I am. I was drunk and it just happened. It was only that one time. I've been fighting her off ever since."

Stephanie bore down on Mo. "You know, I defended you to my mother today. She saw you with your new love on the news last night. She knew. She saw you with Michaela for seconds and she figured it out. PJ knows too, doesn't she? God, I was so stupid to trust you."

Mo pulled herself into standing position. "No, you weren't stupid, I was, and the guilt has been eating me alive. Please, Steph, you have to believe me. I love you, only you. I don't want this to destroy us."

"It already has."

Mo reached out for Stephanie. "I made a mistake."

Stephanie fell into the rage she had been holding at bay. She jerked away from Mo, seething. "A mistake? I don't think fucking around on your wife fits in the mistake category. It fits in the 'I just threw away my fucking family for a piece of pussy category,' but no, this wasn't a mistake."

Mo tried again to come nearer, but Stephanie lashed out. "Don't you ever fucking touch me again!"

Stephanie ran down the stairs. Mo followed.

"Steph, listen to me, please. I'm already trying to get out of my contract. I called a lawyer. He's trying to find a way out."

Stephanie was crying now. She lost all control of her rage and turned on Mo. "Well, call him back and tell him you need a divorce. I won't fight you. She can have your sorry ass, but Colt and I are keeping the house. I want you out of here tonight."

Mo kept her distance. They never fought like this. Mo appeared stunned by the venom in Stephanie's words.

"I'm so mad right now, I could kill you!" Stephanie shouted.

"Calm down, before the neighbors hear you and call the police."

"Fuck the neighbors and fuck you!"

They were standing next to the dining room table, still set for dinner. Stephanie - mild mannered, don't rock the boat Stephanie - picked up the platter with the prime rib and threw it at Mo. It splattered against the wall and bounced off, the platter shattering at Mo's feet. Mo came toward

Before It Stains

Stephanie and tried to grab her before she could throw anything else. She wasn't fast enough. The china plates flew across the room into the wall, followed by the glassware. This activity fulfilled Stephanie's rage and she couldn't stop. She was sobbing and out of control.

Mo fought her way through the flying crystal and captured Stephanie from behind, pinning her arms to her sides. "Stop it! Stop it!"

Stephanie crumpled and fell away from Mo onto the floor. She heard a deep moan and realized it came from her own mouth. Mo landed on her knees beside Stephanie.

Tears tangled with Mo's words. "Oh, God. What have I done?"

"You've ruined everything," Stephanie managed between gasps.

She crawled away from Mo and into the corner of the room. The sobbing turned to wailing. A part of her wondered if she was truly having a breakdown. Stephanie struggled to regain control, but it was no use. She glanced at Mo.

"Get out!" Gasp. "Leave now!" Gasp. "I don't want to look at you."

Mo stood up slowly. She looked down at Stephanie, saying, "I can't leave you alone like this."

This broke Stephanie's crying jag, just long enough to say, "You left me a long time ago. Get the fuck out!"

Mo walked away slowly. She disappeared into the office and emerged a few minutes later with her laptop bag. Stephanie watched, still a quivering ball in the corner. Mo came back into the room, more composed than before.

"Steph, I'm going to go now, because it's what you want, not what I want. I never wanted you to know what happened. I never wanted to hurt you. I know you don't believe me right now, but I do love you. If you'll let me, I'll do whatever it takes to win you back."

Stephanie was calmer now, her breathing almost normal between the shudders from the crying. She looked up at the love of her life.

"This isn't a movie, Mo. There isn't going to be a happy ending."

#

Stephanie was on her hands and knees, wiping up the juices from the prime rib that had exploded all over the room. She'd already picked up the shattered dishes. Stephanie could barely see the floor through her tears, but she just kept cleaning. She wanted something normal to do, something to distract her from the aching. She heard a key in the front door and panicked. If Mo came back, she'd just throw her out again, but if it were Colt, how would she explain all the mess?

PJ's voice was unexpected, but welcomed. "Steph, are you okay?"

Stephanie answered, her voice still shaky. "I'm in the dining room."

PJ came into the room. "Oh, honey. Here, get up off that floor. I'll clean this up."

PJ helped Stephanie into a chair and took the rag from her hand.

Stephanie looked at PJ. She had no more energy to cry. The tears just leaked out onto her cheeks, a continuous faucet she wished she could turn off.

"PJ, you knew didn't you?"

PJ went to work on the floor. "No, Steph, I didn't know. I suspected, but Mo never told me, at least, not until a few minutes ago."

Before It Stains

"She went to you? I thought she'd run into the arms of that little bitch," Stephanie spat out.

PJ looked up and smiled. "She probably wishes she had. I didn't provide the support she was looking for. In fact, I left her crying on my couch and came over here."

"When I heard the key in the door, I thought it was her. I was trying to decide what to throw next."

"Looks like you took care of most of the china."

Stephanie laughed despite her misery. "Yeah, the dog next door is my new best friend. He's having prime rib for dinner." She saw the look on PJ's face and added, "Don't worry, it bounced out into the hall before the glass started flying."

PJ looked at Stephanie, taking in her current state. Her clothes were covered in food stains. Her hands were bloody from picking up glass. PJ put the rag down and stood up.

"Why don't you go clean yourself up? I'll take care of this mess and then we'll sit and talk, or not talk, whatever you want to do, but I'm not leaving you here alone. Okay?"

"Okay," Stephanie said, glad for the help.

She moved up the stairs slowly, not wanting to go into their bedroom. Images from the previous night's love making flashed in her mind. Stephanie shook her head to make them go away. There would be no more nights like that for them. No more waking to watch Mo while she slept. No more hugs and soul melting kisses. This was the beginning of many lonely nights. Stephanie knew she wouldn't sleep in that bed again. She'd move into the guest room in the morning. Tonight she was too exhausted to do it, but she would never go into that room again after tomorrow. As soon as she could sell this house, she and Colt would move to a new one and start over, without Mo.

#

Before It Stains

Stephanie showered quickly and dressed. Everywhere she looked, there were reminders of Mo. Her favorite shampoo was in the shower. A pair of her earrings rested in the dish by the sink. Her robe was on the back of the bathroom door. Stephanie buried her face in the robe, taking in Mo's scent. This began another wave of tears, so she rushed to get out of the room.

Stephanie found her cellphone on table at the bottom of the stairs. She dialed her office and left a message, letting them know she wouldn't be in to work tomorrow, and went back to the dining room. PJ had finished cleaning and removed all the debris. The only signs of the confrontation were the bloody stains from the rib juices that ran down the wall. Stephanie hadn't known she was capable of that kind of rage. Until today, she'd never had a reason to know it.

"Remind me never to make you mad," PJ said, coming out of the kitchen with a wine bottle and two glasses. "Let's go sit in the den."

Stephanie followed, glad to let someone else make the decisions for the moment. PJ sat on the couch and poured the wine. She handed Stephanie a glass as she sat down on the other end of the couch. They both took a swallow and sighed almost simultaneously.

"Damn, I can't believe this. You two were always the ideal couple. From the first time she saw you, Mo has been head over heels in love with you. I had hoped to find a relationship like yours. Now, I know even the perfect relationship can have its pitfalls."

"Why didn't I see this coming? I thought the stress from all the recent attention was getting to her. I never dreamed she was having an affair."

"Don't throw anything at me," PJ said, holding her hands up in surrender, "but I need to clarify something. An

Before It Stains

affair is a very different beast than what Mo did. There was no emotional attachment. It happened once and she was mortified by her behavior. I know you have a hard time believing that, and it does not diminish the magnitude of what she did in any way, but she never stopped loving you. She's heartbroken, as are you."

"I hope it hurts like hell. I hope she can't sleep, or eat, or work. I want her to hurt like this, even worse, because she deserves to feel the consequences of her actions."

"Steph, you're mad and you have every right to be, but don't make decisions now, not when your emotions are running so high."

Stephanie swallowed the rest of her wine and held her glass out for more. She was going to get drunk. At least it would dull the pain, she hoped. PJ poured more wine, while Stephanie spoke.

"I know you're not suggesting that I forgive her and let her come home. You can't possibly think this can be fixed." The wine glass now full, she took a swallow and continued. "Mo betrayed me. I gave her all of me, every ounce of my being. I trusted her to keep it close and safe. Where was that trust while she was fucking another woman? Tell me that."

PJ sat back. "I don't have an answer for you."

The wine disappeared from Stephanie's glass and she held it out again. PJ hesitated.

"Pour me some fucking wine or I'll drink it from the bottle. I'm going to drown my sorrows tonight and then try to make sense of my life in the morning. You can stay and watch, or you can leave, but I'm getting blind drunk."

PJ stood up. Stephanie thought she was leaving, but then PJ walked toward the bar in the corner of the room. She took down two shot glasses and a bottle of tequila from the shelf. She returned, set the glasses on the coffee table, and poured them both a shot. She handed one to Stephanie and took the empty wine glass from her.

"All right, girl. Let's throw down, but tequila is quicker and the hangover won't last for days like the wine."

Stephanie smiled. "Ah, the voice of experience."

PJ laughed. "Unfortunately, that is so damn true."

They tipped up the glasses and slammed back the fiery liquid. It burned Stephanie's throat and she gagged. She really wasn't much of a drinker.

"Don't worry, the rest of them will go down easier," PJ said.

Stephanie coughed. "Aren't we supposed to chase this with limes or something?"

"Lemon wedges. You got any lemons?" PJ laughed again. "What am I saying? Of course Martha Stewart has lemons."

It was a term of endearment Mo and PJ used for Stephanie, because they said she was the perfect hostess. This time it stung, a little.

"Is that what you really think of me, that all I worry about is keeping a nice home and throwing dinner parties? Did I bore Mo? Did she tell you she wanted more out of life? Was her family holding her back? Is that what she said?"

PJ seemed to realize the error she made. "No, Steph. Mo was always so proud of you. You're an accomplished businesswoman, a great mother, and a wonderful wife, not to mention beautiful. Mo had it all, everything we single women are looking for. She found it in you."

"It wasn't enough though, was it? She obviously found something in that other woman she couldn't get at home."

Before It Stains

"What she got was a hot, young lesbian with more money than God, who would not take no for an answer. She wore her down, got her drunk, and took advantage of her."

Stephanie stood up. "Please, tell me you're not defending her."

PJ stood up too. "No, I'm not defending her, but I saw it from a distance. I warned her. She knew she was flirting with danger… uh, poor choice of words, but her career was attached to Michaela, after she signed that contract. She couldn't get away from her without letting her dreams go."

"What about my dreams? What about Colt's? Did she stop to think about that? I wish she'd never made that fucking movie. What a crock. 'Just Fine.' How fine does she think our kid is going to be when he finds out what she's done?"

"Are you going to tell him?"

"No, I told her she had to. I'm not doing the dirty work. I'll just be the one dealing with his anger and hurt, while she's off living the dream."

PJ cocked her head to one side. "Does that mean you're going to give her a chance to put things right?"

"With Colt, yes. He is her son and I can't do anything about that, but with me, sorry that was a deal breaker."

Stephanie walked toward the kitchen.

"Where are you going?" PJ asked.

"Martha Stewart is fetching the lemons, a dish of salt, and some snacks. This is going to be a long night."

PJ's cellphone jangled in her pocket. She pulled it out, looked at the screen, and said, "It's Mo." She answered, "Hello."

Stephanie called over her shoulder. "Tell her I said stop moping on the couch. I'm sure her girlfriend would love to make her feel better. They can fuck guilt free, now."

Before It Stains

Stephanie put up a good front, but once she was out of sight, she felt the tears burning again. She listened to PJ's part of the conversation.

"Yes, she's okay. Still really pissed, but she's okay... Well, this has to be the stupidest stunt you've ever pulled, Mo. You deserve to feel like shit... Go on to bed. I'm staying with her until morning... That's entirely up to you. I don't give a damn about the movie or your career at this point... I'll always love you, Mo, but I don't like you very much right now... I really don't give two shits what you do... Yeah, well you fucked up your life all by yourself, now you can fix it all by yourself, too."

Stephanie couldn't resist calling out, "She can't fix this!"

PJ laughed and then listened again. Finally she said, "No, I won't tell her anything. If you want to talk to Stephanie, then you talk to her. I'm not your friend tonight. I'm hers... Well, first you need to figure out how to explain this to your son. He's more important than your job... No, I don't know you know that. Sometimes, I don't think I know you at all... Yeah, well life's a bitch and then you die. I'm hanging up now. If I were you, I'd get down on my knees and pray. Pray that you haven't totally fucked up the best thing that ever happened to you... Good night, Mo."

Stephanie wiped her tears, before PJ joined her in the kitchen.

"Damn, I hate this. You two were supposed to be together forever. This is going to suck, if you can't work things out."

Stephanie reached into the refrigerator for the salsa she made a couple of days ago. It was Mo's favorite snack. Stephanie always had some freshly made. Since Mo wasn't going to be around to eat it, Stephanie thought it would go well with tequila shots. She handed the bowl to PJ along with a bag of tortilla chips. She talked as she cut up a lemon.

"I heard some of what you said. Thank you for being my friend. I know you love Mo. I appreciate your staying here with me, but if you need to go, I'll understand."

"I'm not going anywhere. She can wallow in misery by herself. I'm not up for the Mo pity party tonight."

"I was going to ask you last night why you were so upset with her. Are you sure you didn't know what she was up to?"

"No, Steph, I didn't know, really. I was upset with her, because I saw what was happening and I called her on it. All this Hollywood shit just grates on my nerves. I left that world to come teach with her. I told her she didn't know the soul stealers she was getting in bed with-- uh, another poor choice of words."

Stephanie smiled. "It's okay. I know what you're saying. I saw it changing her too, but I didn't know how to do anything but keep peace here at home and hope she found her way back to us. I should have said something, anything, but it's too late now. I was worried about keeping our family intact, while she was off gallivanting around the country. I just never saw this coming. It never crossed my mind."

PJ was skeptical. "Never? I saw that look on your face last night, when that bitch grabbed Mo practically out of your arms. You thought about it then, didn't you?"

Stephanie piled the salt, lemon wedges, and napkins on a tray. She headed back to the den with PJ close behind.

"I saw her hand in the small of Mo's back and I knew it meant something. I ignored it, because I didn't want to believe it."

Before It Stains

Once they were seated back on the couch, PJ poured two more shots. This time they used the salt and bit down on a piece of lemon, before the conversation continued.

"Really, last night was the first time it crossed your mind that Mo would cheat?"

Stephanie was taken aback. She answered, "Yes. What are you getting at? Have I been blind all along? Has she done this before? Tell me the truth."

"No, no," PJ waved her hands in the air. "She never cheated on you, not that I know of, but she must be a better at covering her tracks than I thought."

"What do you mean? Just spit it out. It can't be worse than what I already know, can it?"

PJ poured another shot. She seemed to need the fortification as much as Stephanie.

"It's just that even I knew, when she came back from the LA film festival in June, that something was wrong. She couldn't look me in the eye, anymore. I thought she'd made some deal and it was going to fuck me over, but now I know that's not what it was."

Stephanie dipped her tongue in the salt on the back of her hand and downed another shot. She bit into the lemon, but it didn't dull the burning in her throat. Mo always said Stephanie was a lightweight. Mo did the heavy drinking and Stephanie did the driving, but tonight Stephanie was determined to find out what drinking herself blind really meant.

She asked, "Is that when it happened?"

PJ squirmed a bit. "I shouldn't have said anything. You need to hear this from Mo."

Stephanie was beginning to feel the alcohol. She said, "Fuck Mo. Like you said, you're here as my friend. Tell me what you know," she grinned, "or I might start throwing china at you, too."

"Okay, but don't shoot the messenger."

Stephanie laughed. "I don't have a gun, but I'm dead aim with a prime rib."

PJ gave in. "You're already well on your way to being drunk, so you'll probably forget this conversation." She hesitated only a moment, and then said, "Remember we had a party that night, waiting for Mo to call."

"Yeah, she called and said the documentary was a smash hit. She was plastered, as I recall. I was worried she wouldn't make it back to her room."

PJ nodded. "Yes, and then we tried to call her about an hour later."

Stephanie remembered. "She never answered. I tossed and turned all night, not knowing if she was okay. She didn't call back until the next morning."

"Yeah, some shit about forgetting to plug her phone in, when she got back to the hotel."

"Oh, my God. It was that night." Stephanie felt the rage rising, again. "I laid there wondering if she was dead in a ditch and she was fucking all night."

"Now, to be honest, she was so drunk, I doubt there was an all-nighter. She woke up, realized what she had done, and fled the scene. At least, that's what she told me, tonight."

Stephanie poured her own shot this time. She threw it down her throat, not bothering with the salt or lemon. No wonder Mo had been uptight for two months.

"How un-fucking-believably naïve I am. Here I was, scrambling around trying to make everything perfect and stress-free for Mo, and she had already betrayed me."

Before It Stains

PJ was feeling the tequila too. "You know what they say, love is blind."

Stephanie stood up and paced the room. "I just want to hit something. I'd prefer it be Michaela with my car, but I don't want to go to jail."

PJ tried to inject some levity. "We could go kidnap and terrorize her. You know, that little princess would be scared to death of my black ass."

It sounded like a plan to Stephanie. "Let's do it."

"I wasn't serious, Steph. Damn girl, have another drink. I want to make sure you pass out, so if I do, you can't sneak off and do something stupid."

Stephanie took the glass, knocked back the shot, and then threw the glass into the fireplace, shattering it into a million pieces. This time, the alcohol did not cause the tears that burned her eyes. She felt the pain creeping in and then it overwhelmed her. Her body started to shake and then the racking sobs took over. Stephanie fell back down on the couch and cried, while PJ patted her back and whispered, "It's okay, let it out."

When Stephanie finally spoke, she just asked, "Why? Why did she ruin it all? I hate her, PJ. I hate her. I don't want to love her anymore."

PJ kept patting her back. She answered, "Let it out. Go ahead; scream if you need to, just get all that hate out, now. Don't let it linger. You'll never heal if you hang on to it."

Stephanie took PJ's advice. "Damn her! And damn that little bitch. If I could get my hands on her, I'd strangle her."

"If Mo doesn't kill her first," PJ muttered.

PJ's declaration surprised Stephanie. She sat up and looked at PJ. "What?"

"Mo said she threw that napkin away last night, as soon as Michaela handed it to her. She said, and I quote, 'I know that bitch put it in my pocket. The more I pushed her away, the harder she tried.' She was kind of blackmailing Mo, not overtly, but the threat that she would tell you what happened loomed in the air all the time. At least, that's how Mo saw it."

That bit of information didn't placate Stephanie. "She should have just fired her."

"She tried, but Michaela waved the contract in her face. The lawyer Mo contacted said the bitch owned her for the remainder of the contract, which means Mo has to finish the next project before she can get out of it. He also said, if Mo did not do the project, then Michaela could file a lawsuit, come after the house, your business, and anything else Mo cared about to get her cut."

"How could she come after my business?" Stephanie asked.

"Remember, you gave Mo shares last year. It was to protect her should something happen to you, but it's there on paper. Anything with Mo's name on it is fair game."

Stephanie was drunk and confused. Her MBA couldn't cut through the alcohol, but she understood enough. "Why does she want Mo so badly, if Mo wants nothing to do with her?"

PJ laughed. "Honey, Michaela doesn't want Mo. When she's done with her, the little leech will try to suck the life out of someone else's wife or husband. I know her kind. It's the chase that turns her on. She has to win."

"She won, PJ." Stephanie crumbled back down in the pillows on the couch, bawling.

PJ patted her back again, saying, "Only if you can't find the strength to let Mo back in your life. I'm not asking you to. I know she broke your heart, but if you let that little bitch end your relationship, then she does win."

Before It Stains

Stephanie felt the walls crashing in, as she began to pass out, still crying. The last thing she thought she heard was PJ say, "Mo isn't perfect, but she loves you more than her dreams."

CHAPTER FOUR

Stephanie woke to smell of bacon frying. It made her ill immediately. It reminded her of the morning sickness she had when she was pregnant. PJ must have covered her with a blanket at some point. Her neck was stiff from the awkward way she had been laying. Stephanie stood up quickly, which was the wrong thing to do, causing her to run to the downstairs bathroom. She noticed PJ asleep in the recliner, but it didn't register that someone else was cooking in her kitchen, until she was sitting on the tile floor of the bathroom, trying to focus. A soft knock on the bathroom door startled her.

Her mother's voice came through the door. "Stephanie, are you all right, honey?"

"Yes, just give me a minute."

Stephanie looked at the clock on the wall. How did her mother come in the house without waking her? Stephanie remembered the tequila and instantly threw up again. If this was what blind drunk did to her, she wanted no part of it, ever again. When she could stand, Stephanie rinsed her mouth out and wandered toward the kitchen. Her mother was standing over the stove cooking scrambled eggs. Stephanie rolled her eyes at the food and grabbed a bottle of water out of the refrigerator.

Her mother took it from her, saying, "You evidently are not an experienced tequila drinker. You need eggs with hot sauce and some toast. Trust me." She reached in the refrigerator and pulled out one of Colt's sports drinks. "Here, drink this. You need the electrolytes."

Stephanie usually didn't drink Colt's preferred beverage, but she did as she was told. The cold liquid hit the bottom of her stomach and threatened to come right back up, but she held it down and managed to drink half the bottle.

"Mom, how did you get in here without me hearing you?"

"I came in the back door. Luckily, it was unlocked. I could have used my key, but I left the house so fast, I forgot it. I found you two passed out in the den and decided a rescue breakfast was in order."

"Why are you here?" Stephanie asked.

"Well, to make a long story short, I got a call from Mo this morning."

"Oh."

"She didn't give me any details, but I gathered from our ragged conversation, between the crying jags, that she royally screwed up and you were breaking china."

"She cheated on me, Mom."

"Yes, and you're not the first wife that has ever happened to, or husband for that matter."

"Wait, Mo called you this morning. Her flight left at six o'clock. How did she call you from the air?"

Before It Stains

Her mother shrugged her shoulders. "She told me she was at PJ's."

"Did someone say my name?" A bedraggled PJ walked into the kitchen. The rectangle shaped hair on her head looked more like a pyramid.

"Good morning. I'll have the eggs ready in a minute. You two go wash up and we'll have a nice little breakfast."

PJ and Stephanie groaned, but left the kitchen. Stephanie climbed to the second floor, while PJ took the bathroom downstairs. The absence of Mo hit Stephanie hard, once she was back in the master bedroom. She never noticed how much of Mo was in that room, until she didn't want to see it. Pictures of their wedding in Canada, with four-year-old Colt as the ring bearer, and other memories of a happy family filled the walls and the dresser. Her favorite stared back at her from the bedside table. It was of Mo, in hospital scrubs holding brand new baby Colt, beaming at the camera as if she'd found the secret to life.

Stephanie wanted to wake up from the nightmare. She'd do things differently, if she had the chance. Her hopes and dreams would not have been centered on Mo. She would not have spent all of her time making sure Mo was happy. There was no telling what Stephanie could have made of herself, if she had put her needs before Mo's, but then she may not have had Colt. He was as much a part of Mo as Stephanie. Stephanie gave birth to him, but Mo had been there every step of the way. Mo was a good parent. She loved Colt with all her heart. A stabbing pain bent Stephanie over. She thought she was going to be sick. She balanced herself on one arm, leaning on the bed, before she gave in and ran to the bathroom. When she had nothing left but dry heaves, Stephanie leaned against the glass shower door and cried.

Before It Stains

In a few minutes, her mother's voice filled the room. "Stephanie, I know this hurts like hell, but you've got to pull it together. Colt called your cell and I answered it. I told him you decided to take the day off and we were having breakfast. He'll be here in a few minutes. He has practice and forgot his cleats. You don't want him to see you like this."

Her mother's hands gently gripped Stephanie's shoulders.

"Come on, honey."

Stephanie was placed on the stool at the make-up counter.

"Stephanie, I'm going to give you one piece of advice, unsolicited, then if you want more, you'll have to ask. This isn't my burden to bear. I've carried my own for all these years. Your heart is broken. It will heal. What you have to realize is this isn't all about you. This is a family crisis, not a personal one. Other lives are at stake here. You cannot let your pain overshadow that."

Stephanie searched her mother's face. She saw it there in her eyes, long since buried pain, a heartbreak Stephanie had never known existed.

"It's all out on the table now. The hard part is over. The agony will lessen with each passing day. If you choose to wallow in your grief, well, that's your choice, honey, or you can look at this as a fresh start. I'll stand behind you, whatever you decide to do, but take this week to think about it. Colt already thinks Mo's in LA. I can tell by the stains on the wall in the dining room that you haven't had a rational conversation with her. You two need to talk, put your feelings aside, and decide what the rest of your son's life is going to be like, then you can worry about your own."

Before It Stains

Her mom patted Stephanie's shoulder and left her alone to get dressed. Stephanie stared at her haggard image in the mirror. She concentrated on her mother's words, not fully comprehending, but it was all Stephanie could focus on, at the moment. Her hand reached mechanically for the brush and started pulling her shoulder length hair back into shape. Her eyelids were puffy and bruised. No amount of make-up would obscure that from view, but a pair of sunglasses would.

Stephanie made herself presentable, changed her clothes, and went back downstairs. She helped her mother move all the breakfast things to the deck. PJ cleaned up the den. When Colt arrived, Stephanie and the others were seated at the table. The large dark sunglasses she wore hid the pain from Colt.

"Hey, baby boy. You want some breakfast?" Stephanie asked, smiling as if it were just another day in paradise.

"Yes, sit down. I'll fix you a plate," his grandmother offered.

"Hey, Mom. Hey, Grandma. PJ." He hugged his relatives and settled for a fist blow-up with PJ. "I already ate."

Business as usual, on Stephanie's part, she corrected him, "Thank you, but I've already eaten."

He repeated her words exactly, while snatching a piece of toast, then added, "Trev's mom is waiting. I just came to get my cleats."

"Do you want me to pick you up after practice? We can go for pizza." Stephanie was holding it together, despite her emotional state.

"No, we're going to Wyatt's house to swim. Then Trev's mom will drop me back off. I told her you were probably having a bad day, with Mo leaving. She said for you to just relax and enjoy yourself."

"That was sweet of her, and you. Come give me a kiss before you go."

He leaned down, kissed her on the cheek, and said, "I'll hang with you tonight. We can watch a movie."

"Okay, sweetheart. Don't forget to ice your arm."

"You sound just like Mo." Colt grinned. "See you guys later."

Stephanie watched him bound into the house, a happy boy with no clue that his world was teetering. Her mom smiled at her. Stephanie dug into the eggs. She would need fortification to keep this up and there was that other thing. Mo had not gone to LA.

PJ's phone rang on cue. Her expression said Mo was on the line. She excused herself to take the call. Stephanie put her fork down and stared off into space. She felt a hand grip hers and turned to see tears welling in her mother's eyes.

"If I could take the pain from you and hold it myself, I would."

"Oh, Mom, don't cry," Stephanie said, but she was crying too. "I'm sorry this is dredging up old memories for you. I take it our conversation in the bathroom comes from experience."

Her mother dabbed her eyes and regained her confident, "I am Woman," appearance. Debra Austin had shown Stephanie just a peek in the vault where she kept her deepest pain. She cleared her throat.

"Yes, your father and I went through this. I'm not going to explain the circumstances. That really isn't anyone's business but ours. What I will say is, faced with losing my family, I chose to stay."

Before It Stains

Stephanie leaned forward. "How, Mom? How did you forgive him?"

"You mean after I wanted him dead?" Debra laughed.

Stephanie smiled. "That, I do understand."

"Honey, your father is the love of my life. He is also a human being. People do the damnedest things, with no earthly idea why they did them. He was devastated by what he'd done. He's a good man. He loves me. He loves his family. Believe me, he paid dearly for his dalliance."

"And you trusted him after that?"

"I had no choice, Stephanie. He couldn't live with my doubts, and neither could I. Now, I did step up surveillance and I never let a woman in the room wonder who he belonged to, but I had to trust him. My belief in him made us stronger."

"I never knew."

"We wanted it that way. Our kids didn't make the mess, we did. It was ours to clean up."

PJ walked back over to the table. "Mo didn't go to LA. She said she's not leaving here without talking to you first."

Some of what PJ said last night filtered through to Stephanie. She stood up suddenly.

"She has to go to LA. She can't breach that contract."

PJ sat down, shaking her head. "She isn't budging until she talks to you, period. I reminded her that those folks out there have lawyers that do nothing all day but file lawsuits against people like her."

Stephanie was adamant. "Mo doesn't have a choice, at least until we can find a way to get her out of that agent contract."

PJ and Stephanie's mother exchanged grins.

Stephanie said, "What?"

Before It Stains

Her mother smiled up at her. "You said, 'we' have to get her out of the contract."

"I'm not taking her back. I just don't want to lose my house."

PJ shoveled up a fork full of eggs and said, "Well, she's not living at my house, so you go on over there and have your talk. I'm going to stay with Mrs. Austin here and have polite conversation over coffee."

Stephanie looked at her mother for help.

"Go on. Put your big girl panties on and have your say."

Stephanie's shoulders slumped and she felt like a teenager being sent to do her homework. The dread of what was to come weighed heavy in her steps, as she started for the door.

PJ called out to her, "Hey, don't start throwing things at my house. That china belonged to my grandmother."

#

Stephanie sat in her car, outside of PJ's little white house. She checked the make-up she applied back at home, not because she wanted to look nice. She didn't want Mo to see how much she'd been crying. The concealer had done magic, but the puffiness still remained. Too bad they couldn't just sit on the porch, where Stephanie could keep her sunglasses on. The conversation they were about to have needed to take place behind closed doors.

Stephanie looked back at the house and saw the front door now stood open. She had been spotted. Somewhere inside the house, Mo was pacing. Stephanie knew her wife so well she could predict what she would be wearing, a pair of old gray sweat pants and a blue tee shirt, with the University logo almost illegible from wear. These were her comfort clothes. Stephanie had made sure to put them in

Before It Stains

Mo's suitcase, before she threw her out. Even at her most enraged, Stephanie had still been taking care of Mo.

Peering in the mirror on the visor, Stephanie considered her options. There were not many. She couldn't drive back home, crawl in bed, and hope it all worked itself out. This wasn't going away and putting it off would just postpone the inevitable. Stephanie and Mo had to sit down and talk about Colt. Like her mother said, the rest of it could wait, but their son was going to want answers. Stephanie took a deep breath and let it out slowly. She spoke to her reflection.

"Okay, just keep it together, Steph. You can do this."

When she walked through the open door, she found Mo in the front room, wearing the gray sweat pants and old blue tee shirt, as predicted.

"Hey," Mo said, shyly.

"Hey," Stephanie replied.

Neither spoke for a moment. Mo's hair was a mess and she looked like she hadn't slept at all. She was pale and Stephanie could see she was trembling. She probably had not eaten since yesterday. Mo never ate when she was stressed. Stephanie used to have to force smoothies on her when she got like that. Stephanie always looked out for Mo.

They both started talking at once.

"Can I get you something to-"

"Why don't we sit d-" Stephanie stopped, and then said, "No, thank you. Let's just sit down."

Mo held out her hand, indicating Stephanie should sit on the couch, which she did. Mo took the armchair across from her. More moments of silence followed. Stephanie searched Mo's face for an answer. She only had one question, why? Their eyes darted back and forth, locked on each other, until

Before It Stains

Mo dropped her head and began to cry softly. When she spoke, her words were whispers.

"I'm so sorry, Stephanie. I know you hate me. I don't blame you."

They were both crying now. A tear rolled down Stephanie's cheek. The pain rose in her chest, shortening her breath.

Her calmness belied the tempest growing inside her, when Stephanie responded, "I'm hurt, I'm angry, and I feel betrayed, but I don't know that I hate you. I have loved you so long, I don't know that I can hate you. I wanted to. I even said it. I'm definitely not your biggest fan right now, but I don't hate you."

Mo looked up from the floor. "I don't know what to say to you. I can't lose you. I can't lose our family. I'll do anything you want. I'll stay home. I won't go to LA. I'll ..."

Stephanie held up her hand. "Just stop. Before we go any further, there is one thing you need to understand. I won't let that bitch take my house or part of my business. You're going to go to LA and fulfill that contract."

Mo tried to interrupt, "But-"

"Don't. Just don't. You lost your right to have a say in this when you put our home and family in jeopardy. We will get you out of that contract somehow, but until we do, you are holding up your end of the bargain. Go do your job. Unless I'm mistaken, and remember I did read the contract, she simply gets you jobs and takes her cut. It doesn't say anywhere in there that you are required to have personal contact with her."

"How do I do that when she's my agent?"

Stephanie leaned forward to make her point. "If you have one inkling that I'm letting you back in my life, you will cut all ties with her this minute. Ban her ass from the set, lose her number, and keep your fucking pants on."

Mo almost smiled, but covered it by saying, "Done."

Stephanie realized she had given Mo hope and wanted to make sure she understood that this was just the tip of the iceberg.

"Don't think you're getting off that easy. I'm simply taking care of Colt. This isn't about you and me. It's about making sure his home isn't ripped out from under him, because you fucked around. That's not a lesson I want him to learn at this age."

The smile faded from Mo's face. "Is he okay? Did you say anything to him?"

"I told you I wouldn't, and I haven't. That's your hornets' nest. You deal with it."

"I will," Mo said, weakly. "I don't know what to say to him. I don't want to hurt him."

Stephanie narrowed her eyes. "You already hurt him, he just doesn't know it yet."

Mo's tears began to cascade down her face. She buried her head in her hands, her body jerking with silent sobs.

"Why, Mo? Why did you do it? What was so wrong with our lives that you slept with another woman? Are we holding you back? Is there somewhere else you'd rather be? Have you just been waiting for something better to come along?"

Mo shot out of the chair. "No! None of that's true." She wiped her cheek with the back of her hand, but it was no use. Her tears were coming hard and fast. "Stephanie, I never once thought any of that. Don't you get it? I wasn't thinking. I was drunk and to tell you the truth, I don't remember very much of it at all. I don't even know if I really had sex with her. I know I did enough to feel guilty as hell and scared." She shuddered, her diaphragm fighting her attempt to take in air. "Scared you would find out and this would happen."

"Don't give me that shit, Mo. You know exactly what you did, drunk or not. You were scared I would find out? If I hadn't, would you be feeling less guilty? You got caught, Mo. Fess up, tell the truth. No use lying anymore."

Mo spoke, almost in a whisper, "I don't know how this happened."

"I do." Stephanie wasn't letting up. "You started believing your own hype, Mo. She stroked your ego and you liked it. Don't try to put this off on being drunk. You put yourself in an inappropriate situation, something bad happened, and you're surprised? You crossed the line long before you actually slept with her. If you don't realize that, then there's no need to continue this conversation."

Mo stared at Stephanie.

"Admit it. It was exciting and new. It wasn't the same wife and kid at home. Was it worth the few hours you were free of us?" Stephanie's words were hurting Mo. She could see it, but she didn't care. She wanted to say it all. "I'm sure she did look good without any responsibilities tied to her, no mortgage, no car payments, no kid, nothing but time and money to spend on you. I guess, in comparison, your humdrum, day-to-day life with me just didn't stack up."

"Stephanie, it wasn't like that. Don't you know how much I love you, that I love Colt, that you're my world? None of this means anything, if you aren't with me."

Stephanie shot off the couch. "Were you thinking about me when you were flirting and playing grab ass with another woman?"

Mo came toward Stephanie and grabbed her elbows, desperately pleading, "Listen to me, please, listen to me. I betrayed your trust. I know that. I'm trying to tell you I know what I've done. I don't know how to make you see, I know, God, I know." She backed away and fell against the wall. "I'm sorry. I'm so sorry."

Stephanie stood frozen in place, unable to maintain the rage that had bubbled just below the surface. She couldn't look at Mo. Stephanie had never known strong, confident Mo so shattered, so distraught. She'd never heard Mo keen with grief. The audible pain tore at Stephanie's soul. It was all she could do to stand there and not take Mo in her arms, hold her, and soothe her broken heart. Once again, faced with the decision to put Mo's needs before her own, she would choose Mo. Maybe that was the problem all along.

Stephanie reached out and helped Mo steady herself. She walked the completely helpless woman to the bathroom. Mo had given over to Stephanie's touch with no resistance. Stephanie put the lid down on the toilet and sat Mo down. She got on her knees and pulled Mo's chin up from her chest, so they were eye to eye.

"Mo, you never once had to wonder where I was or what I was doing. You never had to sit through a dinner I didn't show up for. You never had to wonder if that dinner would still be waiting for you when you came home. You never had to explain to a little boy why his MoMo was too busy to play with him, again. You took us for granted and I let you. I'm not letting you anymore."

Mo tried to speak. Stephanie placed her fingers over Mo's lips.

"Shhh. Just listen. Take a shower and get yourself together. You're going to LA. You'll have some time to think about being alone, on your own, without me hovering over you. Maybe you'll decide that's the life you want. We're tied together forever by Colt. I couldn't leave you if I tried. You'll always be in my life, but, after Colt, I have to think about me, not you. I have to put me first, do you understand?"

Mo nodded that she did.

"Maybe I spent so much time trying to make our lives perfect, I lost sight of me. That's my fault. You were my universe. That's an awful lot of responsibility for my happiness in someone else's hands. The cheating was just a symptom of something bigger. We have to find out the cause, before we can fix it. I love you, Mo. I've loved you from the first time I saw you. I think I may have loved you too much."

Mo reached out and smoothed stray strands of hair from Stephanie's face. "When I get back, I'm going to spend the rest of my life making sure you know you're everything I ever dreamed of."

"If that's how this ends, then I can live with that, but what I can't live with is the prospect this would ever happen again. I have to trust you. Give me a week to figure out if that's possible, because if I have to tell you today, the answer is no."

Stephanie leaned in and kissed Mo with the full knowledge that this could be the last kiss she ever shared with the love of her life. Mo pulled Stephanie closer, pressing into her lips. The moan that escaped Mo's chest wasn't sensual, it was desperation and longing for things lost. The sound clutched Stephanie's heart and the kiss deepened, their tears mingling on each other's cheeks. Mo slipped to her knees on the floor. They held each other too tightly, too passionately. Stephanie had to break free or she would give in right there on the bathroom floor. Mo's kiss always held some mystical power over Stephanie; at this moment, it threatened to ruin her resolve.

Before It Stains

Stephanie gently pushed Mo away and left the bathroom without another word. She heard Mo speak, as she closed the door behind her.

"I love you, Steph. That's never going to change."

The old Stephanie would have stayed. She would have arranged Mo's flight, as she normally did. She would have made Mo eat something. She would have checked that Mo had everything she needed in her suitcase. She would have driven her to the airport and kissed her goodbye. The new Stephanie walked out the front door without doing any of those things. Mo was on her own.

CHAPTER FIVE

After finally shooing her mother and PJ away, Stephanie was alone for a few hours. She promised to call them both just to check in. Stephanie didn't discuss the details of her conversation with Mo, other than to say, as far as Colt was to know, nothing had changed. It was three-thirty when she finally sat down in the home office and flipped on the desktop computer. Stephanie was a businesswoman by trade. She knew a little about business law, but not a lot. She did, however, know someone who did. Colt's father, or the man he called Dad anyway.

She intended to do a little web surfing on her own. Before she started, she texted Randy Ransom, asking him to call her. Randy and Stephanie were best friends since high school. They dated back then, slept together a few times, even went to the same college, but they realized what drew them together was their sexuality. They were both gay. Randy introduced Stephanie to her first girlfriend and picked up the pieces when it fell apart. He was there when she met Mo and stood by Stephanie's side when she married her. He was Stephanie's maid of honor, decked out in full white tails and matching top hat, claiming if Stephanie could wear white, he could too.

Randy went on to law school and coincidently worked in the firm owned by the female law student Stephanie was in a relationship with when she met Mo. That law student went on to be one of the most successful defense attorneys in the Southeast. Stephanie broke off the relationship when it became obvious to her, she and Mo were meant for each other.

Randy worked in the civil law division of the firm. His specialty was suing insurance companies when they refused to pay a legitimate claim. When Randy got through with them, they usually paid more than it would have cost to do the right thing in the first place. Stephanie enjoyed watching Randy butch up for court, because he told her, "There are twelve people on the jury. My sexuality does not matter to the lesbians. I am already ahead with the gay guys. It's the straight ones I have to play to. It's all in the game."

Stephanie glanced down and saw the napkin with Michaela's note, wadded in a ball, and resting on the top of the trash. She shoved the trash down further and put a piece of paper over it, so she could no longer see the lipstick and faint curl of the inked "*M*." Stephanie turned back to the computer screen and typed "sexual harassment" in the search engine. The phone rang on the desk. Distracted by the search results, Stephanie did not look at the caller ID.

"Hello."

The voice on the other end sent a white-hot bolt of lightning down Stephanie's spine. She went rigid, her rage growing with every syllable on the line.

"Stephanie, this is Michaela. I'm at the LAX. We just landed. I'm sure you know by now Mo did not get on in

Before It Stains

Raleigh. She knows how important this meeting is tomorrow. I can't imagine what would have kept her off that plane. Is she at home? Did something happen? She won't answer her phone. Hello, are you there?"

"She had to catch a later flight," Stephanie said, through clinched teeth, her knuckles turning white from gripping the phone so hard.

"Are you kidding me? What time will she be here? I'm not waiting around the airport for hours."

Stephanie, unlike Mo, was not in the least attracted to or impressed by Michaela. She never liked her, but the young agent came highly recommended. A recommendation Stephanie intended to address in the near future, but right now she had the "other woman" on the phone, and this was not an opportunity she was going to let pass. She laid the gauntlet down.

"Mo's a big girl. She was travelling without your assistance when you were still in braces. I don't see in her contract where it says she has to depend on you for a ride from the airport, or anything else really, other than whoring her out to jobs so you can get your cut."

Michaela revealed just how frequently she had been involved in situations like this. She picked up the heated tone in Stephanie's voice and went straight to the point.

"I guess you found my note."

Stephanie was skilled in the art of handling difficult people. She had to in her job, where she dealt with irate contractors and outraged property owners. She stood toe to toe with guys in hardhats and building inspectors without losing her cool. However, Stephanie could drop her cultured exterior and get down to the nitty-gritty, when the situation called for it. Michaela was flaunting her conquest and disregard for anyone's feelings but her own. Stephanie narrowed her eyes and sat up straighter. If she could have reached through the phone, Michaela would have had a handprint across her face. A verbal slap would have to do.

With the superior tone intended, Stephanie said, "You wanted me to find that note. You're really quite the little bitch, aren't you? Are you so pathetic that you have to get your thrills wrecking other people's lives? Is this what you do to get daddy's attention?"

"I believe your problem is with your so-called wife. She wouldn't be fucking me, if she got what she needed at home."

"Let me ask you a question, Michaela."

"Go ahead, but you might not like the answer."

"Oh, it's not about Mo. I know everything I need to know about Mo. I know what she likes on her hamburger. I know what size shoes she wears. I know what brand of toothpaste she prefers, what she's allergic to, her momma's name, where she had her first girl kiss, her favorite color, I even know what thread count she likes in our sheets. I know her annoying habits and endearing quirks. So, no Michaela, I don't need you to tell me a damn thing about Mo."

Michaela sounded bored. "So, what's your question?"

"I want to know if you love anything. Is there one thing you just can't live without? And I know it's not Mo. You're caught now. The game is up. No more thrills for you. So, tell me, what could you not stand to lose? Let me guess, it's daddy's money. No wait, it's daddy's approval, isn't it?"

Michaela dropped the attitude, when she asked, "Why do you want to know?"

"Because when this is done, and it will be done, I want to make damn sure you realize what kind of games you've been playing at. You seem to forget that I run quite a large business. I know a few things about sexual harassment laws."

"It's not sexual harassment, if she consented."

Stephanie laughed. "I think you better read that part again. That napkin alone is enough to bury you. Have daddy's lawyers check on that for you."

"I'll do that," Michaela snapped.

"I'm going to save some other woman the trouble of dealing with you. After I'm done, you'll think twice about going after something that isn't yours to have. I want you to lie awake at night, wondering where it all went wrong. I want you to remember this moment, when I promised to take the one thing you love more than anything and destroy it. This is my family you're fucking with. I think by now you're wondering what can she do to me? You just keep wondering, honey. Your day is coming, you can bet all your daddy's money on that. You may already have."

"You don't scare me." Michaela laughed, but it was faked to cover her distress.

"I should," Stephanie said, calmly in control of the situation. "I don't have anything else to lose."

Stephanie hung up, reached in the wastebasket, and pulled out the wrinkled cocktail napkin with the lipstick stain that destroyed her world. It was now a weapon and she intended to use it to clean up the mess.

#

Stephanie carried the bowl of popcorn and Colt brought the drinks. They piled on the couch in the den, together. They settled on "True Grit," after Stephanie nixed all the horror movies Colt wanted to watch. Love stories were out. Colt hated them and Stephanie wasn't in the mood for romance. So, a shoot 'em up western was the choice for movie night. Stephanie loved that Colt still wanted to spend time with her. She knew the days were numbered when eating popcorn with his mother would win out over some other activity.

"When's Mo going to call?" He asked, picking up the remote.

"I don't know, honey." Stephanie said, truly not knowing when or if Mo would call.

"I can't wait to tell her about that homerun I hit at practice. I bet that sucker went four-fifty easy, and it was off Coach Reese. He was a minor league pitcher."

Colt's excitement was infectious. Stephanie smiled over at him.

"I wish I could have seen it. I'm sure Mo will be thrilled to hear about it."

"Are you coming to the game tomorrow night?"

"When have you ever played a game without one, if not both of us, in the stands?"

Colt grinned. "Just checking. You've been kind of down."

Stephanie had tried hard not to let her pain show. Colt saw through her act.

"I'm just tired, honey. Aunt PJ and Mom had a bit too much to drink and it's been a very long day."

"Where was Mo? I thought you had to take her to the airport early this morning?"

Stephanie thought fast. "She took her car and let me sleep." It wasn't a lie, really. Mo had taken her car and Stephanie had slept. "Let's watch the movie, before I conk out on you."

Colt, satisfied with the answer, hit play on the remote. He slid over close to Stephanie, not quite snuggling, because he fancied himself too old, but still boy enough to want to be close to Mom. They lost themselves in the old west. With twenty minutes left in the movie, someone rang the front door bell. Colt hit pause and Stephanie went to the door. She opened it to find a floral deliveryman holding a giant arrangement of lilac colored roses.

"Sorry to be so late with the delivery ma'am, but the sender paid extra to have them brought here right away. Are you Stephanie Austin?"

"Yes."

"Then these are for you." He handed her the vase. "Somebody must love you an awful lot. That's nearly three dozen right there, every lilac rose we had in the store. Sorry we didn't have more."

"This will do fine. Thank you, they're lovely."

The deliveryman knew to delay his exit long enough for a tip. Stephanie put the vase on the foyer table and reached into her purse. She handed the folded bills to the man, repeating, "Thank you, again."

He tipped the bill of his baseball cap. "Y'all have a good night, now."

Stephanie closed the door and realized Colt was standing in the foyer with her.

"Are those from Mo?" he asked.

"I assume so," Stephanie said, carrying the roses to the dining room.

"What did she do this time?" Colt was right on top of things. "She always sends you flowers when she screws up."

"We just had a little disagreement. Nothing for you to worry about."

Colt laughed. "Must have been more than a little disagreement. Look at the size of that thing. She must really be sorry."

Before It Stains

"I'm sure she is."

Stephanie placed the arrangement on the dining room table. Lilac roses were her favorite. Mo gave Stephanie a single lilac rose the night she met her, trying to pick Stephanie up, by telling her the color meant love at first sight. Mo was all swagger and rascal back then. Stephanie, who was in a relationship, had laughed at Mo and walked away. She was intrigued but unattainable, which was apparently irresistible to the young Mo. It didn't take her long to win Stephanie's heart. Lilac roses had a special meaning to them both. Stephanie opened the attached card and read it out of Colt's view.

"Whatever it takes, Steph, I will do. I have never stopped loving you, since the first moment I saw you."

"What does it say?" Colt asked, trying to see the card.

Stephanie put it back in the envelope and tucked it in the back pocket of her jeans. "Colt, this is between Mo and me. I'm going to ask you to respect that."

"Oh, she really screwed up this time," he said, laughing.

Stephanie smiled. "You could say that. Now, let's go watch the rest of the movie."

The doorbell rang once more. Stephanie and Colt exchanged looks and shrugs and went to see who was at the door together. Colt pulled the door open and Randy Ransom burst in, already talking before he made it across the threshold.

"Why do I have to hear things second hand? Am I not your oldest, dearest, and of course most attractive friend?"

Colt laughed and offered his fist for a shared rap of the knuckles. "Dad! What up?"

Randy lowered his voice and did his straight butch routine. "Son. How's it hanging?"

"A little to the left," Colt answered.

Before It Stains

"Boys, there is a lady present." Stephanie stopped them before the testosterone fest got underway.

Randy engulfed her in his arms. "How are you sweetie?"

Stephanie pulled back to look in Randy's face. He was gorgeous, always had been. Randy had thick blond hair, brown eyes, and a year-round natural tan before the advent of tanning beds. They had been a striking couple back in the day. She stared into those deep-brown eyes, willing him to see she didn't want Colt to know.

"I'm fine. Mo is in LA. We're just waiting for her call. All one big happy family. Come on in. Colt needs to tell you about his homerun."

Randy got the hint. He turned to admire Colt. "See, Steph, I told you I was a good judge of sperm. Look at him. He's a young Greek God."

When Colt was old enough to understand, Stephanie and Mo sat him down, explained the whole procedure they went through to have him, and told Colt he could know who his father was when he was eighteen. Colt chose to call Randy "Dad." Randy helped find the donor, vetted him, checked his medical records, and had every available test run on the young minor league baseball player. He delivered the sperm in a brown paper bag, fresh from procuring it himself, a fact they did not discuss with Colt. Randy invested so much time in Colt's donor selection he really was the stork that brought the baby.

Stephanie tried to rescue her son. "Stop it, Randy. You're making him blush."

Randy looped his arm through Stephanie's and led them back to the den, all the while listening as Colt told the story of his booming homerun that afternoon. Stephanie went to the kitchen to bring Randy a glass of tea, while the boys

Before It Stains

talked of summer ball and the upcoming school year. The phone on the wall rang. A quiet night at home with her son was turning into anything but.

"Hello."

"Hey." It was Mo.

"I guess you made it to LA."

"Yes, I'm here. I don't want to be, but I am."

"Just do what you need to do, Mo. This is your moment. It's what you've worked so hard for."

"No, Steph, it's what we worked hard for and if you're not a part of it... It just feels so wrong for me to be here when my life is falling apart back there."

"Whatever it takes, Mo. Isn't that what you said? Well, part of it is cleaning up the mess you made. You got yourself into this, now figure it out."

"The flowers came?"

"Yes, that was very sweet, but not very smart. Colt knows you've done something. You always send flowers when you've been an ass."

"I guess I should try to be less of an ass or more creative."

"I don't want flowers, Mo. I want my life back. Unfortunately, we can't undo what's been done. I'll always know you cheated on me. I don't know if I can ever forget. I don't know if it would be fair, to either of us, to take you back and then not be able to get beyond that."

"I don't care, Stephanie. You can rag me every day for the rest of my life. At least, I'll be with you."

"You say that now, because you're scared. Five years down the road, you may not feel that way. Why postpone the inevitable?"

Mo's voice cracked with emotion. "Don't give up on us, Steph."

Before It Stains

Stephanie felt the tears begin to burn again. She couldn't let Colt see her. Meaning it as much for herself, she said, "Mo, pull it together. You have to talk to Colt. He's been waiting for you to call."

"Okay." Stephanie heard Mo exhale loudly. "Steph, will you promise me one thing? Promise you'll try to remember the good in me."

"I see it in our son, Mo. He's really the best thing we ever did together."

They were both quiet for a moment. Then Stephanie said, "All right, are you good? Can you talk to him now?"

Mo exhaled loudly, again. "Yes, put him on." She paused before saying, "I love you, Steph."

Stephanie wanted to say, "I love you, too," but she didn't. She did love Mo with every fiber of her being. That was not the problem they were dealing with. Stephanie knew she would love Mo for the rest of her life, but would she ever trust her again? Those doubts, coupled with the rising tide of tears she was about to let spill over the dam, caused Stephanie to put the receiver to her chest and call out to Colt.

"Honey, Mo's on the phone."

He answered back from the other room, "Okay, I got it."

She waited until she heard him say hello and then hung up. Randy entered the kitchen.

He tried to whisper, but he was still too loud. "What the fuck is going on? You haven't told him you threw Mo out."

"Shhh. Keep your voice down." Stephanie said, holding a finger in front of her lips.

Randy scrunched down, as if that would make him quieter. He did lower his volume, when he said, "He's going to flip out."

"I know," Stephanie mouthed and rolled her eyes.

Before It Stains

"What are you going to do?"

Stephanie answered in a whisper, "I really don't know at this point. Can you stick around until Colt goes to bed?"

"Are you kidding? This is a girl-talk opportunity from hell. It's time to plot your revenge, my specialty."

Stephanie couldn't help but laugh. She hugged Randy. "I love you, Randy Ransom. I really do."

Randy dropped the affected voice and flamboyant personality. He looked deep into her eyes. "We'll get through this. We always do. Whatever it takes."

Stephanie smiled. "That's what Mo said."

Randy released her from his arms and reached in the refrigerator, taking out a bottle of wine. "I saw the roses on the table. Nice try."

"Yes, they are beautiful, but even Colt saw it for what it was, a feeble attempt to make up for, as he said, her screw-up."

Randy went straight to the drawer where the corkscrew was stored. He knew their house as well as his own. "He's not only pretty, he's smart. He smells something. You're going to have to face him sooner or later."

"That's Mo's burden, not mine. We aren't saying anything to him until she gets back from LA on Sunday."

"Good luck with that," Randy said, pulling the cork out of the bottle with a pop to punctuate his statement.

Stephanie changed the subject. "Colt should be going to bed anytime. He has early practice and then a game tomorrow night, which by the way you must attend, and then we'll talk. I have a legal question for you."

Randy held up his hand and ticked off items as he spoke. "I can get you anything you want, the house, the cars, the underwear on her ass. Change the locks, before she gets back. Possession is a position of power."

Before It Stains

Stephanie grabbed two wine glasses from the cabinet. They looped arms and went laughing back into the den, two old friends faking not a care in the world. Colton was still talking with Mo. He was holding his cellphone, looking at the screen, and talking into the house phone.

"Yeah, I got it. Cool... Hey Mo, can you bring me a Hard Rock hat... Yeah, a black one... Okay, I will... I love you, too. Hey, you want to talk to Mom... Mo?" Colt shrugged his shoulders, turned the phone off, and put it back in the charger. "She hung up."

Stephanie answered nonchalantly, "That's okay. I already told her goodbye."

Randy nearly spilled the wine he was pouring. The double meaning was not lost on him. Colt handed Stephanie his cellphone when she sat down on the couch. He talked excitedly.

"She sent me a picture of the palm trees beside the pool. That's where she was. Look how tall those suckers are. It's still daylight. Cool huh?"

Stephanie said the first thing that came to mind, "It never rains in California," and she finally understood the lyrics.

Randy sang the rest of the verse, ending with, "...it pours, man, it pours."

This totally confused Colt. "What does that mean?"

Randy sat back in Mo's recliner. "It means, the sun always shines in California, except when it rains."

"That's lame. It would have to rain sometime for the trees to grow so tall," Colt observed.

Randy winked at Stephanie. "He's got you there."

Stephanie chuckled. "It's an old song, honey." She handed Colt back his phone. "Let's finish the movie. You have to go to bed early."

Before It Stains

Colt picked up the remote, but hesitated. He looked back at his mother. "I know there's something going on. I could hear it in Mo's voice. I can tell you've been crying a lot."

Randy raised his glass. "Gotcha again."

Stephanie glared at Randy, and then turned to her son's questioning expression. "Colt, Mo and I had a disagreement. That's all you need to know. This is between us, it has nothing to do with you."

Colt was all boy, rough and tumble, but he also possessed a sensitive side. It showed, when he said, "I just wish she wasn't way out there, all alone. She tried to act like everything was fine, but I could tell she was bummed."

Stephanie saw the harsh reality of what Mo's betrayal was going to do to Colt. She reached out her arms to him and he fell into her hug.

"It's going to be all right, Pony Boy. She'll be home Sunday. Don't worry about it, okay? You just be a teenager and let the adults figure things out."

He lifted his head and searched Stephanie's eyes. If he asked the right question, she knew she couldn't lie to him. She reached out and wrapped her finger in one of his stray curls.

"Colt, we both love you more than anything. You just remember that."

Colt's depth of understanding amazed Stephanie. He said, "That's what Jordan's parents said the last time they separated. And the stains on the walls in the dining room, how did they get there?" He was on a roll, infused with teenage moxie, venturing into adult territory, pushing boundaries. "When I put the trash in the can outside, I saw all that glass and the plates. That must have been a lot more than a disagreement."

Before It Stains

Stephanie looked at Randy for help. She got none.

Randy shrugged his shoulders, saying, "He's observant. Don't lie. It will just make it worse."

Stephanie threw daggers at Randy with her eyes. She faced Colt and told the truth, just not all of it.

"I lost my temper and threw the prime rib at Mo. I broke some dishes. I am not proud of it and hope you don't think it is acceptable behavior."

"Wow, I would have paid money to see that," Colt said with enthusiasm, then just as quickly added, "Mo didn't get hurt did she?"

Stephanie laughed. "No, honey. I do not have your aim."

Colt smiled. "Never seen you that mad. Glad it was Mo, not me. Bet she's sorry she did whatever she did."

Stephanie answered honestly. "I'm sure she is."

Luckily teenage boys have an attention span of about fifteen seconds. Randy, understanding that, suggested, "Hey, you two, let's watch the movie and take our minds off life's travails, shall we?"

Colt pushed play on the DVD. Rooster Cogburn distracted him right away, challenging the outlaws in an open field. Stephanie mouthed, "Thank you," to Randy. She picked up the wine he poured for her and took a sip. They settled in and watched the "one-eyed fat man" put the reigns in his teeth and charge full steam ahead into the fray.

#

Colt went to bed after the movie. He was quiet and hugged Stephanie tightly, before slowly climbing the stairs. Randy poured himself another glass of wine. Stephanie put her hand on top of her glass, indicating she wanted no more.

"More alcohol is not going to help," she said.

Before It Stains

Randy moved to sit beside her on the couch. "I don't know. If I was dealing with this, I'd be shit-faced, twenty-four seven."

"Not with a kid you wouldn't. We're hurting him already and he has no idea how bad things are."

"How would you like to handle this?" Randy asked.

"I'd like to crawl in bed and sleep until this nightmare is over, but I can't do that to Colt."

"Well, he's not here now, so fall apart. It's cathartic."

Stephanie turned her body to face Randy, pulling her feet under her. "How did you find out? Did Mo call you?"

"No, I got your text, but before I could call you back, your mother called me. She said she thought you needed a shoulder to cry on, so here I am shoulder ready. I even brought another shirt in case you stained this one."

Stephanie chuckled. "Of course you did."

"Tell me what happened. Your mother only said there had been a breach of trust. In case you don't know, that's what gentile southern women like Debra Austin call, the fucker cheated on me."

"Mo slept with her agent."

Randy waved a hand in the air. "Oh, who didn't see that coming?"

His words wounded Stephanie. "I didn't," she whispered.

"You were too close to it. I only met the trollop once, and I read her beads in sixty seconds. I knew right away she was poison."

Stephanie's face flushed hot. "It doesn't matter what she was. She wasn't the one wearing the wedding ring, Mo was."

"Touché. I can't argue with that."

Before It Stains

Randy was the keeper of Stephanie's secrets. He knew things about her even Mo didn't know. They shared deep conversations into the night, the kind of talks old friends have when there's nothing left to hide. Randy had a way of looking at the world from both sides, weighing the evidence, and making judgments unfettered by blame. It was simply the right thing to do. His integrity was one of the things that attracted Stephanie to him all those years ago. He wouldn't judge her for what she was about to say, and she let it all fly for the first time in twenty-four hours.

"Mo betrayed me. She betrayed Colton. Am I just supposed to pretend it didn't happen? It has to cost her something. It's cost me everything. Every dream I ever had just vanished, poof, it's gone." Stephanie's tears flowed freely now. "I'll never forget this. I'll never forget how it feels to have your whole world shattered. I can't forgive her, Randy. I just can't."

He reached out and smoothed the tears from her cheeks with his thumbs, caressing her face.

"Steph, your heart is broken. You can't see beyond that right now, but there will come a day when you can. Don't say you can't forgive her, you can, and you will. Whether it's now, ten, or even twenty years down the road, one day you'll let it go. You can't hold that kind of pain forever. It's all in the timing, sweetheart."

"Her timing sucks."

Randy laughed. "There's my girl. There's still some fight left in you. That's a good sign."

"I was good to her. I gave her everything I had to give and this is the thanks I get."

"She gave you something too, Steph, don't forget that. All you ever wanted was a family. Mo made sure that wish came true for you." Randy scooted closer and let Stephanie lean against him. He put an arm around her shoulder. "Remember how we made you stay at your mother's overnight, while Mo and I painted the nursery in that first little house? It was so small there was nowhere you could get away from the fumes."

"Yes, I remember. I loved that nursery."

"It was all Mo. She'd listened to you talk about what your fantasy nursery would look like. She tore through magazines, cutting out pictures. She saved them in a shoebox. She showed it to me. Mo knew you two didn't have the money for all the things you wanted, but she saved for that crib without you knowing."

Stephanie smiled at the memory of walking into the nursery for the first time, seeing the exact crib she coveted and knew they couldn't afford. Her parents would have bought it for her, but for some reason Stephanie and Mo had it in their heads they were going to do this on their own. They were comfortable, but an extravagance like that crib was out of reach. It was one of the sweetest gifts Mo gave her. Stephanie hadn't thought of it in years.

Randy chuckled. "Mo and I got pretty drunk that night. She told me things I've never told you, because it wasn't mine to tell."

Stephanie lifted her chin so she could see Randy's face and asked, "Like what?"

"Well, you know Mo knew she was a lesbian when she came out of the womb, unlike some of us later bloomers. She knew who she was and what she wanted out of life, when the rest of us were trying to figure it out. Mo was headed to Hollywood to make movies and screw as many beautiful women as possible. She told me being a wife and mother was not in her game plan."

Before It Stains

Stephanie's mouth opened to speak, but Randy stopped her.

"Just listen."

He handed her his wine glass. Stephanie took a sip involuntarily, while he continued.

"That all changed when she met you. Mo said she never told you she had not planned on a baby, because when you asked, she couldn't tell you no. She made up her mind to stay in school and not take an offer in LA, because she couldn't take you with her. You would have had to quit your job. Her position would not have supported you both, let alone a baby. She didn't want you working in a retail store on some corner until that MBA got you a job, while she was learning how to edit for pennies. It wasn't a great job, but it was the break she had waited for. It was Mo's answer to a lifetime of hoping for a career in the movie business and she gave it up for you."

Shocked was an understatement. Stephanie sat up on the edge of the couch, turning to face Randy. "Mo never told me about a job offer."

"She never wanted you to know. Mo said you would have forced her to take it, because you always put her first. She wanted you to have your dream, Steph. So, she painted the nursery and fell in love with that kid the moment she laid eyes on him. I reminded her of our conversation on your wedding day. I asked if she had any regrets. I'll never forget the way her face lit up. Looking at you across the room dancing with Colt, she said, 'Not one regret. Look at them. They're all I could have hoped for.' She loves you, Stephanie, probably more than you will ever know."

"Then why did she do it? Why did she sleep with her?"

Before It Stains

"I believe the circumstances are a bit shady on that issue," Randy said, leaning up to fill the wine glass they were now sharing.

Stephanie was confused. "How do you know all that if you only talked to my mother?"

"You asked me if Mo called me, not if I called her."

"That's splittin' hairs," Stephanie complained.

"I split hairs for a living. I tell my clients, answer the question you're asked, not the one they meant to ask you."

Stephanie took his wine glass and gulped this time. Alcohol might just be necessary to get through this. She handed Randy the glass back, saying, "Well, is there some kind of confidentiality in place here, or can you tell me what she said?"

"Mo gave me permission to answer any of your questions; of course, this was after I got through berating her for being so fucking stupid. How much do you know?"

"Not much," Stephanie answered. "Mo said it happened once, in LA, and she doesn't remember much of it. I'm not sure I believe that."

"I do. In my line of business, it pays to be able to detect a lie. I honestly think she blacked out for a while and when she woke up she found herself in a very compromising position."

Stephanie reacted angrily. "It's like I told Mo, she crossed the line way before then, or she never would have been in that situation. If she had made it clear she wasn't interested, Michaela wouldn't have gone after her."

"Oh my dear," Randy said, chuckling, "how naïve you are. Unavailable is much more attractive to her kind. They traveled all over the country for months. Why do you think it took a drunken night to get Mo in bed? That home-wrecker seized the opportunity to, if nothing else, make Mo think she did something."

Stephanie smirked. "I hate to break it to you, Randy, but there's going to be evidence left behind if they had sex. Mo knows if parts of her were places they shouldn't have been."

Randy wrinkled up his nose. "Eww."

Stephanie laughed. "I could say the same about swallowing."

Randy waved a hand. "To each his own, I say. Anyway, one night of drunken debauchery does not a cheater make, especially one who is so destroyed by her behavior. Honey, Mo fell in the trap, the trap of being up-and-coming. It happens all the time. Perfectly levelheaded people lose their balance when success rocks their world. The flirting was exciting. Having someone chase after you can be exhilarating. Mo lost sight of some boundaries, she got too close to the flame, and she got burned."

Stephanie was incensed. She sat up and glared at Randy. "You're not making excuses for her, are you? I don't care how hard someone came after me. I would never cross that line. I would never cheat on her."

"No? You've never been intrigued by someone since you met Mo?"

Stephanie quieted and sat back hard against the couch. She knew what was coming.

"I seem to recall a certain conversation we had about a little blonde in your *Mommy Dearest* group. Mo was gone for a month on a shoot in the mountains, you had a toddler in tow, and you were lonely. It didn't take much to get your heart thumping fast."

"Nothing happened."

Randy pointed a finger at Stephanie. "Nothing happened. That's an interesting thing for you to say. So,

Before It Stains

you're little infatuation wasn't the same as what Mo did? You said Mo crossed a line way before that night in LA. Is her line somehow different than the one you drew for yourself?"

Stephanie sulked. "That happened a long time ago."

"It did happen, though. You had a moment of weakness. It happens to everyone. We're human. When someone feeds our egos, the lines can get blurred."

"But Mo crossed that boundary, Randy. I didn't."

"She knew she was in trouble. Did she not beg you to go on that LA trip with her, in June?"

"Yes, but Colt was playing ball that weekend. One of us had to be here."

"Stephanie, he's a big boy. Your missing one or two games would not have bothered him. He has a huge support system. We would all have been at the games. You could have gone with her. You say you put Mo's needs above your own, but that's not true, is it? You put what you think are Colt's needs above everything, even Mo."

"That's as it should be, Randy."

"Not when the relationship that frames his world is in trouble. You pride yourself in taking care of your family, but you were so busy trying to make everything perfect, you couldn't see Mo was drowning."

"Why didn't she just tell me what was going on? I think I could have handled it better than this."

Randy tilted his head to one side and said, "How was she supposed to come down off that pedestal you put her on and admit she was human?"

Stephanie sat in silence. She had no earthly idea what to say. Randy waited for an answer. Finally, her voice almost a whisper, she said, "I didn't expect to be blamed for this, not by you."

Before It Stains

"There's no blame, only truth. There's no room for pride in this situation. You each have your own cross to bear here. You've sheltered and coddled Mo like a child. She's a grown woman. Treat her like one. Don't forget that you're her lover, not her mother. Mo let her recent successes go to her head. I think she's come back to earth, now. In fact, I'm pretty sure she's getting her act together as we speak. She's not going to lose you, Steph."

"Don't I get some say in this?" Stephanie asked. "What makes you think I'm ready to let her walk back in here, like nothing ever happened?"

Randy put up his hands in surrender. "I am not suggesting that at all. What I do recommend is, if you decide it's worth a try to reconcile, you and Mo sit down and re-evaluate your needs and wants. From what I see, strictly as an observer, you are both satisfied with the goals you set for each other seventeen years ago. That's a long time. You're older now. Your experiences have changed you. Look at you, Steph. You used to be a wild child. You could pass for a Republican housewife."

Stephanie was taking a sip of wine when Randy made the Republican crack. She nearly spit in the glass. "Oh, now that's low."

Randy didn't try to soothe her. "A very attractive housewife, but conservative. You've got the hair, the clothes, the house in the burbs."

"What's wrong with my hair?"

"Nothing, if you're Hilary Clinton's age and, by the way, Laura Bush wants her wardrobe back."

Stephanie popped Randy on the arm. "Oh, now you're just being mean."

"I'm serious, Steph."

Before It Stains

"I have you know I wore a sexy red dress Saturday night."

"I bet I know which one. It's your 'fuck me' dress. Only you've been saying it with the same ensemble for several years. You can afford an occasional new 'have your way with me' outfit. You've stayed in shape. You have a nice body. Show it off. When was the last time you whipped out the garters and bustier?"

Stephanie tried to recall the last time she wore any sexy lingerie. She was currently wearing old cotton underwear and a sports bra.

Randy interrupted her thoughts. "If it takes that long to remember, it's been way too long."

Stephanie put the wine glass on the coffee table and dropped her head in her hands.

Randy rubbed her back in gentle circles. "Honey, I know this is a lot to take in. If you'll let me, I'll help you. The first thing you need to do is go to work in the morning and make arrangements for the rest of the week off. You have vacation time built up, because you never take any."

He pulled her up, turned her head toward him, and said, "It's time for a makeover and a fresh start. You game?"

"Do I have a choice?"

Randy smiled. "Nope."

#

After Randy left, Stephanie locked up, turned off the lights, and took her wearied body up the stairs. She stopped at Colt's partially opened bedroom door. He didn't like to sleep with it shut, probably because Stephanie never shut his door or theirs. He went through a stage where they would find him in their bed every morning. Stephanie thought that was when she stopped wearing sexy things to bed, and sleeping naked ended long before that. Colt had complained, at five-years-old, it wasn't fair that they slept together and he had to sleep alone. That was a tough one to explain. He finally got it and quit sneaking in, and through it all, Stephanie insisted that they could not shut their door. She needed to be able to hear him. Mo said that's what the baby monitor was for, but Stephanie wouldn't budge.

She peeked in. He was asleep with his iPod blaring loudly enough for her to hear. She tiptoed into his room, removed the ear-buds, and turned off the iPod on the nightstand. She ran her fingers in his curls and kissed him lightly on the forehead. He didn't stir, sleeping peacefully through her intrusion. Stephanie quietly left the room and started across the hall.

Her hand was on the doorknob when Stephanie remembered her proclamation never to sleep in the master bedroom again. She could take the bed in the guest room downstairs, but she was too tired to walk all that way. Besides, her clothes were up here, her toiletries. It was just too much to deal with right now. She opened the door and the scent of Mo filled her head, a familiar scent that always said home. She stepped into the room just as the phone rang by the bed. It was eleven-thirty.

"Hello."

"I hope I didn't wake you," Mo said.

"No, I was just going to bed."

"It's been a long day, hasn't it?"

"Yes, it has. Randy just left. I've talked to PJ, my mom, and now you. I am about talked out. I just want to sleep."

"I just called to say good night. I won't keep you."

"Good night, Mo. I love you." It was pure habit, something she said all the time. It just came out and she couldn't take it back.

Before It Stains

"I love you, too. Sweet dreams."

Stephanie hung up. She slipped out of her clothes and dropped them on the floor, not bothering with the hamper. She grabbed the first old tee shirt she could find and crawled beneath the sheets. Stephanie thought she would have trouble sleeping, but she was bone tired and drained of emotion. Stephanie closed her eyes, sinking into the down mattress top. Without looking, she reached for Mo's pillow and pulled it tight against her. Stephanie caught a whiff of the perfume from Saturday night, the one that wasn't hers. She tossed the pillow across the room.

"Damn you, Mo, why didn't you just talk to me?"

The well of tears, she thought had dried up, began to fall. Stephanie buried her face in her pillow and cried herself to sleep.

CHAPTER SIX

Stephanie didn't feel like cooking when she awoke the next morning, but she had to feed Colt. She let him drive, which kept her attention away from her worries. He had his learner's permit a few months and, after the initial white knuckled rides, settled in to be a good driver. Still, Stephanie was on alert in the heavy morning traffic.

After arriving at the restaurant, Stephanie congratulated Colt. "Good job. I only flinched once."

They ate a quiet breakfast. Luckily Colt was like Mo, not much of a talker in the mornings, and he was starving as usual. She couldn't seem to feed him enough. He filled several plates at the buffet and consumed more food than Stephanie thought humanly possible, while she read the paper. Neither seemed to need nor want to discuss the family crisis.

She dropped him at Trevor's house. Trevor's home was ball team central. His mother, Marlene, relished the position as team Mom. Her life revolved around her five sons' activities. Stephanie used to envy her, even tried to emulate

Before It Stains

Marlene's efficiency in running her family's grueling schedule. Today, when she hugged Marlene at the door, Stephanie looked into another broken woman's eyes and decided it was true; it takes one to know one.

The drive into work was uneventful. Stephanie's mind raced with what she needed to accomplish before leaving the office today. Twenty-six people worked at Cleggland Property Management in the tall white-granite building on West Main Street. Stephanie barely spoke to anyone, simply offering a smile or a wave, as she ambled down the hall to her corner office. She did tell her assistant, Amber, to hold her calls. When Amber tried to follow her into the office, Stephanie waved her off.

"I just need a few minutes. I'll call you when I'm ready," she said, and closed the door.

Amber Hughes had been with Stephanie for two years. She was competent, and always at work, even if her hair color changed frequently. Today, it was magenta and blond, but it looked great. Amber did what was asked of her competently. That was all Stephanie cared about. Stephanie fetched her own coffee, typed her own correspondence, and generally did many of the things another boss would have expected of an office assistant. Stephanie didn't ask people to do things she was capable of doing. Like most of Stephanie's employees, Amber was happy with her job. Stephanie ran the business like she ran her home, always concerned that everyone's needs were being met.

She learned a valuable business lesson from her mentor, Royce Cleggland, the man who sold her controlling interest in the business when he retired eight years ago. He hired the best, paid them well, and treated them with dignity. Mr. Cleggland had taken a special interest in Stephanie when she was a part-time employee, working her way through business school. He taught her the business, tutored her through the real estate exams, and attended her wedding to Mo. He and his wife moved to Florida. Stephanie missed him.

Stephanie's status as managing partner afforded her the most prestigious office in the building. After taking care of her calendar and answering emails, she sat at her large oak desk, gazing out the windows, overlooking downtown Durham. Life below her went on, as if nothing had changed. Once her head had cleared somewhat, she pushed a button on the office phone.

Amber answered, "Are you ready for me now?"

"Yes, and if you would, please ask Bailey if he could join us in my office?" Stephanie hesitated. "And Amber, would you please bring me a cup of coffee?"

A few minutes later, Lance Bailey tapped on her door. He entered looking as clean-cut and tightly pressed as Stephanie expected. He was handsome with dark black hair and blue eyes. Bailey was thirty-five, married with two kids, and so deeply in the closet he could barely breathe. He was Bailey to his friends and co-workers, but Lance in his idyllic family home. Stephanie hired him away from a real estate company in Raleigh five years ago, after interviewing him at Randy's suggestion. She didn't know just how well Randy knew Bailey. Uncharacteristically, Randy danced around the issue, which said a lot in itself. Bailey was Stephanie's second in command now, and he was about to earn his money.

"Come on in," Stephanie said, standing to greet him.

Amber followed with her tablet computer and Stephanie's coffee.

"Would you close the door behind you, Amber?"

Before It Stains

Stephanie waited for Amber to hand her the coffee cup, said, "Thank you," and then sat down.

Amber and Bailey took the two leather chairs in front of Stephanie's desk. Bailey crossed his legs, with his tablet computer resting on one knee, ready to answer any of her questions. He was very good at his job and would probably leave to run his own company one day. Stephanie was about to give him that opportunity. It was not an extremely difficult thing to do. Cleggland Properties ran smoothly. Sitting in Stephanie's desk was not stressful, if everyone did his or her job as expected. The test would be how Bailey handled the bumps in the road. She had no choice but to trust he would succeed. Stephanie had her own bump laden path to walk this week.

She went straight to the point. "I'm going to take the rest of the week off."

Bailey expressed concern. "Are you okay? When you were out yesterday, I wondered if you weren't feeling well."

"You do look a little tired." Amber chimed in, never one to keep her thoughts to herself. "Are you coming down with something? I thought you were inhuman. You never get sick or take time off."

Stephanie reassured them. "I'm fine. I just have some family stuff to deal with. Colt is in a tournament this week and Mo's out of town. I'm stretched a little thin."

"Oh, praise Jesus," Amber said, raising her hands up to the heavens. "You are not perfect. I thought you could handle the world coming down around your ears and never have a hair out of place. Halleluiah, there is hope for the rest of us."

Stephanie was sure Amber meant that as a compliment, but it didn't land that way. Instead, it was just one more dig at Stephanie for being too perfect. She was anything but, in

Before It Stains

her mind. Did she come off as unflappable, even now, when it took nearly every ounce of her strength to get up off her knees and show up today? Stephanie played off the hurt with a chuckle and continued.

"I'm leaving at lunchtime and I won't be back until next Tuesday," she paused and added, "if then. Bailey you are in charge and I mean really in charge. Do not call me, text me, or email me one bit of information from this office. I do not care if the biggest client we have has a meltdown or a building crumbles, you will not look to me to find the answer. Is that clear?"

Bailey sat up a little straighter in his chair. Amber's mouth hung open. Stephanie was always available to solve a problem, rarely demanding, and never asked anyone to do her job. She'd do an employee's job, so they could have a vacation, but Stephanie never went completely off the clock. Even when she and Mo took Colton to visit Mo's mother in Florida, she was in touch with the office. Severing all ties was completely out of character. A stunned silence hung in the room.

Stephanie looked from one to the other, making sure they understood her completely. Bailey was the first to speak.

"Are you sure nothing's wrong? You're not going into the hospital or anything?"

"Oh, my God. You have cancer!" Amber exclaimed.

Stephanie started laughing. She was teetering on the edge of sanity and threatened to go into full-blown hysterics. "No," she managed to say between breaths. "I'm really very healthy. It's not cancer."

Amber clapped her hands together. "Well good, then whatever it is it can't be all that bad."

Before It Stains

Stephanie laughed even harder. Amber's interpretation of things made complete sense. She smiled at Amber, who still had the sparkle of innocence shining brightly in her young eyes. Stephanie picked up her purse and keys, still chuckling.

"I don't think I'll wait until lunch to leave. You are absolutely right, Amber. How bad can it be? At least I don't have cancer."

#

Stephanie drove around Durham aimlessly, down tree-lined streets filled with students arriving for the start of the new semester at the area's many colleges and universities. To most people it would have been a waste of time, but it was somehow freeing to know she should be at work and wasn't. Stephanie's days were measured out carefully, each task completed in turn. She was always where she should be, right on top of things, the loving wife, the caring mother, with the perfectly timed out life. What would her family do if she didn't run their lives? How would the business fare without her there to hold it together? Would the world fall apart, if Stephanie took care of herself for a while?

She pulled into the parking lot of the Sarah P. Duke Gardens. Dedicated to the woman who funded the original gardens back in 1935, the present-day gardens were considered a national architectural treasure. Five miles of paths and walkways wound through acres of carefully maintained flora and fauna. Stephanie and Mo brought Colt here to feed the ducks, but not since moving to the new house.

How long had it been since Stephanie took a leisurely stroll in the middle of the day? She really couldn't

Before It Stains

remember. Stephanie slipped off her high heels and exchanged them for tennis shoes she kept in the trunk, once again, always prepared. Stephanie began to wonder if her need for order and planning wasn't a symptom of fear, the fear that she really wasn't worth much to anyone, if she somehow wasn't prepared for everything.

Stephanie ended up on the boulder-strewn beach of the large pond, inside the Culberson Asiatic Arboretum portion of the gardens. Exotic species of water lilies, covering the color spectrum, sprouted from the still water. It was peaceful here. Stephanie sat down, letting the August mid-morning sun beat down on her. Her jacket was in the car, but Stephanie still had to roll up her sleeves, as the temperatures began to climb. She loosened a few more buttons on her silk blouse. A bullfrog jumped in the water's edge. Dragonflies buzzed the surface above the lily pads. She was surrounded by beauty with no one to share it with. It was a strange sensation.

Stephanie realized she was never really alone, never still, always moving, always planning. Even sitting with Mo and Colt, watching a movie, her mind was constantly on the move. Had she done everything she was supposed to? What about tomorrow, was it lined out for maximum productivity? Were Colt and Mo happy, had all their needs been met? Wasn't that how you showed people you loved them? What if she stopped being "the perfect" wife, mother, boss? What would be her worth? Why would anyone want her around? She rolled her neck, relaxing her tired muscles. A huge sigh left her chest.

She felt the vibration and heard the ring tone from her skirt pocket. Her phone was never far away and she always answered it, but not this morning. She pulled it out and saw Mo's smiling face on the screen. For the first time in

Before It Stains

seventeen years, Stephanie refused to take Mo's call. She was going to have to get through the day without hearing Stephanie's voice. Let Mo wonder where Stephanie was and what she was doing.

"Stephanie, it's time for a change," she said to herself.

She stayed there in the sun, shaking the breeze through her hair. Stephanie watched the swan couples and their babies float along the surface. If swans could mate for life, why did humans find it so difficult? Of course, Stephanie knew that wasn't true. She read that some female swans would select new mates, if they did not feel safe and secure with their first choice. Wandering, unfaithful mates that didn't safeguard the family were cast aside for better candidates. Stephanie's safe and secure nest had been scattered to the wind by an intruder. Any good mate would have protected their home. Stephanie was beginning to wonder if she was as smart as a swan.

Her phone vibrated in her hand and the text message tone sounded, bling-bling. Stephanie looked at the screen. She could see the message, or most of it, in the preview window. It was Mo again.

"R U OK? Called work. Amber said you…"

Stephanie slid her finger on the screen and the message window opened. She read on.

"…left and you don't have cancer???"

Stephanie laughed. Bling-bling. Another message popped up.

"What is she talking about? Where are you?"

Stephanie stared out at the pond. Her mouth curled into what Mo called her crooked grin. She aimed the camera at the pond and focused on a single white duck near her. She snapped the shot and sent it to Mo with a message.

"Duck U"

Before It Stains

Stephanie giggled as the send bar slowly turned blue. She gave it a few seconds after the message went through and sent the following text.

"Damn auto correct. I'm at Duke U, but that should have said…"

She cut off the message and sent it, waited for it to complete, counted to ten, and then sent another.

"Fuck U"

Stephanie cackled so loud it startled the ducks at the edge of the pond. They squawked loudly and batted their wings, some skimming out over the water away from the crazy blond human. Bling-bling, Mo was responding.

"Have you been drinking?"

Stephanie was enjoying this. No hazel eyes to distract her, no pouting lips to turn her heart, just a small screen and raw emotions. She typed fast.

"No, just enjoying this time free from responsibilities. #1 being, taking care of your ass."

The message went through seconds before Stephanie's phone rang. Mo's picture popped up. Stephanie declined the call. She waited. Bling-bling.

"Please, answer the phone."

Stephanie typed, "Nope, we're playing by my rules now."

Mo responded, "I see you've had time to get good and mad."

Stephanie exclaimed the words as she typed them, sending more birds to flight. "You're right. Fuck off!"

Mo was persistent. "Just tell me if you're OK. Are you sick?"

I'm fine. Never better." Stephanie hit send. Then she quickly typed, "Gotta run. Meeting with a lawyer. She's taking me to lunch. Have a nice day," and hit send again.

Before It Stains

It wasn't a lie. She was meeting with two lawyers, Randy and his boss. Let Mo worry about who Stephanie was meeting and why. Mo needed to know what it felt like to wonder, to have the seed of doubt placed in her mind. Mo had unleashed a long buried side of Stephanie. It was Mo that chased her. Stephanie was in a relationship when they met. She paid Mo no attention, even though she wanted to. Stephanie played hard to get and it drove Mo crazy. Mo was going to get all of that and more. This time Mo was dealing with a grown woman, not some twenty-three-year-old, and this Stephanie knew all the right buttons to push.

Molly Kincaid was a huge button.

#

How appropriate that Stephanie would be having lunch at the Washington Duke Inn and Golf Club, located on the campus of Duke University. Washington Duke was a prime example of starting over. He lost his first wife to typhoid fever, married another, and lost her to the same disease. He returned from the Civil War a widower with children to feed. A tobacco barn and a mule were all that were left on the Duke homestead, in Orange County, North Carolina. He had fifty cents in his pocket. That was the sum total of his worldly possessions. Washington Duke and his sons turned his misfortunes and a simple family business into one of the most influential and powerful corporations in the world, the American Tobacco Company.

Washington's son, James, was influential in moving Trinity College to Durham, in 1892. Four years later and ahead of their time, the Duke family endowed the college with what today would be millions, with the stipulation that women would be allowed to attend. Trinity College was renamed in honor of the Duke family in 1924 and stood today as a leader in academics and athletics. Washington Duke started over with mere pennies. Stephanie wasn't broke or in dire straits. If a beyond poor, broken down, widowed, wounded soldier could pull it together, Stephanie figured she could too.

Stephanie valeted her car and stepped into the sumptuous surroundings of the lobby. The inn, nestled in long leaf pines and the rolling landscape of the Duke University golf course, opened its doors in 1988. It was much newer than the interior décor led one to believe. The English antiques and fine paintings inside gave the feel of a traditional English country inn. This was what money looked like, old money, and there seemed to be plenty going around. The lobby was busy with men and women in suits and granddames dripping diamonds.

Stephanie crossed the lobby to the ladies room. She took off her jacket and fussed with her hair and blouse. Leaving the buttons open down to her cleavage was a bit sexier than her usual daytime appearance. She touched up her makeup, freshened her lipstick, and checked herself in the mirror. After her hours spent by the pond, Stephanie's cheeks were glowing from the sun and she liked the untamed way her hair fell around her face. She put her cellphone on vibrate, so Mo wouldn't disturb them with a barrage of text messages, and headed out to meet her old flame. Stephanie was feeling a bit untamed herself, as she walked toward the hostess in the Fairview dining room and gave her name.

"Stephanie Austin. I have a luncheon with…"

The woman smiled brightly. "Ah yes, Ms. Austin. You're with Ms. Kincaid's party. Please, follow me."

The hostess led Stephanie into the dining room and down toward the terrace overlooking the golf course. Just inside the terrace doors, Stephanie spotted Randy seated with the sandy-haired blonde from her past. Her stomach suddenly filled with butterflies, batting their wings furiously. Even though Molly was Randy's boss, Stephanie had not seen her in person for at least fifteen years. Mo liked it that way. Of all the women Stephanie encountered, only one could send Mo into a jealous fit at the mention of her name, Molly. Stephanie thought it was silly. She obviously chose Mo from the beginning. Approaching the table, she got a good look at the now famous defense attorney. Mo had reason to be jealous. Little Molly had grown up.

"Ms. Kincaid, your guest is here," the hostess said, with the appropriate deference to the woman she was speaking with, and then stepped away.

Randy and Molly both stood up to greet Stephanie. Randy gave her a quick hug.

"You look fabulous," he said, pecking her on the cheek.

Stephanie and Molly took each other in from head to toe. What Stephanie saw before her was the twenty-one-year-old, freckle-faced girl of her past transformed into a beautiful woman. People said she resembled Jodie Foster, but to Stephanie she was all Molly, the feisty little softball player she had fallen in love with. Molly's grin and dimple had not changed. Stephanie hesitated for only a moment and then opened her arms.

She said only, "Molly," but it meant so much more.

"Stephanie, you look wonderful," Molly said, stepping into the slightly taller woman's embrace. "It's really good to see you."

"You, too," Stephanie responded, releasing Molly from her arms. They took their respective seats. "You look amazing. Being a high powered attorney agrees with you."

Before It Stains

Molly blushed, but ignored the compliment. Her steel-blue eyes sparkled, as she grinned at Stephanie. "I can't say that it's a bad life. How's your son?"

"Colt is great. He's growing so fast. He'll be sixteen in a couple of months."

"Wow! Has it been that long? I saw you right after he was born. Remember? You and Mo were in the grocery store."

Stephanie remembered, no question about that. Mo had not liked running into her old rival. Especially since Stephanie and Molly spent the whole time in the store walking up and down the aisles together, talking as if Mo wasn't there, or at least that's how Mo had seen it. After that, any invitations to parties or activities including Molly were conveniently inconvenient for Mo. Stephanie thought it was cute and had no real desire to see Molly, so she played along.

"Yes, I'm sorry I haven't been a better friend," Stephanie replied. "I did follow your career through Randy, though. You're quite accomplished for a thirty-eight-year-old."

Molly laughed. "Oh, I had my fair share of breaks. Look at you, running the company now. I'd say you're quite successful in your own right."

"I guess we both got what we wanted," Stephanie said.

Molly lowered her voice just a touch and said, "Yes, I guess we did."

Molly's phone vibrated on the table. It saved them from the awkward silence that was about to take place.

"I need to take this call. Would you excuse me for a moment?"

Molly walked toward the lobby. Cellphone conversations were not allowed in the swank establishment.

Before It Stains

Stephanie looked over at Randy, who was beaming from ear to ear. She cocked her head to one side and said, "I know that look, Randall. What are you up to?"

"Not a thing, darling, not a thing. I just enjoy watching you two. The sparks still seem to be flying, don't you think?"

"No, I don't think. I'm not interested in Molly any more than she's interested in me. Old flames, that's all."

"Just imagine if you had stayed with Molly. You would be so rich you couldn't spend it all."

"I am rich, Randy, just not that kind of rich. I have a family. Molly has a big old empty house from what you've told me."

"Well, her bedroom doesn't stay very empty. You should see the one she's been dating. She looks like Charlize Theron. She's a veterinarian. Lives in the southwest, I think, a long distance relationship. That appears to be the way she likes them, at a distance. Still pining for her first love, you."

"That's your fantasy, Randy, not hers. If I was single, I would probably be the same way."

Randy patted her hand. "Ah, but you are single, at the moment anyway. Give it a whirl, it might be fun."

"I'm not going to sleep with Molly to get back at Mo. That is not a very mature way to handle things."

"You don't have to sleep with her, but if you tell Mo you've seen Molly, she'll snap to attention, that's for sure."

"You're the one that always brings Molly up around Mo. You do it because it drives her crazy."

"I think Mo needs to be reminded on occasion that you had other options. Since you don't seem to be capable of that, I do it for you. I bet she is climbing the walls right now. I just sent her a picture of you hugging Molly."

Before It Stains

"You didn't!"

Randy smiled mischievously. "I most certainly did. Don't tell me you don't want her wondering what you're up to. She texted me just before you got here, wanting to know what female lawyer was taking you to lunch. Now, how did she know that unless you told her? I know you, Steph. You didn't have the guts to tell her outright. You told her you were seeing a lawyer, but stopped short of saying it was Molly. Chicken shit!"

Randy's phone vibrated on the table. "Ah, and here comes the reply."

Stephanie leaned over trying to read the message on the screen. Randy moved the phone so she couldn't see.

"What did she say?" Stephanie asked, more interested than she thought she'd be at Mo's reaction.

"I believe she's telling me to kiss part of her anatomy and then she would like to have sex with me."

He turned the phone around so Stephanie could see. The picture had done its appointed duty. Mo was livid.

Mo wrote, "Kiss my ass, Randy. FUCK YOU!"

Randy put his finger to his chin and looked up at the ceiling. "Hum. How should I respond?"

Stephanie had to admit she was glad Randy had done what she wanted to do, make Mo worry. She delighted in Mo's reaction to the picture, but tried to hide it.

"Tell her it's just a meeting to go over her contract."

"Oh, hell no," Randy said, a little too loudly. Other patrons turned to look at them. He lowered his voice. "She needs a dose of reality and if you're not going to give it to her, I will."

He started typing fast. Stephanie couldn't see his response, but with his wit, it was sure to be a stinging retort. He hit send, laughing.

Before It Stains

Stephanie was almost afraid to ask. "What did you say?"

Randy showed her the message on the screen. "They always did make such a cute couple. Look, even their hair color matches."

Mo's answer popped up, before Randy took the phone away. "Tell her to answer the phone. I know she's there with you."

Stephanie's phone started vibrating. She pulled it out of her pocket and once again declined the call.

"Good girl," Randy said, and then read aloud as he typed into his phone. "Sorry, no cellphone calls in the dining room. I can send more pics if you want."

Stephanie laughed. Randy brought out a devilish streak in her and encouraged her to do and say things she wouldn't normally, like now, when she held up her middle finger and said, "Hey, send this."

"Now, we're talking." Randy snapped the picture and sent it, just as Molly walked back to the table.

"I see you two have not changed in the least," Molly said, as she took her seat. "Let me guess, you're antagonizing Mo. I don't know how she survived all these years with the two of you ganging up on her."

Randy waved a hand in the air. "She'll live. It's nothing she doesn't deserve, at the moment."

Stephanie suddenly wondered how much information Randy had relayed to Molly. Her answer came with Molly's next statement.

"That brings us to why we're all here. First of all, Stephanie, I'm sorry. I never imagined this would happen to you and Mo. I hope things work out for the best. Now, about this contract with the agent, I made a few phone calls.

Before It Stains

I don't think there will be any problem getting Mo out of it."

"What makes you say that?" Stephanie asked, forgetting that Randy had discussed her personal life with, of all people, Molly.

"I Googled this woman and found out who her father is. He's a big time agent with a huge clientele. The last thing he wants is a sexual harassment suit against his daughter, not good for business. At least, that's what one of his lawyers told me, in confidence. We went to law school together. It pays to know who you're dealing with."

"So what do we do now?"

Randy reached under the table, picking up his briefcase. He opened it, pulled out an envelope, and handed it to Stephanie. "This letter went out to Michaela, today. It was also faxed to her father's office, as he has interest in her vanity agency. It appears the business is a way to keep Michaela out of Daddy's hair."

Stephanie opened the envelope. On Kincaid Law Firm stationary, the letter stated Mo's intentions of suing Michaela for the entire amount of her studio contract, as well as asking for damages caused by the stress Michaela put Mo's family through. Molly had signed the letter.

Molly waited for Stephanie to finish reading. When she raised her eyes from the paper, Molly spoke.

"It won't be long, now. We'll be hearing back from them very soon. They'll want to stop us from actually filing the suit, to keep it out of the media. I was assured that once Daddy saw the letter, Mo's contract would be null and void, probably with a healthy offer to hush Mo up. I wish Mo had come to Randy, before it went this far. We could have ended this a lot sooner, but I'm sure she had her reasons for using a different law firm."

Before It Stains

Stephanie smiled. "Yes, she had her reasons." She and Molly exchanged looks of understanding. "Thank you, Molly. I don't know how to repay you."

A grin lit up Molly's face. "No repayment necessary, but if things don't work out with Mo give me a call." Molly winked and then stood up. "I have to go, now. It was really good to see you."

"You're not staying for lunch?" Stephanie asked.

"No, I have some business to take care of in Texas. I should have left this morning, but I wanted to see you."

Stephanie stood and hugged Molly tightly.

Molly returned the embrace and then whispered into Stephanie's ear, "I should have fought harder for you. Tell Mo she has every reason to be jealous. I'd take you back in a minute."

Molly walked away without another word, signaling to the waiter that it was time to approach the table. Stephanie slowly retook her seat after watching Molly leave. The waiter asked for their order and sensing Stephanie's current confusion, Randy ordered summer salads for them both. After the waiter left, Randy leaned forward, taking one of Stephanie's hands in his.

"See, I told you. Mo's not the only woman out there who wants you. Molly, for one, is still in love with you."

Stephanie looked at the letter, lying open on the table in front of her. "That must have been hard for her to write that for Mo."

Randy smiled. "She didn't do it for Mo. Quite frankly, I think she's hoping you throw Mo out on her ass, but Molly doesn't want to see you hurt by this contract. She was protecting you, not Mo."

Before It Stains

"That was really sweet." Stephanie said, while folding the letter and placing it back in the envelope. "I hope Mo appreciates it."

"I hope Mo appreciates you. It was your idea to go after Michaela for sexual harassment. After we talked last night, I approached Molly this morning. She said you were a smart girl."

Stephanie blushed from Randy's statement and the realization that Molly really did admire her, did respect her, maybe even still loved her. She glanced at the path Molly had taken out of the room.

"Molly's a smart girl, too," Stephanie said. "She knew when it was time to walk away."

Randy asked, "Then or now?"

Stephanie sighed and gave a one-word answer. "Both."

CHAPTER SEVEN

Colt was with his teammates at the coach's house. Stephanie had nothing to do until time to go to the ballpark. After lunch, Randy made her promise to do something for herself with the rest of her day. All Stephanie wanted to do was go home and take a nap. That was something she rarely did and considered it a treat to have the time alone to do it. All the way home she fought the urge to think, what if? What if she had picked Molly over Mo? She spoke to her reflection in the rearview mirror.

"Don't go there, Stephanie."

Just as she unlocked the front door, the vibration in her pocket made her stop and pull out her phone. It might be Colt, so she had to look.

It was Mo again, texting this time. Her message, "Please, please, check your email."

"Dammit, Mo! I just don't want to talk to you right now," Stephanie said aloud.

Stephanie's hurts were turning to anger. She was swiftly moving through the stages of grief. Slamming the front door

Before It Stains

behind her, Stephanie stormed into Mo's office. They shared it, but it was mostly Mo's, filled with editing computers and the trappings of Mo's profession. Books lined the walls from the classics to textbooks. Stephanie had her own laptop and preferred to sit in the den to work, but she occasionally used the desktop computer, as she had yesterday. The napkin still lay inside the file folder where she placed it on the desk. She lifted the folder without opening it, crossed to the safe in the corner, and put the file inside. Molly may have confidence that Michaela was done, but Stephanie wasn't taking any chances.

She turned on the computer and left to change clothes. Returning in flannel pajama pants and a tee shirt, she felt more relaxed and less angry at Mo's insistence that she speak with her. She typed in her password and the home screen appeared. After waiting to let the computer finish the boot up, she hit the email button. Stephanie checked and cleared the inbox this morning that was now showing five messages from Mo, all sent in the last few hours. The subject line of each message read, "Please, talk to me."

She went to the earliest message on the list and clicked on it. The email was sent right after Stephanie's text messages from the pond.

> *Steph,*
> *I deserve your anger, but please don't do anything until I get home. I need to talk to you. I need to know you're all right. Amber said you took off work until next Tuesday. I'm worried. I hope you just need the time to think. I know you're trying to make sense of all this, but please wait for me. I'll be there as soon as I can get away from here.*
> *I love you.*

Before It Stains

Mo

Stephanie snorted her displeasure. "You think I give a rat's ass, if you're worried?"

She clicked on the next email, which would have arrived about the time she entered the Inn.

Steph,
I have an idea who you're meeting and I really hope it's not her. I don't stand a chance of keeping you, if she gets involved. Just remember you chose me once. You must have had a reason.
Mo

"Ooo… I bet that picture really hacked you off after that, huh?" Stephanie taunted the screen, before clicking on the next email, which had arrived at the time she was talking to Molly.

Dammit Steph! Could you show just a little bit more cleavage? Did Randy set this up? Are you going to pay me back by fucking your old girlfriend?

"Hum. No salutation that time. Pretty pissed, aren't you? Good. I hope you think I went upstairs at the Duke Inn and fucked Molly's brains out. I hope you see it very clearly, because I see you with that bitch every time I close my eyes."

The following email had arrived seconds after the last one. Stephanie opened it, her level of anger climbing with each successive click.

Stephanie,
I'm sorry about the last email. I wish I could take it back. I would leave here this minute, if it

Before It Stains

wouldn't cost us everything, but staying here is costing me more than possessions. I'm caught here, trying desperately to get back to you. I'm talking to the studio about re-working my contract. It's hard to negotiate without an agent and Michaela is missing in action. I'm working on it, Steph. I'm getting out of here.
I don't blame you for wanting to hurt me. Like I said, I deserve it. I have no right to accuse you of anything. I guess I really don't have any right to say anything at all.
You said I took you for granted. I know I've let you take care of us, our family. I know I've let you bear the responsibility for nearly everything in our lives. I know I need to step up. But you have to know I never took you for granted. I guess I didn't tell you enough how the things you do for Colt and me, big and small, mean so much. I promise you, not another day will go by when you don't know how much you mean to me. I meant what I said, whatever it takes.
You say you'll never forget what I did. I won't either, but I'm sure telling you it won't happen again is useless. What if I said I am ashamed and disgusted with my behavior? What if I said I don't want our son to think it's okay to betray a trust? What if I said the most important thing in the world to me is my family? Would any of that matter?
I'm going to call Colt on his cell, so I won't bother you anymore. I hope that you will call me. I'd really like to hear your voice and know that you're okay.

Before It Stains

I love you.
Mo
PS. I got the pic of you shooting me the bird. I smiled. At least you're still wearing your wedding ring.

Stephanie looked down at her left hand. She twirled the diamond around her ring finger with her thumb. She'd never thought about taking it off. It was a part of her and it symbolized so much. Except for her yearly mammogram, when she had to remove all her jewelry, the wedding band and engagement ring had not been off her finger since Mo put them there. Stephanie knew if she took them off, it would be over. She wasn't ready to take that step, yet. She clicked on the final email. Mo sent it just before Stephanie got home.

Steph,
I just received a fax from Randy with the letter to Michaela. I really don't know what to say. He explained what you did and I am grateful beyond words. I sent Molly an email thanking her. I am now thanking you. Once again, you came through for me, for us. I'm going back into the studio in a few minutes. I just wanted to tell you how much I love you and how unbelievably lucky I am that you loved me for seventeen years. I wouldn't be here without you, but the thing is, I don't want to be here anymore. I belong with you and Colt. The rest of this, well, the sooner I'm done with LA, the better. I hope you can love a college professor with time on her hands. I'm done with all this,

Before It Stains

*Steph. I want to come home. I hope I still have
one when I get there.
I love you.
Mo*

Stephanie reread the message. She blinked back tears. Mo had dreamed of being a movie director her whole life. Mo's mother told Stephanie, Mo would have made a movie of her own birth, if someone had handed her a camera. Now, she wanted to give that up to save their marriage. Stephanie didn't want Mo to wake up one day, down the road, and blame her for ending a life's dream. She hit reply and wrote.

*Mo,
I appreciate your thanking Molly. I know that was hard for you. You must know it was hard for her, as well. Now that Michaela will soon be out of our lives, I think we can have a rational discussion about our future together. That said, I don't want you to quit your dream of directing a feature film some day. You'll resent me later. Our problems have nothing to do with the movie business. You let a touch of notoriety go to your head and I stood around and let you. We both made mistakes. We can't blame an entire industry for our shortcomings. We were in trouble long before this happened and neither one of us saw it. I see it now, and I need some time to figure out what went wrong. I'm not talking to you, because I've never been able to resist you. I need to figure out what's best for Colt and me. I will not deny you access to him, but I may have to deny you access to me. Back*

Before It Stains

off, Mo, and give me time to think. I'll have Colt call you after the game.
You can't expect me to just take your word that this would never happen again. Once you've done it, there is no saying, "I wouldn't do that," now is there?
Steph
P.S. They have perfectly good movie studios in Wilmington.

Stephanie sent the email, closed the program, and shut down the computer. She went to the den and curled up on the couch. Stephanie set the alarm on her phone, so she wouldn't be late for Colt's game. Then she closed her eyes and said a soft prayer.

"Please, may I have a moment without dreams? Can I just sleep here for a while without the pain? I really need a nap. I think my plate is full, so you can stop heaping things on it. And oh, by the way, I am thankful for all I've been given and equally thankful for those things I have not had to suffer, but I could use a break here, just so you know."

Stephanie breathed an enormous sigh and faded off to sleep.

#

Stephanie awakened to the doorbell ringing and knocks on the front door, just before her alarm was set to go off. She ignored it at first, not really awake, but the second knocks were louder and the ringing more persistent. Stephanie pulled herself out of the daze of sleep and went to see who it was. When she entered the foyer, she saw her mother and PJ through the beveled glass in the door. She opened the door and then turned without speaking, heading for the kitchen. The two women followed her.

Her mother spoke first. "I hear you've taken some time off."

"Good Lord, don't people have anything to do, but get in my business?"

"You are my business," her mother said.

"Sorry, Mom. It's been a long day."

PJ pointed at Stephanie's hair. "Looks like you took a nap. That's good. I'm sure you needed the rest."

Stephanie stopped at the refrigerator door and saw her reflection in the stainless steel. Her hair was smashed flat on one side, pushed up about three inches, forming half of the McDonald's arches. She snatched the door open and pulled out a pitcher of sweetened tea.

"Here, let me pour the tea," her mother said, taking the pitcher from Stephanie. "You all go on and sit down. I'll bring it to you."

PJ followed Stephanie back to the den. "I talked to Mo today. She was pretty upset about you seeing Molly. She's afraid, I mean really afraid."

"She should be," Stephanie snapped.

"Oooo, girl got some attitude today," PJ said, backing away in mock fear.

"It's been quite an uplifting experience not to be the cheerleader in the room," Stephanie said.

"That's what I'm talkin' about. Get righteous."

Debra Austin entered the den as if she was serving afternoon tea in the garden, all smiles, and politeness. She was Stephanie's role model, the perfect wife, and mother. Stephanie clenched her jaw and tried to hold the words back, but they spewed out.

Before It Stains

"How could you not tell me my father cheated on you? How could you act like nothing ever happened?"

PJ put her hand up, her once smiling face slackened to a frown. "Damn girl, I said righteous, not hateful."

Debra smiled. "It's quite all right, PJ. It's a legitimate question." She handed Stephanie a glass of tea. "Here, drink this. It'll cool you down a peg."

Stephanie fell back against the couch, pouting. She knew she was doing it, but it felt good. Maybe that's why kids rolled their lips out and sulked for hours in front of anyone that would watch. The outward expression of enormous disappointment Stephanie felt cleansed her soul somehow. There was no doubt and no words necessary for the people in the room to understand, "Hell yes, I'm mad! I'm pissed, I'm hurt, and I just want to wallow in my misery, thank you!"

"You had that same look on your face when I said you could not go to the Bahamas for spring break, at barely seventeen. What sane adult would volunteer to take a group of teenagers to a tropical island?"

Stephanie recalled being left out when all her friends went on the trip. She brooded the entire break and for some time afterward.

"I remember, you ignored my distress and acted as if nothing was wrong. I eventually moved on to something new and we never spoke of it again. Was that the key to how you got by, Mom? Just pretend it isn't there and it will go away."

PJ stood up. "I think I'll go outside and let you have some privacy."

Debra waved PJ back down on the couch. "No, stay. What I'm about to say might benefit you, one day." She turned back to her daughter. "Stephanie, there was no need

Before It Stains

to discuss our decision to keep you home. It was a done deal. The trip was already happening while you moped around the house. Had I given into your teenage lament, we would have spent hours with you in tears and me trying to make you understand that we could not let a child your age go to another country with a gaggle of teenagers. You're a mother now. You know exactly how futile that would have been. Life's too short to waste on things that just don't matter anymore. You figured it out and moved on."

Stephanie stiffened. "Is that how you handled the affair? Just moved on?"

Debra's voice dropped to a less accommodating tone. "Okay, we'll have this conversation, but only once, so listen up. You think less of me, because I didn't throw a big fit and involve the kids in the mess your father and I made. And yes, we made that mess together."

Stephanie tried to say, "I didn't -"

Her mother raised her hand for silence. "You wanted to know, so here it is. Judge me if you want to. I did what I thought was best for all of us."

Stephanie sank further back into the couch, as her mother continued.

"You don't pick who you fall in love with, it just happens to you. I fell in love with your father and he with me over a spilled glass of milk. I know you've heard this story, but PJ hasn't. I was in a little drugstore downtown, working the lunch counter after school. I was delivering a glass of milk to a table and ran into Stephanie's father. The milk went everywhere, but he caught the glass. I was so impressed, I fell for him on the spot."

"That's so sweet." PJ said.

"We got married while he was in college, just after I graduated high school. Those first few years were very hard, but we had so much fun with nothing, I wonder why we need so much now? He got his degree and went to work, providing for his family. I stayed home and had babies. That was our life, work and family. Somewhere in there we both got lost in our own little worlds, his at work and mine at home. We were happy, but it wasn't fun anymore. That's when it happened."

Stephanie sat up, incredulous. "So you blame yourself for not keeping him entertained?"

"I blamed myself for not knowing something was wrong. Don't misunderstand, there were plenty of angry words and tears, but when I got beyond the hurt I felt, I could see his pain, too. We hurt each other, but we couldn't stop loving each other. As hard as I tried, I could not imagine my life without him. I forgave him, slowly, but I forgave him. To have continued to drag out the fighting, let it escalate, grow a life of its own, would have been fatal to our marriage. Rehashing and bringing up old hurts just sucks the life out of things. It was spilled milk. We wiped it up before it stained and moved on."

Stephanie sat very still, but her mind was racing, searching her mother's eyes for the answer. Debra saw the question, sensing what her daughter wanted to know.

"Honey, nobody can tell you what to do. It's all up to you, what you can sit with, and what you can't. What I will tell you is this, if you stay in this marriage, you have to let go of the hurt and anger. It will eat you from the inside out and all of it will have been wasted time, best spent elsewhere, for everyone concerned."

"Amen to that," PJ said, quietly.

"It would help if I wasn't thinking about it all the time." Stephanie was still irritated, but she was cooling down. "I'm sorry, Mom. I shouldn't take my frustrations out on you."

Before It Stains

The warmth returned to Debra's voice. "You're just venting. Better me than some unsuspecting stranger at the drive-thru."

PJ looked at her watch. "You better get moving, unless you're wearing a ball cap. That's what we call bed hair, not your best look."

Stephanie twirled a lock of her shoulder length hair between two fingers. "I'm thinking about cutting it off. What do you think?"

"I think that would be a good start," her mother answered.

"Go ahead, Steph," PJ said. "Changing your hair can change your attitude."

Stephanie looked at the three inch tall, Grace Jones like, boxed hair on PJ's head, and smiled.

"Yes, PJ, I think it's time for a change of attitude."

#

Stephanie tried to brush her hair into shape, but it was no use. She pulled it back into a short ponytail and stuck one of Colt's spare team caps on her head. She wore shorts and a team logo tee shirt, and large dark sunglasses. Stephanie wanted to be comfortable and invisible. She was in no mood for girl-talk. She just wanted to watch her son pitch a game of baseball. Stephanie realized this was going to be impossible almost immediately upon sitting down.

Randy was waiting by the stands when Stephanie arrived with her mother and PJ in tow. Stephanie stopped to talk to Colt at the fence, while the others found seats.

"How are you feeling? Did you eat enough? Remember to stay hydrated and keep your arm warm."

Colt looped his fingers through the fence and grinned. "I got this, Mom."

Before It Stains

"Okay, just checking," Stephanie said, looping a finger through one of his. "You'll be great. Everybody's here."

"Mo called," Colt commented. "She said all the same stuff."

"Good, I'm glad you were able to talk to her."

Colt had to go when the coach called the team together. He jogged backwards away from her, grinning. "Take some pictures and send them to her. Coach won't let us have our phones out."

Stephanie smiled and waved. "I will. Have fun!"

When Stephanie joined the others in the stands, she was left sitting on the open end of the group, next to PJ. Randy was at the other end of the row. Her mother was sandwiched between Randy and PJ. On Stephanie's right were a couple of empty spaces before the aisle. In the next section over sat "the mothers." Stephanie and Mo supported Colt in his athletic endeavors, but they were not fanatical about it. Their hopes and dreams for Colt did not hinge on his prowess on the field. "The mothers" were the ones who knew everyone's batting average and most definitely had an opinion on which boys "deserved" to play. They took being supportive to the next level. While appearing mild mannered and caring, these women could turn into a pack of wolves if things went against their sons on the field. There were also "the fathers," but they tended to band together down by the fence. Stephanie was one of "the other mothers and fathers," the ones who cheered for everyone and were proud, win or lose. They were scattered around the stands, distancing themselves from "the mothers and fathers." All except Stephanie, whom her family had left woefully exposed.

Stephanie was glad when Marlene, Trevor's mom, sat down beside her. Marlene had too many sons in too many

Before It Stains

sports to invest as much energy in their games as "the mothers" did. Colt and Trevor were the youngest players on this All-Star team. They came as a set, Colt the pitcher and Trevor the catcher. They were best friends, since meeting at age nine in little league, and a match made in baseball heaven. Colt never tired of pitching and Trevor never tired of catching. Colt took the mound and the two proud mothers watched their sons warm up. No one spoke. The steady pop in Trevor's glove grew crisper, as Colt began to bear down. After one particularly loud pop, Colt smiled and looked in the stands for his extended family. They all waved back.

Randy even got in touch with his old ball playing butch days and shouted, "Atta boy, Colt!"

"He looks really good tonight," Marlene said. "You wouldn't know he had the weight of the world on his shoulders."

Stephanie turned to face Marlene. "What are you talking about?" she asked.

Whispering conspiratorially, Marlene said, "Colt told Trevor you and Mo were splitting up. I guess I can tell you now, I've always been jealous."

Evidently, Marlene hadn't whispered softly enough. PJ let out a giggle and covered it with a cough.

Stephanie responded to Marlene's prying with, "He told Trevor what, exactly?"

Marlene looked around, checking to see if anyone was listening. "Trevor said that Colt said you and Mo had a huge fight. Dishes were broken, and Mo sent lots of flowers. He even said there was blood on the walls, but that it was probably from the prime rib you threw."

"And from that you got we are splitting up. Marlene, you know how dramatic teenage boys can be."

Before It Stains

"Well, like I said, I was always so jealous of how you two got along. I never imagined you ever had a fight. From the sounds of what happened that was no small disagreement. That usually means money or a woman. My bet is a woman. Someone like Mo - out in LA - all alone. I'm just sayin'."

"What do you mean, someone like Mo?" Stephanie had gone beyond disbelief at Marlene's intrusion into her personal life. She now wanted to know what Marlene knew.

"You know," Marlene said, punching Stephanie lightly in the thigh. "She's Mo. She's attractive and funny. I'm sure she has to fight the women off."

PJ started having a coughing fit and the umpire yelled, "Play ball," saving Stephanie for the moment. She wasn't sure how she was supposed to respond to Marlene's thinly veiled attraction to Mo. Colt threw two balls out of the strike zone, before he settled down and struck out the first two batters. The third batter flew out to centerfield. Colt let that pitch get too high in the strike zone. He shook his head coming off the mound, before Trevor greeted him with a slap on the back. His worried look faded and Colt disappeared into the dugout.

Marlene jumped right back into the conversation, as if no time had gone by. "I know how difficult these things can be, not that I've experienced it myself."

Stephanie didn't believe that for a minute, but she kept her eyes focused on the end of the dugout. It worked and Marlene stood to go.

"Well, if you need anything, just let me know. That goes for Mo, as well. You're both my friends."

Stephanie managed to smile at Marlene and say, "Thank you, I'll be sure to tell her."

Before It Stains

Marlene was just too dumb to walk away. "She has my number. We used to talk all the time - about the boys, you know."

The daggers Stephanie shot with her eyes were hidden behind her oversized sunglasses. Her smile belied her true feelings, which were to come right out and ask Marlene if she was looking to get Mo in bed, now that she was free of the wife.

Instead, she said, "I'm glad Colt has someone to confide in, like Trevor, but really, we have not split up. I hope you'll help by not letting this misunderstanding go any further."

Marlene looked over her shoulder toward "the mothers," saying, "Too late. Jordan knows and she was sitting with Wyatt's mother. We all know what a rumormonger she is."

Stephanie was thinking the same thing about Marlene. PJ finally came to the rescue.

She pointed at her throat and said, in a dry whisper, "I think I swallowed a bug." Cough - cough. "Need water."

"Excuse us, Marlene. I need to help PJ find some water."

Stephanie was up, pulling PJ along, before she finished her sentence. Colt was fifth up to bat so they had time to get back before he hit, if they even made it that far down the batting order. The guy throwing against them was the best in the league. Colt had never had so much as a base hit off the guy. Stephanie nearly pulled PJ down the steps, not stopping until they were behind the stands, where she began to pace.

"Can you believe the nerve of that woman? She practically drooled over the prospects of a single Mo."

Before It Stains

PJ was laughing, even after the harrowing descent she'd just been through. "Lord, girl, if you don't take Mo back, she'll be hounded by Marlene. You have to save her."

"Why should I save Mo?" Stephanie asked. "I didn't do anything and I'm here fending off the rumor mill, while she's out doing God knows what in LA."

"She has no idea what she's missing," PJ said, still laughing. "The look on your face was priceless." She mimicked Stephanie, "Thank you, I'll be sure to tell her."

"Shut up, you," Stephanie said. "You were absolutely no help."

"I got you out of there, didn't I?"

Stephanie smiled. "Yes, you did."

The crack of the bat on the ball drew their attention to the field. From what they could see through the legs in the stands, Trevor was safe at first base.

Stephanie rushed PJ. "Let's get you that water and get back. Colt might make it up to bat."

Luckily, there was a short line at the concession stand. Stephanie and PJ made it back to their seats in time to see Wyatt take his third strike, much to his mother's displeasure.

She screamed, "Are you blind? That was down around his ankles. How much did his daddy pay you to make that call?"

Stephanie shook her head. Wyatt did not argue the umpire's call. He walked slowly back to the dugout, while the rest of his team took the field. Stephanie was sure his mother's behavior embarrassed him. God help the child with the overzealous parent in the stands. One of the coaches put his arm around Wyatt and must have said something funny. Wyatt beamed and hustled for his glove. At least some of the adults involved had things in perspective. Stephanie was pondering this when Geri Lee sat down beside her.

"Hey, Steph. Colt looks good tonight."

Geri Lee Strand was a very pretty woman. She had long brown hair and green eyes. Tall and thin, Geri Lee turned heads. That apparently was the problem in her marriage. Marlene, the infinite fountain of gossip, told Stephanie and Mo that Geri Lee and her husband were swingers, but Geri Lee liked it a bit more than her husband. It caused their recent separation and impending divorce.

Stephanie nodded, but didn't take her eyes off Colt as he warmed up. "Yes, he does."

Geri Lee leaned in so her shoulder was touching Stephanie's. In a hushed voice she said, "I heard about you and Mo. I would have thrown a chair through the dining room window, too. I'm not surprised there was blood shed. Of all things for Mo to do, I would never have imagined she'd sleep with a man."

Geri Lee had been leaning a bit too heavily into her conversation. Stephanie nearly toppled the woman, when she sat back quickly in astonishment.

Tension clearly rising in her voice, Stephanie asked, "What are you talking about?"

"I know it's hard to take it all in, I mean, unless you had some agreement that you could see other people."

Stephanie cut Geri Lee off. "I don't know what you think you know, but none of it is true. I did not throw a chair through a window and Mo did not sleep with a man."

Geri Lee looked surprised. "Oh, I must have misunderstood. I was told you threw her out and she moved to LA to live with this guy. So does that mean my coming to ask you to coffee at my house," she paused and batted her eyelashes, "was a lost cause? You're still not available, I take it?"

PJ sprayed the water she was drinking down the front of her shirt. She was laughing so hard she fell over on Stephanie's mother, who had no idea what was happening. Stephanie swallowed hard, smiled, and looked Geri Lee straight in the eye.

"I'm flattered by the invitation, but no, I am not available."

This sent PJ into slapping her thigh guffaws. Stephanie's mother, having heard her reply to Geri Lee, was chuckling as well. Geri Lee looked around Stephanie at PJ, shrugging her shoulders.

"What's the matter with her?"

Stephanie looked at PJ and said, "Oh, I think we got her out of the hospital a little too soon." She turned back to Geri Lee. "She's been off her meds."

"Oh, I understand that. When I forget to take mine I can be a real weirdo." Geri Lee snorted a very unpleasant laugh and stood up. "Well, if you change your mind, my number's on the team roster."

Stephanie could barely keep from laughing, when she said, "I'll keep that in mind."

Geri Lee walked back to her seat, but not before she waved and winked at Stephanie. PJ was still immersed in convulsive laughter, leaning on Debra when Stephanie turned around.

"I'm so glad you're enjoying yourself, Patrice." Stephanie only called her that when PJ was being an ass. Even her hated name didn't break PJ's amusement. "Is it that funny that someone would hit on me?"

PJ panted to get air and fanned herself. Tears were running down her cheeks. She finally managed to say, "No,

Before It Stains

it was you throwing the chair through the window first." She was overcome by the giggles and had to take a break, before adding, "Then the thing about Mo with a man." More giggles were followed by, "I'm sorry, I could not stop myself," before PJ lost it entirely.

Randy leaned up and said, "Would you behave down there? Their big hitter is first up to bat."

Stephanie elbowed PJ in the side, for good measure, and turned her attention to the game. The opposing team's fourth hitter in the lineup was a man-child at six-foot-three and a good two hundred and fifty pounds. He hit Colt's pitches hard a couple of times during the regular season. Stephanie crossed her fingers.

"Ball!" The umpire called the first pitch outside.

Stephanie could tell Colt thought the pitch was a strike, but he went right back to the rubber. He prepared to throw again, nodding at the signal for the next pitch from Trevor. Colt rocked back and let go of a sweeping curve that buckled the batters knees and crossed the plate for a strike. Stephanie saw the slight grin Colt was trying to hide.

"Nice pitch, Pony Boy!" She yelled.

Just before Colt let the next pitch go, Stephanie saw Trevor move inside. They were going to brush the big guy off the plate. The pitch came so fast, Stephanie didn't have time to finish the breath she took when she realized what the boys were doing. Brushing a guy back was a legitimate tactic in baseball, but if Colt miscalculated slightly, things could go bad in a hurry, and they did.

Colt threw another curve ball, but this one didn't break. At least that's what it looked like. The batter, having fallen for the first curve, dug in. The ball smacked him in the thigh, which thoroughly enraged him. He charged toward the mound, but was stopped by the umpire who ran out in

Before It Stains

front the batter. To Colt's credit he stood his ground. Stephanie saw him say, "Sorry, man," to the red-faced batter, who in all likelihood could have snapped Colt in two.

The batter went to first base without any further bravado. He was big and slow, not much of a threat to steal, but he kept dancing off first base far enough to draw a few throws from Colt. Trevor called timeout and went to the mound. The boys talked secretly, with mouths covered by their big leather gloves. A strategy agreed upon, play resumed.

Randy yelled out, "Come on, Colt. Fire that ball in there!"

Colt reared back and let fly with a fastball, but it wasn't a strike. It was a chest high throw, off the plate, straight to Trevor who caught the pitchout in full stride and threw his own strike down the first base line. Wyatt, the first baseman, caught it and tagged the runner, as he slid face first back to the bag.

"Out!" The umpire behind the bag shouted. The stands erupted both pro and con. Colt snuck a look in the stands after congratulating Trevor on the throw. He grinned just for a second, but he had to keep his cool exterior intact for the opposition. Mo told him never to show up the other guy. It was bad sportsmanship and could get your ass kicked. Colt hit a home run once and mimicked some overpaid jerk in the major leagues, by dropping his bat and watching the ball go over the fence, before taking a leisurely stroll up the base line.

When Mo got him in the car after the game, she lit into him. "That was disrespectful. You're a pitcher, you should know better. Not only that, it reflects badly on your

Before It Stains

character. Are you out there for personal glory or to help your team win?"

Colt, who was all of twelve said, "You don't understand. It's a guy thing."

Mo had turned so she could look at Colt in the back seat. "No, it's a jerk hung up on his own ego thing. It's so much classier to drop the bat and start to first base, than stand there and preen for everyone. Act like you've been there before. Put your head down and come around the bases. Players will respect you more for that than being a self-serving asshole."

Mo had talks like that with Colt often. She was the character builder, the one concerned that he knew the way to be a good man. Stephanie wanted the same things, she just didn't have the same bond with Colt that Mo had. Mo was straight up - here are the facts - with Colt. She pulled no punches. They had a mutual respect for each other that Stephanie envied at times. Mo would have liked that last play. Stephanie suddenly remembered she needed to take pictures.

She excused herself. "I'm going down to field level and take some pictures."

Randy, who was never good at sitting still for very long, offered, "I'll come, too."

The batter at the plate grounded out to the shortstop for the second out, before Stephanie and Randy reached the grass behind the backstop. They joined all the other parents filming from ground level, finding a spot near their team's on-deck circle. Stephanie took shots during the next series of pitches. The first two were fastballs the batter swung at and missed. The next two pitches were balls. Colt was trying to get the batter to swing at a bad pitch. The last was a curve ball that landed in Trevor's glove for strike three.

Before It Stains

Colt ran by them to grab his bat. He smiled and high-fived Randy through the fence.

"Good job," Randy said, and then warned, "Don't dig in, you know they're going to throw at you."

"Yeah, I know," Colt said, and then grinned mischievously. "But their pitcher gets tossed if he does hit me, so it's all good."

Colt jogged into the dugout to retrieve his bat. Stephanie took pictures while he loosened up in the on-deck circle, all the while praying this pitcher wouldn't hit Colt in the face, or in the chest and stop his heart.

"Stop it," Randy said. "I know you want to say something motherly, just don't."

"Okay, I won't say anything, unless he gets hurt. Then I'm going to say what a macho asshole tradition it is for the pitcher to purposely retaliate for a player being accidently hit with a pitch."

Randy laughed. "You think he accidently hit that guy? You really don't understand baseball. The last time he hit off Colt, he crowded the plate. He's also prone to losing his temper. What better way to get rid of a potential homerun hitter and mess with his head for the rest of the game? He may not have thrown at him, but he's not sorry he hit him. Coming inside like that, he knew it was a distinct possibility."

Stephanie answered, "At least it was an off-speed pitch, no intent detected by the umpire."

"Ah, so you do comprehend more than you let on."

"Yes, Randy. I let Mo do the coaching and I watch, but I do understand the game and all its nuances. I am not clueless. Don't let the blond hair fool you."

"Wow. Where did that come from?" Randy asked, taking a step back from her.

Before It Stains

"Oh, it's been an interesting evening already," Stephanie said, looking over her shoulder at the stands. "It's amazing how a neighborhood can be so much like a small town."

"What did the team moms want?"

"Well, apparently, Mo and I have split up, she's living with a man in LA, and I throw furniture through windows. Also, we both have prospective dates if this doesn't work out."

"Damn, I knew I should have sat by you. I saw PJ dying over there, but I couldn't hear any of it."

Stephanie changed the camera on her phone to video mode and prepared to film Colt's at-bat. She kept talking while she fiddled with the phone.

"Thankfully, the two of them were almost discreet, except for letting PJ hear them. Still, I believe Mo and I are now the center of team gossip, thanks to our son's need to share."

Stephanie aimed the camera at Colt, when he stepped into the batter's box.

Randy chuckled. "At least you have options if your marriage does fall apart. Molly made no bones about how she felt. She'd take you back tomorrow. Just say the word. Which one of the mothers was after you?"

Stephanie kept the camera focused on Colt. The first pitch was inside for ball one. They were going to hit him, no doubt about it. She was concentrating on Colt, but she answered Randy.

"Geri Lee would like me to come over to her house for coffee and a romp, if I'm so inclined."

The next pitch was even further inside. Colt was in the back corner of the batter's box, not his usual stance. He

Before It Stains

anticipated the pitch correctly and moved before it nailed him.

Randy was watching closely, even though he kept talking. He yelled, "Good eye, Colt!" and then lowered his voice again. "Who knows, Steph, maybe that's what you need, a good ol' non-emotional romp in the hay?"

Stephanie's laugh shook the camera, so she quieted it before saying, "If I was going to sleep with someone, it would be Molly, not Geri Lee. No telling where that thing has been."

"So, you have thought about it," Randy said, in an accusing tone.

"Yes," Stephanie said, giving up the fight. "I did think about what Molly said. Are you satisfied?"

The third pitch came toward the plate and there was no doubt it was meant to hit Colt. He turned at just the right second and took a glancing blow across his left shoulder. He did not look toward the mound. Colt simply dropped his bat and jogged to first base, while the umpire tossed the pitcher and the coach from the other team. Retaliation was strictly forbidden in the league, especially such a blatant throw at a player's head. The other coach had deemed it necessary to lose his ace pitcher over nothing more than pride. Stephanie understood the game, but sometimes not its egocentric behaviors.

Colt never rubbed the spot where the ball hit him. He stood on first base suppressing a grin. Randy left her alone for a few minutes while Stephanie typed a text message and sent the video to Mo. She then sent the stills she took of Colt, which took almost the whole time the new pitcher warmed up. Just as she hit send on the last photo, a text message from Mo popped up on the screen.

Before It Stains

"You do know that your camera records audio with the video, don't you?"

The second player stepped into the batter's box just as Stephanie reacted to Mo's text. "Oh, my God!" Stephanie shouted so loud a few people turned to look. She smiled and said, "Big bug, sorry."

She held the phone up so Randy could read the message.

"How much of what we just said did I record?" Stephanie asked.

"I don't know, play it back."

Stephanie hit play on the video and held it up so they could both lean close and listen. The next batter was up, but this was a pressing issue. Stephanie wanted to know what Mo heard. About halfway through the video, she turned it off. She knew Mo heard her say she thought about sleeping with Molly, without listening to any more. She typed in a reply.

"Sorry, you were not supposed to hear that."

Randy looked over her shoulder and said, "Oh, you just missed a golden opportunity to mess with her."

"I don't want to mess with her, Randy, not like that. I don't want her thinking about me with someone else. I want her thinking about why this happened in the first place."

"It happened because she found someone else sexy and exciting. Maybe finding out other women think you are desirable will remind Mo you are all that and more."

The batter struck out swinging, momentarily drawing Stephanie's attention before another text arrived from Mo.

"Thanks for the pictures. Is he all right? That didn't hit him too hard, did it?"

Stephanie replied, "He's fine. The pitcher got tossed."

Randy was quiet during the next few pitches. Colt was now wearing a jacket to keep his arm warm, while he

Before It Stains

waited just off first base. The batter hit a line drive back at the pitcher. Colt dove back into first to avoid the third out.

Another message from Mo vibrated Stephanie's phone. "I'm trying to pretend I didn't hear all that, but I did. I guess the rumors are flying. I haven't been gone forty-eight hours and they're after you already. I don't blame them for trying."

Stephanie smiled and replied. "That's okay, since you left me for your new boyfriend in LA, I guess they think I'm in need of comforting."

The third batter of the inning struck out on three pitches and the teams exchanged places. The next message from Mo arrived just seconds after Colt retook the mound.

"What? Are you kidding me? LOL"

Stephanie had fallen back into talking to Mo with ease and realized it. She typed, "Colt pitching now. Will send more pics later."

Randy read over her shoulder, as she typed. He chuckled. "Remembered you were mad, huh?"

"Just hush and watch the game."

With the opposing team's best pitcher out of the game, Colt's team started to hit the ball. He had a three to nothing lead going into the fourth inning. Stephanie took pictures and sent them to Mo, but refused to answer any text messages from her. Finally, Mo gave up and commented only on the pictures with no reply expected. Colt had given up three hits, but no runs. His team played good defense behind him. This inning he faced the top of the order again.

The first batter laid down the perfect bunt and beat out the throw to first. The next batter went down swinging, but the runner on first stole second base. The third hitter connected with the first pitch, sending it whizzing toward Wyatt at first base. Wyatt fielded the ball and tagged the bag, holding the runner on second. Two outs, with the guy Colt hit earlier up to bat. They couldn't walk him and put the tying run at the plate. Colt had to pitch to him.

"Colt can't overpower this guy," Randy said. "He's going to have to out think him."

"Yep," Stephanie replied, the tension evident in her voice.

The coach called timeout and walked to the mound. The infield players ran in for the conference.

"Hello, Stephanie," a male voice said.

She was so concentrated on Colt, Stephanie did not see Jordan's father walk up beside her. Todd Ressler gave Stephanie the creeps. He was good looking, but a sleazy womanizer that always looked at her and Mo as if he were imagining a threesome. Stephanie suppressed the desire to shudder. She faked a smile.

"Hello, Todd. Are you here to pick up Jordan?"

Todd had no boys playing ball. He rarely picked up his daughter. More than likely, he was trolling for a lonely woman, which he did often. Stephanie didn't have to wait long for verification.

"No, I was looking for you actually. I did talk to Jordan today. She told me Colt was pitching. She also told me you and Mo split up, and I wanted to offer to take you to dinner. I know how stressful this part of a breakup can be."

Randy sang under his breath, "Word gets around in a small, small town."

The meeting on the mound broke up and the players resumed their positions. Stephanie kept her eyes on Colt, while responding to Todd's comment.

"Since my personal life has become the topic of the day, I guess I have no choice but to respond. Mo and I did not split up. She is in LA working on a project. We had a disagreement. My son is overly concerned and the rumor mill of wolves in the stands has blown this completely out of proportion. Now, if you'll excuse me, I would like to watch my son pitch."

Todd bounced on the balls of his feet. "No problem. You know I used to pitch in high school."

Stephanie ignored Todd and watched as Colt threw the first pitch. It was the same sweeping curve that buckled the big guy's knees in the first inning. It also looked like the pitch that hit him, until it broke across the plate for a strike on the inside corner. The batter stepped out of the box and glared at Colt. The next pitch was a fastball low and away, sucker pitch for a guy with a big swing and pent up frustration. The batter nearly twisted in two, missing the ball for another strike. Stephanie and the rest of the team supporters cheered loudly. The next two pitches were two-seam fastballs out of the strike zone on the outside of the plate, making the count two and two.

Todd added his unwanted commentary. "Smart kid. He's trying to get him to swing at bad pitches."

Stephanie forgot she didn't like Todd for a moment. "Now, he has to throw a strike. He doesn't want to go full count on this guy. The runner would take off on the next pitch."

"Wow!" Todd said, grinning seductively. "Pretty and you know baseball. My dream woman."

Stephanie was in no mood for Todd. She faced him and said, "Todd, I am sure there are women who would be flattered by your attention, but you're wasting your time here."

Todd's ego was bigger than his brain. "I just thought you might need a little company. I heard you were looking for a man."

Before It Stains

"Jordan told you I was looking for a man?" Stephanie said, a little too loudly. Heads turned in her direction.

Todd looked around and spoke in a hushed voice. "No, Geri Lee said you and Mo had decided to go back to men."

"Oh, for the love of God!" Stephanie exclaimed, just as Colt threw the next pitch.

Colt came inside on the batter with an off-speed pitch. The bat made a whooshing sound, as it cut through the air. At the sound of the ball slapping the leather of Trevor's glove, the stands erupted in cheers. Stephanie missed the whole thing, still staring at Todd with her mouth open.

While the rest of the spectators were occupied with celebrating, Stephanie recovered enough from the shock to lean close to Todd, and whisper, "Just for future reference, if Mo and I did split up, you can rest assured a man would be the last thing I'd be looking for. I'm a lesbian, Todd. I don't do dick, so go wag yours somewhere else."

Todd's expression was one of utter surprise. "I'm sorry. I seem to have offended you. I was simply offering my services."

"No service required. Now, do you mind? I would like to watch my son play baseball."

Todd shrugged his shoulders and walked away, as if he were the one offended. Randy held his cascade of laughter long enough not to do it in Todd's face. Stephanie elbowed him hard, just as Colt walked by to get his high-fives.

"Great pitching, honey," Stephanie said.

Colt asked, "Was that Jordan's dad?"

Randy, who was trying to rub away the pain in his ribs, added, "Yeah, he was hitting on your mom."

Colt laid his head back and laughed. "Jordan's right. That guy is totally clueless."

Before It Stains

"You have no idea." Stephanie replied. "Now, go get a hit."

Colt didn't get a hit, nor did anyone else. The inning closed with the score still three to zero. Stephanie took more pictures of Colt pitching and sent them to Mo with no message attached, other than the score. Colt pitched well and all three batters for the other team went down swinging. Blake, who had a wicked fastball, pitched the sixth and seventh innings. After all the off-speed pitches from Colt, the opposition could not catch up to Blake's steam. Colt's team didn't score any more, but the three runs were plenty to win the game. Stephanie couldn't remember ever being as happy to see a game end.

Stephanie was hoping to avoid dealing with any more gossipmongers, as she waited for Colt to come out of the dugout. When he emerged with the rest of the team, Colt was beaming, exchanging hugs and high-fives all around.

"I'm proud of you," Stephanie said, as she hugged her sweaty teenager.

"Did you send Mo some pics?" Colt asked.

Randy answered for her, "Yes, she did. She even sent a movie of you getting hit with the pitch, audio and everything."

"Cool," Colt responded. "I'd like to see that."

Stephanie thought quickly. "I accidently erased it. I'm sorry."

"That's okay. Coach's wife probably got it. She tapes our at bats." Colt said, and then asked Stephanie, "Can I stay and watch the second game? Trev's mom said she'd bring me home."

"May I stay," Stephanie corrected him.

"May I stay, please," Colt asked again.

Before It Stains

"Yes, you may. Call Mo. I'm sure she's waiting for the play by play. Do you have money for food?"

Colt answered, "Yeah," and then corrected himself. "I mean, yes."

"Would you walk with me for a second? PJ, Mom, I'll meet you at the car. Randy, are you coming back to the house?"

"No, but I'll be there to get you at one o'clock tomorrow afternoon. I have plans for you," Randy said, walking away with the others.

Stephanie led Colt down the fence away from everyone, so they could talk privately. He looked confused, but followed along. When they were alone, Stephanie stopped and looked up at Colt.

"Honey, I know you are upset about Mo and me fighting. I realize you need to talk about it, so please don't misunderstand what I'm about to say."

"What, Mom? What's the matter?"

"Colt, whatever you said to Trevor and Jordan in confidence has now been blown out of proportion. You know the telephone game? Well, it's something like that. I just want you to know that if anything serious were going on, you would be the first to know. Understand?"

"Why are you telling me this? Is there something really wrong?" Colt was confused.

Stephanie smiled to ease his tensions. "Because when you hear that Mo and I are splitting up and she left me for a man in LA, I want you to know it's all just stupid gossip and nothing more."

Colt started laughing, which eased Stephanie's mind a bit. "You're kidding me, right? Someone actually said that?"

Before It Stains

Stephanie rolled her eyes. "Yes, be careful what you say, okay honey? I know it's not your fault, but somehow my breaking a few dishes has turned into chairs flying out of windows and blood on the walls."

"Oh, man. I'm sorry, Mom. I'll straighten it out." Colt was truly remorseful.

Stephanie looped her arm in his and headed them back toward the dugout. "Don't worry about it. I'm a big girl. I just didn't want you to be blindsided by a rumor. Okay?"

"No worries, Mom."

Stephanie hugged him once more and then let him go with his friends. As he jogged away, she watched him for a moment. She had not lied to him, but Stephanie was holding back the truth of how grave things really were at home. She was setting him up to be blindsided by her own actions, if by the end of the week she decided to stick to her guns and make Mo leave for good.

Stephanie whispered, "I'm sorry, Pony Boy."

CHAPTER EIGHT

Stephanie said goodbye to her mother and PJ in the driveway, before entering the quiet of her home. Dragging up the stairs, she passed the happy family photos on the walls and barely looked. In the bedroom, she changed her clothes. She opened the closet door to put her dirty tee shirt and shorts in the hamper. The walk-in was as organized as her life. Mo's shirts, trousers, and the one obligatory black dress hung on the left, with some of Stephanie's jackets toward the back of the row. Stephanie's dresses, blouses, slacks, and business suits hung to the right, according to season. Mo had a few pairs of shoes. Stephanie had many more. It was only right. Stephanie was expected to dress for work in a much different environment than that of Mo's casual academia.

Stephanie turned on the overhead light in the walk-in closet. She stared at her wardrobe. Randy's assessment had been correct. Her tastes had gone from colorful to bland over the years, as witnessed by the neat row of conservative suits in muted colors, with matching shoes. She started

Before It Stains

pulling the out-of-date jackets off hangers first, finding a box in the back of the closet to put them in. Soon Stephanie had to go to the garage for more boxes, which she found neatly folded and stacked, where she placed them after their move into this house five years ago. At least, that particular hoarding practice had paid off in the end.

With packing tape, boxes, and garbage bags in hand, she climbed the stairs intent on removing the color beige from her wardrobe. As she passed the grease stains on the dining room wall, Stephanie chuckled. Losing her temper and melting into a puddle in the corner were so out of character for her; looking back, it felt like an out of body experience. She remembered it all, but from a distance. Her mind wouldn't let her world spin that far out of control again. Back in the bedroom, she called George, a handyman that worked for her company, and made arrangements for him to come over in the morning to repaint the dining room. At least, that stain wouldn't last forever.

Stephanie started packing away everything she thought looked as if it belonged to a sixty-something Texas librarian, albeit a smartly dressed one. When the hangers were nearly bare, she culled the contents of the built-in closet drawers, and then attacked the six-drawer dresser in the bedroom. Old undergarments went in the trash, worn nightgowns followed. Her favorite tattered housecoat met the same fate. For two hours, Stephanie purged her wardrobe of anything remotely old and too familiar. The cleansing did her good, if for no other reason than she didn't think about Mo's betrayal, not once.

The flashing images of Mo in bed with Michaela, though imagined, had haunted her for days, always catching her off guard. Sometimes she couldn't shut the images down and the movie played on in her mind, too long, too

Before It Stains

intimate for Stephanie to watch. Yet, she couldn't look away. Shutting her eyes did no good. It only gave the movie high definition with stereo sound. The few hours of uninterrupted eradication of old Stephanie was a welcome distraction. She looked at all the half-empty drawers and her nearly naked closet and realized, if nothing else, she was getting a new wardrobe out of this mess. That was something she could smile about.

Stephanie hauled three boxes and two large black garbage bags down to the garage. She was thinking of cleaning the spare bedroom, maybe moving Mo's things down there until a decision was made. Stephanie was contemplating how she would explain that to Colt, as she hit the button on the wall to open the garage door. The garbage bags needed to be taken to the curb, or she would be stuck with them for a week. Car headlights turned into the driveway, blinding Stephanie. She turned away and came face to face with what the passengers of the vehicle were seeing.

Stephanie had stacked the boxes near the garage door, so George could run them over to Goodwill in the morning. Stephanie paid little attention to the boxes, simply filling them and taping them shut. Now, under the blazing headlights, the large black letters stood out, screaming the wrong message – "MO'S STUFF." Stephanie had laughed at Mo's choice of labeling when they moved. Now, it wasn't so funny.

Colt was out of Marlene's vehicle before it came to a complete stop. "What the hell, Mom?"

Stephanie ignored the profanity. The stricken look on his face was her main concern.

"Honey, these are old boxes from the move. I was just cleaning out my closet." She winked, to settle him down.

Before It Stains

"Yours is next. Hide your favorite stuff. I'm on a clearing out binge."

Colt smiled and took the two garbage bags from Stephanie, saying, "Maybe you should just eat some chocolate," before he turned away.

"Wow, already understands women at fifteen. You've done a great job with him," Marlene said, suddenly at Stephanie's side.

"I think we'll keep him," Stephanie said, watching Trevor and Colt carry the garbage bags down the driveway.

Marlene peeked around Stephanie. "So, what's with all the boxes?"

"Just some things for Goodwill." To stall the rumors she added, "Those are old boxes from when we moved in."

"Oh," Marlene said, quietly.

Stephanie could tell Marlene didn't believe her, but it was hard enough facing the reality that Mo's stuff might indeed be on the way out the door. Finding their relationship the leading gossip in the neighborhood was making it worse. Stephanie changed the subject.

"The game is at six tomorrow, right?"

Marlene tore her eyes from the boxes. "Yes, six. I'll pick Colt up at four."

Stephanie put her hand on Marlene's elbow, skillfully steering her back to her car. "Have I told you lately how much I appreciate your hauling my kid around?"

Marlene forgot about the boxes and glowed in the praise. "I already have a herd, what's one more? We love having Colt around. He's a good boy."

"Well, you'll have to send the herd over sometime so you and Eric can have an evening out."

Marlene climbed into the driver's seat, her middle-school twins in the backseat, two more tweeners in the rear.

Before It Stains

"Oh, I gave up that pipe dream years ago. I'll see Eric again when the last one is in college."

"Yes, but will he still be there," was what Stephanie thought. What she said was, "Well, think about it. I'm sure I can handle them for twenty-four hours."

Trevor climbed into the car and shut the door. Marlene leaned out the window.

"I hope your troubles pass soon. If you need someone to talk to, I'm a good listener."

Stephanie said, "Thanks," and Marlene's SUV rolled back down the driveway.

Marlene would be the last person on earth Stephanie would share her deepest thoughts with. Marlene was an excellent mother, but an even better busy body. Stephanie liked Marlene, even with her penchant for gossip. She could be counted on in a crisis to organize food, take care of kids, and help keep a person's world from crashing down around them. Those skills might come in handy with the way things were going.

#

When they came inside Stephanie fed him again, even though he told her he had three hot dogs at the game, and now they were both upstairs in their bedrooms, a typical night, no drama. Colt seemed satisfied that whatever was going on with his moms would work itself out. Hunger abated for the moment, he went to his room to play video games. Stephanie decided to clean the bathroom cabinets and closet. Half a garbage bag later and all that was left to go through was a box she couldn't reach at the back of the top shelf.

"Colt, could you help me get this box down?" Stephanie asked, standing in Colt's doorway.

Before It Stains

"Sure, Mom."

Colt smiled. He loved being the tall one in the house. He tapped a few keys on the game controller in his hands and then bounded off the bed. Stephanie followed Colt to her bathroom and waited, while he easily reached and retrieved the medium sized box from the shelf. He carried the box and placed it on the bed.

"What's in there?" Colt asked, studying the outside of the box.

"I don't know. It's been there since we moved in. It's obviously something we don't need."

Stephanie pulled the packing tape back and opened the box. They both sat down and peered inside. The larger box contained a folded baby blanket with several shoeboxes underneath. Stephanie lifted the blanket and smiled. She put it to her face and searched for the baby scents it once held. Whether they were still there or not, Stephanie could smell them. She pulled the blanket down and looked at Colt.

"We brought you home from the hospital in this. Mo gave me this right after we found out I was pregnant with you. She rushed out and bought it that night. I remember laughing at her, because she was so excited."

After her talk with Randy, Stephanie realized Mo had covered her reservations well. That night must have been an emotional roller coaster for Mo, but she made Stephanie believe it was what they both wanted. Stephanie reached out and touched Colt's curls.

"She loves you, you know."

"Yeah, I know." Colt wasn't in the mood for sappy mom talk. He dug in the box and pulled out one of the shoeboxes. "Wonder what's in here?" He read what was written on the tape that held the box shut. "Dirty Santa and gag gifts."

Before It Stains

Stephanie snatched the box from his hands. "Nope, don't think we'll be opening that box."

Colt smiled. "Bet there's some stories in that one, huh?"

Stephanie ignored him and pulled the larger box closer. She needed to see if there were other things she was not prepared to share with her teenage son. Two more shoeboxes were at the bottom. One labeled, "Steph," and one, "Colt." They looked safe enough, so she pulled them out. Colt reached for the one with his name on it. Stephanie didn't stop him. He broke the tape and pulled the lid off.

Colt dumped the contents of the box on the bed. Out fluttered pictures and pages snipped from magazines. Colt held up a picture of a big Tonka truck.

"I remember that truck." He fingered through the stack and pulled out more pictures of toys. "I had all of these. Why does she have pictures of them in a box?"

Stephanie picked up one of the magazine pages. It was an article on playing classical music to babies. Another was on how to approach healthy training for young athletes. Mo had saved pieces of her research on how to be a good parent. Stephanie remembered Mo reading parenting books all through her pregnancy. She had no idea that Mo kept collecting information after Colt was born.

Digging through the pictures, Stephanie said, "Mo used to make dream boards. You did those in school, where you put pictures of things you want or quotes you believe in on a board?"

"Yeah, we did them freshman year for how we saw ourselves in four years."

"I guess she started using shoeboxes instead of boards. It must be things she wanted for you or things you told her about. I never saw this stuff."

"What's in yours?" Colt said, reaching for the other box.

Before It Stains

Remembering the gag box, Stephanie quickly pulled it back. "Maybe I should look first."

Stephanie pried off the tape and opened the lid a bit. She saw nothing alarming and took the lid off. She didn't dump the box on the bed, but pulled the contents out one piece at a time. On top was the real estate ad for the house they now lived in. It was circled with a red pen, something Stephanie remembered doing. She left the ad on Mo's desk one morning and for some reason Mo kept it. There were pages from magazines with pictures of outfits that somehow found their way into Stephanie's closet, after mentioning them to Mo. A picture of the very bed they were sitting on was in the box. She recognized Valentine and Christmas presents given to her over the years. Stephanie hadn't remembered pointing these things out to Mo. It seemed Mo paid attention to everything she said and made sure Stephanie got the things she desired.

Stephanie dug through the box all the way to the bottom, where she found the pictures of Colt's crib. Ten years of their lives together were chronicled there in that shoebox. It appeared to have been last touched just before they moved into the new house. Had Mo stopped listening or caring? Had Stephanie stopped talking to Mo about her hopes and dreams? Had they been too wrapped up in their lives to notice the little things anymore?

"Looks like she loves you, too," Colt said, breaking the silence that had overtaken the room.

Stephanie stared into the box. "Yeah, I know."

Colt sensed the mood change in Stephanie. "Well, I'm gonna go play video games. Trev is waiting for me to get back online."

Stephanie kissed him on the forehead. "Okay, honey. Don't stay up too late."

Before It Stains

"Good night, Mom." He started to leave and turned back. "Can I have my box?"

"Sure. I don't think she'd mind."

Colt gathered his shoebox and left the room.

Stephanie took a few more minutes to look through her box and then put it on top of the dresser. She put Colt's blanket in one of her sweater bags and sealed it shut. It went on the top shelf in the walk-in closet. The Dirty Santa box went back on the bathroom closet shelf, pushed out of sight. It wasn't the kind of thing Stephanie thought she should toss in the trash outside their house. If the broken dishes in the garbage had caused a stir, she was sure the contents of that box would be fodder for some interesting gossip. No need to confuse the heterosexuals any more than usual.

Stephanie finished her cleaning frenzy just after midnight. Colt, exhausted from his day, had long since fallen asleep. Mo texted, "Good night. I love you," around eleven. Stephanie didn't respond. She was caught up examining the last seventeen years of her life with Mo. How much of the real Mo was kept from her? What other secret boxes might there be, figuratively or literally? What other choices had Mo made without telling Stephanie? Was all of what they had together based on a façade of happiness Mo provided? What should have seemed a sweet gesture, the box instead represented something entirely different to Stephanie. Now, sitting in bed, she looked at her phone and decided to send a message of her own.

"I never knew you had so many secrets."

After hitting send, she turned off the phone and the lights. Stephanie didn't want a reply. It was merely an observation.

CHAPTER NINE

Randy came by the house sharply at one p.m. George was still painting in the dining room, so Stephanie paid him, and told him to leave the windows open a bit. Colt was sprawled out on the couch in the den watching a movie. He barely looked up from the screen when she kissed him goodbye.

"My phone will be off. If you need me, call Randy." Stephanie did not intend to speak to Mo today. "George will be finished soon. Just lock up when you leave at four."

"No problem. Hey, can I order a pizza?"

"I just fed you lunch," Stephanie answered, amazed that he could be hungry again.

Colt shrugged. "I can't help it. I'm starving."

"Okay, but eat some fruit or something too." Stephanie pulled some cash out of her wallet. "Here take this." She paused and then added, "I'm going to cut my hair short, today."

Colt was already dialing the phone. "Okay, Mom. See you at the game."

Before It Stains

It wasn't as big a deal to Colt as it was to Stephanie. Her hair had never been short, at least not since she was six or seven. It hung down her back through college. Shortened to shoulder length after she had Colt, she'd worn substantially the same hairstyle for nearly sixteen years. Stephanie had no idea how she wanted it cut, she just hoped she didn't look horrible when it was all said and done. She'd seen bad break-up haircuts before. God help the broken hearted lesbian with hair clippers and a drunk best friend. At least Randy wasn't taking her to get a tattoo.

As soon as she sat down in his car, Randy plopped a stack of papers in Stephanie's lap, containing images of her face with different hairstyles.

"Here, look at the ones I marked with sticky notes."

"How did you do this?" Stephanie said, pulling out the first marked page.

Randy backed down the driveway, talking so fast Stephanie knew he'd had way too much caffeine. "You remember Will. He came over last night. We took pictures I had of you and ran them through his stylist program. These are the ones we liked the best."

"So my make-over has become a community project."

Randy laughed. "Yes, honey. It's going to take a village. We're headed to Day Spa for massages, facials, mani-pedis, and a color and cut for you."

"I like the color of my hair," Stephanie said, pulling out a few strands to look at it.

"Just some highlights, brighten you up, make your eyes pop. You'll also be getting a new look from Will's make-up artist. Waxing is optional, but highly recommended. I'm not privy to your personal hygiene habits, but it's good to trim the bush occasionally, darlin'."

Before It Stains

"I will have some waxing done, but I'm not going for the landing strip or Mohawk, or whatever they call it." Stephanie cringed at the thought of that much hair being ripped from her crotch. "That just seems extreme."

Randy glanced at Stephanie. "So, you have kept up with the modern world whilst hidden behind the walls of suburbia."

Stephanie snapped. "What's so wrong with my life, Randy? You keep insinuating that I'm not seeing the complete picture. Tell me then, what is it that you see is so awful?"

Randy drew back from her. "Wow. Did you get any sleep last night?"

Stephanie took her frustrations out on Randy, because she could. He could take it. He'd been begging for it since this whole thing started. He wanted her to be pissed and shout at the rafters. Randy knew her well enough to know that until Stephanie gave voice to her feelings, she would never heal. He'd listened to her for nearly twenty-five years. He was prepared for her worst.

Stephanie gathered steam. "Answer me, what's so terrible about my life? Everybody keeps hinting that I should have seen this coming - that somehow I am culpable in this, and I'm here to tell you, I am not! Poor Mo, mean ol' Stephanie wants to hold her accountable."

"Well, ol' Stephanie is going out the window today," Randy said, grinning. "You want to know what I'd like to see change? I'd like to see you take care of yourself. You are a beautiful, desirable woman. You have, of late, lost sight of that. You define yourself as a wife and mother first. You've forgotten how to flaunt your assets. Today, you will let life happen to you. You are not in control. Today, you will be reborn."

Before It Stains

"Oh, you are so full of shit," Stephanie said, laughing, her anger subsiding.

"Don't interrupt me. I was just getting to the butterfly from the cocoon part."

"Randy, have I told you how much I love you? Thank you, for all this."

"It is my pleasure. Let's have fun, shall we, drink Mint Juleps and tell ourselves that tomorrow is another day."

"Okay, but I have to be sober enough for Colt's game at six."

"There you go, thinking like old Stephanie."

"Well, Peter Pan, some of us have adult responsibilities. Some things are not going to change. I'll change my hair, my clothes, maybe even my wife, but I won't stop being Colt's mother, and I'm not stumbling drunk into one of his baseball games."

"Who knows, it might get you more indecent proposals."

Stephanie chuckled. "Oh God, don't remind me. Maybe they won't recognize me after my make-over."

Randy pressed down on the accelerator. "Honey, they may not recognize you, but they are sure as hell going to notice you."

#

The facial mask was beginning to lose its appeal. After having her crotch set afire by having a "little waxing," Stephanie enjoyed an hour-long massage, followed by lots of water and a sauna, leaving her feeling like a wet noodle. Now, in the final stages of the facial portion of her day, Stephanie was fighting heavy eyelids and the desire to drift away to the land of no worries. She would have, if the mask had not begun to tickle her nose. Unable to scratch, the

Before It Stains

itching was driving her to distraction. That's probably why Stephanie didn't notice the attractive woman walk up to Randy, who was seated next to her. His face was also covered in a meringue of white cream, but he had talked non-stop to the technician, and anybody that knew Randy would recognize that voice.

"Why, Randall Ransom, you handsome devil. I have now discovered your beauty secret."

Stephanie wrinkled her nose against the tickling in her nostrils. She glanced over to see who was speaking. Randy sat up, grinning like a melting Staypuff-marshmallow-man from under the frosting of his mask.

"Martha Anne Smith! One of my absolute favorite people."

Stephanie recognized one of her biggest clients right away. Not only was she a client, she was one of the film school's largest patrons and the Smith in the Smith foundation that funded much of Mo's movie. Martha Anne Smith wielded lots of financial and political clout. Martha Anne, as usual, was dressed impeccably. In her late fifties, this woman was still stunning, and when she walked in a room people took notice. Stephanie wasn't sure if it was her looks, the way she carried herself, her business shrewdness, or all of the above that made Martha Anne such a force, but that she was. Stephanie looked in the mirror and was horrified at her own appearance. She was Staypuff's maniacal girlfriend. Maybe Martha Anne would not notice her.

Randy called her out. "That's Stephanie Austin hiding behind the face mask."

Stephanie waved, weakly. "Good afternoon, Mrs. Smith."

Before It Stains

Martha Anne walked between the two salon chairs and patted Stephanie on the shoulder. "Stephanie, it's wonderful to see you and how is that charming wife of yours? I've kept up with Dr. Hunt's recent successes. How wonderful for you both."

Stephanie tried to pretend she didn't look like a Halloween costume gone terribly wrong. "Mo is living the dream out in LA, as we speak. Thank you for your support over the years."

"The film school may be losing one of its finest faculty members, but it is a well deserved tribute to her work. I know you must be proud."

Stephanie tried to answer, but the tickling finally won over her attempts to ignore it. The sensation overwhelmed her. She caught the mighty sneeze with part of the terry cloth robe she was wearing, sending facial cream flying in all directions. When she raised her eyes to the mirror, she saw some of the cream was missing from her face. Parts of the flying muck had landed in her hair. Now, she looked like a zombie from the "Thriller" video.

"My goodness, bless you," Martha Anne commented, after stepping back from the exploding facial.

"I'm so sorry. Did I get any on you?"

"No darling, I'm fine."

Randy wiped at the bottom of his terry cloth robe. "I did not fare so well."

Stephanie apologized. "I'm sorry. I couldn't help it."

"It's simply your body telling you that cream is not for you," Martha Anne stated. She turned to the technician. "Kim, the next time Stephanie comes in use my cream."

"Yes, Mrs. Smith," the technician answered demurely.

"It's divine. You'll love it," Martha Anne added.

"That's very kind, thank you," Stephanie said.

Before It Stains

"I called your office to set up an appointment, but I was told you were out until next week. How fortunate to find you here. My daughter is painting again. You remember Lauren, don't you?"

"Of course," Stephanie answered, thinking who could forget meeting the exquisitely beautiful Lauren Smith.

Martha Anne got to the point. "I would like to display some of her pieces at my properties. I would greatly appreciate it, if you could help me select the paintings and facilitate the installation."

"Certainly, it will be my pleasure," Stephanie said, almost forgetting she looked like a horror film character.

Martha Anne dug in her purse, pulling out two ivory colored cards. "I know this is short notice, but Lauren is having a gallery opening tomorrow night. I'm sorry I did not think of this sooner. If you have not already made plans, I'd love to see you both there. There will be a reception with dancing afterward." She handed an invitation to both Stephanie and Randy. "I'm disappointed Dr. Hunt will be out of town. I do love conversing with her. She is so passionate about her art."

"I'm sure she will be sorry she missed you."

Randy spoke up, without consulting Stephanie. "We'll be there."

"Wonderful, then I'll see you tomorrow evening. Enjoy the rest of your spa day." Martha Anne squeezed Randy's shoulder. "And you, handsome, owe me a dance."

Stephanie waited until Martha Anne was out of hearing range. "We'll be there? Don't you think you should have asked me?"

Randy shook his head. "No, we need somewhere to show off your new look. This is perfect. If Colt's team wins tonight, they won't play again until Friday. Your schedule is free."

"What if they lose? I'll be making an apology to one of my biggest clients and Mo's benefactor."

Randy shook his head. "They won't lose. Have faith. This is going to be fun. Besides, it's a great excuse to buy that expensive outfit."

"What expensive outfit?" Stephanie asked.

"The one you owe yourself for putting Mo and Colt first all the time."

"I threw out half my wardrobe last night. I think I need to concentrate on buying some new work clothes."

Randy was becoming excited. "We'll do that too, but you are getting a new 'fuck me' ensemble before tomorrow night, something disgustingly sexy."

"And who will I be wearing it for? Mo is out of town."

"There are other options," Randy said, grinning mischievously.

"I'm not ready for other options. I'm trying to deal with the mess I'm in. I don't need any more trouble."

"Oh honey, trouble is exactly what you need. You need to be the trouble that walks into the room. It's the very cure for what ails you."

The technician, who had been discretely quiet up until now, said dreamily, "He's right. Nothing like making an entrance in 'fuck me' pumps to get your heart racing."

They both turned and stared at the technician. She blushed, quite embarrassed that she had voiced her fantasy aloud.

Randy rescued her with, "See Steph, Kim here knows what I'm talking about. It's even better that Mo won't be there. You've got a free one coming and she can't say a damn thing about it."

Before It Stains

Stephanie grabbed a towel from the table by her chair. She began wiping away the cream on her face. There was little protest from Kim. Stephanie was sending out waves of "back off" in both Randy and Kim's direction.

"As usual, Randy, you think a good fuck is the answer to everything. I am not interested in playing the gotcha last game with Mo. Wild monkey sex with some stranger isn't going to make me feel better."

Randy and Kim looked at each other and then turned back to Stephanie, saying in unison, "Yes it will."

#

By the time Stephanie's spa day was through, she felt more relaxed than she had in months. She thought she would include a spa day in her monthly schedule from now on. There was something to be said for being fawned over for hours and having all your needs attended to by others. Yes, Stephanie could learn to take the time to be pampered, at least once a month anyway. She felt fantastic.

She wasn't completely sold on her hair. The breeze whipping around her neck felt strange. Stephanie kept reaching to touch the hair on her shoulder that wasn't there anymore. Randy and Will selected a style that they said was "sexy and fun." Her shoulder length hair was now jagged cut near chin level. The sides and top were shaped in short layers, with playful uneven bangs over her forehead. Stephanie hadn't had bangs since the eighties. Highlights had been added to "freshen" it up. Will and Randy were quite delighted with the finished product.

"Holy shit, girl! Look at you!" Randy whooped.

Will had a more sedate comment. "You are beautiful."

Others in the salon remarked on how much they liked the new hairstyle, but Stephanie wasn't sure. Her reflection in the mirror looked so different, it startled her a bit. She'd asked the make-up artist to keep her look natural, not too heavy. Stephanie worried when it took so long to look "natural," but the results were flawless. She also thought the shorter hair made her look much younger. The true test would be her son's reaction. Stephanie would know the moment Colt laid eyes on her if she had made a mistake.

With no time left to go home and change - at least that was Randy's excuse - they ducked into a boutique. Randy selected Stephanie's purchases. She was too relaxed to argue. Although the body hugging, scooped neck, white tee and equally tight jeans would not have been her first choice for ballgame attire, Stephanie had to admit the look was flattering. Randy dubbed her outfit, "Casual sexy." Stephanie was actually starting to feel sexy when they hooked arms and walked down the sidewalk together.

"Thank you," she whispered, leaning into Randy.

He patted her hand on his arm. "This is only the beginning. Just hold on tight and watch me work."

#

Arriving at the ball field, Stephanie did not want to draw attention. Best intentions aside, she made an entrance. It had been decided the night before, in order to avoid the gossips in the stands, Stephanie's mother would bring lawn chairs so they could sit along the leftfield fence. Randy and Stephanie climbed down the hill, avoiding the stairs and the main flow of traffic to the stands. She could see Colt and a few of the players warming up their arms on the other side of the fence, near where her mother and PJ were already camped out in chairs. Two empty seats waited for Stephanie and Randy. Stephanie hoped to make it to the chairs without being spotted. It was not to be.

Before It Stains

Trevor sounded the alarm. Stephanie saw it happen. He glanced up in her direction and the kid's jaw dropped. He pointed with his gloved hand, saying rather loudly, "Holy crap, Colt. Is that your mom?"

Colt turned toward Stephanie. She shielded her eyes against the sun to see his reaction. He squinted at her, trying to make sure he was really seeing what was there.

Wyatt chimed in, "Nah, that's not his mom. She's too hot!"

By now, the three boys had come close together, all looking in Stephanie's direction. Colt took a step closer to the fence. Stephanie lowered her hand and smiled at him. Colt grinned and then slapped Wyatt in the stomach with the back of his glove.

"Shut up, man. That is my mom."

Randy chuckled at Stephanie's side. "You've passed the MILF test, my dear. First step to recovery."

"MILF?"

"Adolescent male slang for 'mothers I'd like to f-"

Stephanie cut him off. "Oh God, don't say that."

The three boys' attention brought more eyes Stephanie's way. One of the coaches, drawn to what was occupying three of his players, smiled appreciatively and tipped his hat. Stephanie glanced over at the stands. Marlene was pointing with one hand, and trying to get Geri Lee's attention with the other. Stephanie's mother and PJ were standing, watching her approach. They were both smiling. Stephanie beamed back at them, as a trace of her once youthful self-assurance swept over her. Somewhere along the way, she lost that sense of being anything but someone's wife or mother. The looks she was receiving told her she was well on her way to regaining her identity as a sensual woman.

Stephanie walked up to the fence, where Colt was now standing, fingers draped through the wire mesh. Trevor and Wyatt hung back, still gawking.

"Wow, Mom. You look sick."

Stephanie knew from her dealings with teenage boys that his statement was the highest form of praise. "Sick" was the new "Awesome."

"Thank you. So the hair is okay?"

"It's better than okay."

"I'm glad you approve. Now, go have some fun."

Colt smiled widely again and went back to warming up. Stephanie turned to take her seat with the others, who were all still standing.

Her mother said, "Honey, you look gorgeous. Randy, I applaud your efforts."

Randy took a bow. "Thank you. It was a tough job, but someone had to do it."

Stephanie looked at PJ who had remained quiet, so far. "PJ, what do you think?"

PJ held up her hand. "Steph. I didn't think you could get much hotter, but da-yam."

"Thank you, now would you all sit down. We're causing a scene," Stephanie said, taking her seat.

PJ sat next to Stephanie. She leaned over and said, "I tried to call you earlier."

Stephanie watched Colt take leftfield, his normal position when he wasn't pitching. Without looking away, she answered PJ, "I turned off my phone. Sorry, was it important?"

"No, not really, I guess. Mo was just concerned that she had not heard from you. I told her I would call you."

"That's the very reason my phone is off. I'd rather not deal with her right now." Stephanie paused, and then faced

Before It Stains

PJ. "I know you are in an awkward situation, but I would appreciate it if you would politely decline to be her messenger."

PJ snorted. "Honey, I don't intend to get in the middle of this fight. I told Mo that and now I'm telling you."

Stephanie soothed PJ's ruffled feathers with a pat on the knee. "Thank you for being such a good friend to both of us." She tried to lighten the mood with a laugh. "I'll have to fight for visitation rights in the divorce."

PJ's countenance darkened. The joke had not landed well. PJ leaned closer, so they could talk quietly.

"So, you've made up your mind?"

Stephanie shook the bangs from her forehead. She wasn't accustomed to the hair brushing against her skin. She refocused on Colt in the field.

"No, I haven't made any decisions, though I have come to one realization. If I can't forgive her, there really is no need to continue this marriage."

Intuitive as ever, PJ commented, "And at this point you don't think you can forgive her?"

The umpire yelled, "Play ball!"

Stephanie answered PJ with only one word, "No."

#

The game went well for Colt's team. They were leading by five runs in the fifth inning. Colt had two hits, one a double, and he made a great diving catch in the top of the third. Stephanie remained by the chairs, hoping to avoid Marlene and the rest of the rumor mill, while the others went to the concession stand. Of course, this did not prevent Marlene from tracking her down.

Marlene rushed at her, talking fast. "I saw you come in earlier. Your mother told me you had a spa day. If a spa will do this to you, sign me up. You look fantastic. I love your hair."

Stephanie smiled, but she wasn't happy to see Marlene. Life was normal for five innings of baseball. Now, here was Marlene and trailing not far behind her was Jordan, Colt's little blond Barbie girlfriend. Stephanie and Mo liked Jordan okay, but dared not show signs of disapproval, which would guarantee Colt liked her more. They were hoping his tastes would turn toward girls interested more in the world as a whole than being the center of their own universe.

Mo's comment had been, "He deserves his trophy girl. Trust me, it will be one of many."

This statement came from a woman who had her fair share of trophy girls before she met Stephanie. Mo dated and bedded many women, beginning in her teens. Stephanie was hoping Colt would wait a bit before becoming sexually active, but she wasn't naïve. They both talked to him. She was sure her conversation with Colt had been more about love and commitment than Mo's. Randy had taken Colt to the drug store for a lesson in condoms and safe sex. Between the three of them, Stephanie hoped they covered all the bases.

She stood to give the hug Marlene seemed to be expecting.

Marlene continued to gush. "Mo is going to flip when she sees you. Did you send her a picture?"

"Thank you and no, I didn't send a picture. I'd like it to be a surprise." Stephanie added the last part to keep Marlene from broadcasting her picture all over Facebook. Marlene's team pages included candid shots of the parents.

"Oh, I would love to see the look on her face," Marlene said, sitting down, much to Stephanie's chagrin.

Before It Stains

There was no time to respond to Marlene. Jordan arrived just as Stephanie retook her seat. Jordan was a pretty girl, still growing into the heart-stopper she would be. That didn't make up for her lack of common sense. What came out of her mouth solidified Stephanie's assessment.

"Oh my God! Ms. Austin, you look so much younger. My mother did the same thing when my dad left the first time, cut off all her hair."

Stephanie tilted her head to one side, forcing a smile. "Thank you, I think - but really, Jordan, Mo is in LA on business. I would appreciate it, and I'm sure Colt would too, if people would stop misinterpreting our private lives."

Jordan sat down in one of the empty chairs. Unfazed by Stephanie's words, she continued, "I know. Can you believe it? As soon as I got here, I heard about Mo's stuff being boxed up and put out on the curb. Some people need to get a life."

Stephanie turned to glare at the shrinking Marlene. "Yes, people do need to get lives."

She was saved from any further conversation with Marlene and Jordan by the arrival of the chairs' rightful owners. After quick goodbyes, Marlene and Jordan returned to the stands. PJ handed Stephanie a bottle of water and a bag of popcorn.

"Thanks for the rescue," Stephanie said.

"Your mom sent her this way, because she was going off by the concession stand about how sad it was to see you putting Mo's stuff on the curb."

"I did not put Mo's stuff on the curb. The boxes were in my garage."

PJ raised an eyebrow. "So, you did pack up Mo's things."

Before It Stains

"Oh, for Pete's sake. I used some old boxes from the move when I cleaned out my closet last night. The boxes were labeled 'Mo's stuff' on the outside, but that is not what was in them."

PJ seemed relieved. She chuckled and said, "That's how rumors get started. All it takes is a mislabeled box and a nosey neighbor."

Stephanie didn't think they were talking loudly, but her mother chimed in, "They smell blood in the water. Nothing like someone else's troubles to take small minds off their own."

"Let 'em talk," Randy said, "By the time the truth comes out, Mo cheating will be a minor offense compared to what the rumor mill can stir up."

Stephanie sank back in her chair. "That's what I'm afraid of."

#

The game ended with Colt's team winning six to one. The boys were all going to Wyatt's house for a pool party and sleep over since they did not have a game on Thursday. Stephanie met with Colt briefly after the game. She rushed through finding out when she should expect to see him again, gave him some money, and kissed him goodbye. She escaped to the parking lot, hurrying everyone along. At the back of the car, Stephanie hugged her mother.

"Thanks for bringing the chairs, Mom. I think I would have died if I had to sit in the stands."

With a look only a woman who understood could give, her mother said, "Stephanie, running from them won't help. Hold your head up. They prey on the weak."

Stephanie chuckled. "At this rate, they'll be picking my bones clean by the end of the week."

Before It Stains

"Randy tells me you are going to a gallery opening tomorrow night. I'll pick up Colt tomorrow afternoon. I need some grandson time before he's too old to spend a night with me. I'll bring him to the game on Friday." She climbed into her car. "You need to blow off some steam, so I suggest you have some fun."

"Thanks, Mom. I love you."

A huge sigh of relief filled the air when Stephanie sat down in the passenger seat of Randy's car.

He looked at her. "So, where to?"

"I really just want to go home."

#

Stephanie was quiet most of the way. She stared out the window as they drove through her neighborhood. This part of the drive always gave her peace. The closer she was to home and the people she loved the calmer her spirit would become. Now, it simply reminded her of the troubles that waited for her there. A new haircut couldn't change the fact that her life was in turmoil and the future rested on a decision she had no idea how to make.

Randy was not quiet. He babbled on about the gallery opening and his plans for tomorrow. "... and after breakfast, we have a ten a.m. appointment at The Boutique."

"That's a bit out of my price range, don't you think," Stephanie said.

"You can afford a nice dress."

"Nice, yes, but from an exclusive boutique, no. We're comfortable, Randy, not rich."

"I was going to let Mo tell you, but since you're not speaking to her at the moment, we heard from the agency lawyers. Mo gets to keep all of the money from her current studio contract, no percentage taken out for the home-

Before It Stains

wrecker. She is out of her contract with said bitch and was offered a fifty thousand dollar settlement for any suffering she may have endured. All with the caveat that she never reveals what happened. I think we could get more, but you probably want this over with. I am proposing that part of that settlement is for your suffering and silence, as well." Randy smiled and patted Stephanie's knee. "Honey, you earned a designer dress."

"And new shoes," Stephanie said, grinning.

"That's my girl!"

#

Stephanie walked through the dining room, after changing into more comfortable sweats and a tee shirt upstairs. The new paint brightened the room, the stains no longer visible on the wall. Stephanie closed the windows George left open a few inches. The fumes had almost dissipated. The closed rose buds in the arrangement on the table had begun to open. The scent of drying paint mingled with the fragrance of the blooms. Stephanie gave them no more than a passing glance.

The screen on the kitchen phone handset read, "16 Missed Calls," and "5 Messages." Stephanie only glimpsed it, as she made her way to the refrigerator for a bottle of water. She stopped on the way back out of the kitchen to check the missed calls, in case one of them was Colt. Four calls were from unavailable numbers, probably the usual solicitations. The other twelve were Mo. Stephanie hung the phone back in the cradle, not bothering with the messages. She had the whole night to herself. Why start off listening to Mo whine, because Stephanie wouldn't talk to her?

Not talking to Mo had become easier as the day wore on. Stephanie went into the office to retrieve her laptop. Just as she was leaving the office, the phone rang. She looked at the receiver and saw Colt's name flashing, so she answered it.

"Hey, honey. Is everything all right?"

"Yeah, everything is fine. I just wanted to check on you. Mo called. PJ sent pics from the game. We talked about the game and then she said she couldn't get up with you. I tried your cell. Is it still off?"

"I forgot to turn it back on. I'll do that in a minute. Are you having fun?"

"Yes, we're playing pool basketball."

"Well, be careful honey and enjoy yourself. I'll see you tomorrow afternoon, all right?"

"Grandma called and said I was going to her house tomorrow night. Are you going out?"

"Yes, Randy and I are going to an art gallery opening. I'll be shopping in the morning, but I'll have my phone on, if you need me. I'll pick you up at Wyatt's after lunch. I'm sure you boys won't be up much before that."

"That's cool," Colt said, and then Stephanie heard voices shouting for Colt to get back in the pool.

"I guess you need to get back to the game. Love you, sweetie. Have a good night."

Colt responded, "You have a good night, too." He paused and added, "Hey, call Mo. She's worried about you."

"Okay, honey. I will. Good night."

Stephanie hung up the phone. Leave it to Mo to use their son to get to her. This made Stephanie even angrier. She found her cellphone and turned it on. Once it was up and running she called Mo. After four rings, she started to hang up, but then a female voice came on the line.

"Mo Hunt's phone."

Before It Stains

Stephanie could hear loud music in the background. She hesitated and then said, "May I speak with Mo, please?"

The voice answered, "She's just stepped away. I can go get her or would you rather leave a message?"

Who was this woman and why did she have Mo's phone? The anger swelled into Stephanie's throat in the form of bile. It burned and fueled her growing ire. She spat out the words without thinking.

"Yes, you can tell her that her soon to be ex-wife called."

Stephanie hit the "End Call" button on the phone and slammed it down on the desk. Here she was agonizing over their future and Mo was out at some club.

"That's it! Fuck you, Mo!"

Stephanie began her exit strategy at that moment. She was going to make Mo pay for this, one way or another. She looked at Mo's desk.

"What other secrets have you been keeping, I wonder?"

In the seventeen years they had been together, Stephanie never once snooped around in Mo's business. Times were different and this was war, as far as Stephanie was concerned. She fired up the desktop computer and pulled one of the drawers out of Mo's desk. She dumped the entire contents on the floor. That was so rewarding, she pulled out all the drawers and dumped them on the floor, enjoying it immensely, and then she dug in. She found receipts and read each one, looking for anything out of the ordinary. Stephanie found nothing she didn't already know about. Maybe Mo was too smart to bring any incriminating evidence home.

One folder spilled its contents into the pile. She picked it up, reading the label aloud, "CYA. Oh, now this might be fruitful, the cover your ass folder."

Before It Stains

Stephanie began picking up the things that fell out of the folder. There were cards and notes from women, all addressed to Mo. Mo's handwritten notes were on each item. She picked up a slip of paper and read it.

> *Dr. Hunt,*
> *I was hoping to take you out for coffee so that we could discuss my project. If you would rather do dinner, or anything else, please let me know.*
> *Emily*

Mo had written:

> *Gave copy to dean, 9/19/03. Discussed student's continuing obsession, inappropriate comments and behavior. Dean called student in. Hope she gets through to her.*

Stephanie remembered Emily. How could she forget "The Stalker?" This young woman had followed Mo to their house. She would sit down the street and just watch. It was really creepy. Stephanie remembered now, how she and Randy made Mo document everything. The CYA folder had been Randy's idea. Because Mo was a lesbian, she had to be very careful around the young women she worked with. A false accusation was as damaging as a true one. After that, it seemed Mo kept records of any interactions that she felt might become a problem. The folder had appeared promising for evidence of infidelity, but turned out to be just the opposite.

Two hours into the search through the pile and no smoking gun. Her cell and the house phone rang several times, but she ignored it when she saw Mo's name on the caller ID. Stephanie turned to the computer. She logged on using Mo's password. She knew it, because Mo was always

Before It Stains

calling to have Stephanie send something she'd forgotten to download on her flash drive. The first place she went was Mo's email account. Stephanie scoured every folder and saved message. There were only a few questionable ones from Michaela, but only if Stephanie read between the lines. Not good enough to nail Mo for anything.

She opened the "My Documents" folder. She scanned the titles. One file name stood out, "She'll Ruin Everything." Stephanie clicked the folder open and found only one document. She opened it and read.

> *"She still loved her. Even while the keycard sliced through the lock on the hotel room door, she was not far from her thoughts. As she pulled the other woman into the room behind her, she was consumed by guilt. When she unzipped the woman's black dress and let it fall to the floor, she wished she were somewhere else. But then she knew she would end up back at this same place. Sex with this woman was wild and out of control. That's all it was, just sex; unfettered by relationships and emotions, hot, sweaty sex. She needed that the first time it happened. She had an itch and she scratched it. She regretted ever meeting the woman now standing in the puddle made by the black dress at her feet, but she kept coming back, because if she didn't this woman would ruin everything."*

Mo wrote bits and pieces of screenplays all the time. Her documents folder was full of story ideas and half-written projects. Stephanie read the ones Mo showed her, giving opinions and support. It never bothered her that Mo wrote about fictional women having sex and running amuck, but then she'd never read this particular storyline. In light of recent events and the date on the document, indicating it was written in July, the writing rang more true than fiction. Not only had Mo cheated on her, now she was fantasizing and writing about it.

The text notification sounded from her phone. Stephanie picked it up and slid her finger across the screen. Texts from Mo popped up. There had been several throughout the day. Stephanie went straight to the last one.

It read, "I'm coming home."

Over the last few days, Stephanie attempted to let go of her anger. The harder she tried the more furious she became. Tonight, with no one around to focus her energy elsewhere, the malice grew to the point of no return. For the last several hours, she'd had nothing to do but plot her revenge. Stephanie was consumed by hurt and betrayal. The payback was going to be a bitch. One small part of Stephanie's mind warned her not to go too far. There was an invisible line she had yet to cross. There were words that could be said that once they were spoken, they could never be taken back. She skittered to the edge, her toes just on the line.

Stephanie looked back up at the word document. She copied the paragraph into an email message and sent it to Mo's cell. Picking up her phone again, she typed a text message back to Mo.

"Read your email. And by the way, you'll be needing that hotel key."

Stephanie went back to the computer. She closed the file and looked again at the folder names. She saw one labeled, "Colt 16." She clicked on it and found it contained other folders with pictures, videos, and a movie project file. Mo must have made a movie for Colt's sixteenth birthday party.

Before It Stains

She opened the movie project, pushing play when the window popped up.

Elton John's "Circle of Life" came through the speakers, as Colt's life unfolded on the screen. It began with pictures of the young and in love, Stephanie and Mo. They beamed back at the camera from multiple poses. Soon the images were of Stephanie in various stages of pregnancy and finally in the hospital, where a grinning Mo held Colt to Stephanie's chest, moments after he was born. The rest of the video chronicled Colt's life in pictures and video clips of his friends and family, the activities he loved most, the vacations they took, his whole young existence on film. Throughout the movie, they looked like the perfect family.

Stephanie exported the video to email and sent it to Mo with the subject line, "She did ruin everything."

Stephanie stood up, left the pile from Mo's desk drawers in the floor, and went in search of wine. She took her cellphone with her out of habit. On her way, she stopped to pick up the vase of roses, took them to the kitchen, and threw them in the trash. Still at the kitchen counter, after downing the first glass of wine in a hurry, she was pouring her second when the text notification played on her phone. Sliding her finger on the screen, the phone opened to Mo's message.

"Look all you want. I have nothing to hide. You know it all now. By the way, I did not write that paragraph. It was a student's pitch exercise from summer school. Also, I was on a tour of the sound studio when you called. The assistant who answered the phone thought she was doing me a favor, because she knew I was expecting a call. Believe me or not, it makes no difference. I never wanted anyone but you. I'm done talking to you through messages. I'm coming home so I can talk to you face to face. You're going to listen to what

I have to say. Then if we're done, you make the call. I'm not the one walking away, you are."

Stephanie drank from the glass and contemplated her reply. She sipped and seethed. How dare Mo turn this on her, as if it were Stephanie's fault they were in this mess? She set the glass down and typed.

"Watch me walk."

CHAPTER TEN

Stephanie spent the night on the couch. She watched old movies until she finally fell asleep near dawn. She woke just in time to shower and meet Randy for breakfast. She drug through the morning, barely enjoying spending way too much on new shoes and a daring black dress that Randy said was "sex in crepe." He complained about her lack of enthusiasm, until she explained the interaction with Mo and not getting much sleep. He dropped her off at her car just after noon.

"Steph, honey, go home and take a nap. We're going to have a marvelous time tonight. You can't be rocking a dress like that with bags under your eyes."

Stephanie got out and stood by the car door. "I'll be all right. Mom is picking up Colt in a few hours. I'll lie down after he leaves. Don't worry; I'll look good on your arm. I'm looking forward to going out as a free woman for the first time in seventeen years."

Randy's smile slipped a little. "Sounds like you've made up your mind. When is Mo getting here?"

Before It Stains

"I don't know. I didn't ask."

Randy leaned a bit farther over, so he could see her face better. "What if she comes home before you leave tonight?"

Stephanie smirked. "Guess she'll have to go back to her hotel and wait until I feel like talking to her."

"Yeah, like she's going to watch you walk out the door in that dress." Randy chuckled. "I see a massive lesbian drama about to unfold before me. It's like watching a train wreck. I can't avert my eyes."

Stephanie leaned in and kissed him on the cheek. "You just be there at seven and don't be late. If she does show up, I'd hate to ruin a good parting line by not having a car waiting for my escape."

"Oh girl, you know I'll be there on time. I'm going to be filming this exit, you can bet your sweet ass on that one."

#

Stephanie picked Colt up and stopped to get sub sandwiches on the way home. She was starving and, even though he had already eaten lunch, Colt was still hungry. After a quick lunch, Stephanie washed his uniform and other funky things from his gym bag. Colt only raised an eyebrow when he saw her unzip the dress from the hanging bag and walk upstairs with it. Stephanie hung the dress on the bathroom door and went back down to spend time with Colt in the den. He was lounging on the couch, watching ESPN. He leaned up on one elbow when she sat down in the easy chair next to the couch.

"Is that dress for tonight?" he asked.

"Yes, do you like it?"

"New hair, new dress - What's up, Mom?"

Before It Stains

Stephanie dodged the truth. "Just wanted a different look and I haven't had a new dress like that in years - well, ever."

Stephanie waited for his questioning to continue. He was too smart not to know something was not quite right around the household. She held her breath, hoping he would not ask what she feared most - When is Mo coming home? She didn't want to be the one to tell him never. Colt sat up and turned the TV down.

"I have to ask you something," he said.

Here it comes, Stephanie thought. She swallowed hard and said, "Okay."

"Mo and I talked this morning. She said I had to ask you, so here goes."

Great! Mo was dumping this on Stephanie too.

Stephanie stopped him from continuing with a hand up in the air, saying, "Honey, Mo should be here too. I shouldn't be the one to tell you what happened, but I guess she's too much of a coward to even do that."

Colt's eyes widened. In his whole life, he never heard Stephanie speak of Mo that way. Stephanie was pretty sure he'd never heard more than a smart remark between them, and that she explained once he was old enough to understand PMS. She thought it only fair for the lone male in the house to be forewarned when the females were hormonal.

"I'm sorry, Colt," Stephanie said, moving to slide in next to him on the couch. "I'm just so mad at her right now. Just remember we both love you and nothing will change that."

Colt's Adam's apple bobbed with a swallow. His voice was dry, almost a whisper, when he said, "Okay."

Before It Stains

Stephanie took a deep breath and began the dismantling of her son's perception of the world.

"I wish I knew how to tell you this, so it wouldn't hurt, but it's going to. Promise me you'll talk to me. Don't hold it in. It will just make it worse. Promise me."

Colt stared at her, his brow wrinkling, eyes pinching together. He picked up this quizzical puppy expression from Mo. It amazed Stephanie the number of mannerisms he adopted from each of them. He was truly their child. It went way beyond genetics. Colt only nodded his head in agreement, unable it seemed, to speak.

"All right then, I'm not going to sugarcoat this." She hesitated and then blurted out, "Mo had an affair, and I asked her to leave."

Colt's expression went from questioning to total confusion. He regained the ability to speak, but not his ability to censor his language in front of his mother.

"What the fuck!"

Stephanie's reaction was automatic. "Hey, watch your mouth."

At that moment, they both heard the front door open. Stephanie's heart leapt into her throat. She wasn't ready to face Mo and she had a confused teenager to deal with. This wasn't going well at all. She and Colt turned toward the archway leading to the foyer. Stephanie realized Colt was frozen too, anticipating Mo's entrance. Huge sighs of relief escaped them when Stephanie's mother's voice cut through the air.

"Hey, where are you two?"

Stephanie called out, "In the den."

She looked at Colt, who was now searching her eyes for answers to the questions flooding his young mind. Stephanie could only imagine what he must be thinking and her eyes began to fill with tears. Debra Austin made her entrance, noticing right away that something was most definitely wrong.

"What's going on in here?"

Stephanie turned to her mother. "Mo told him to ask me what happened and I had to tell him."

Debra plopped down in the chair across from Stephanie. She looked on her grandson with compassion. "I'm so sorry, honey. I was hoping they'd leave you out of this."

"I can't believe she made him ask me." Stephanie said, defending herself.

Colt startled both women, when he said, "She didn't."

Stephanie faced Colton. Now, she was the one with the confused look. "What?"

"She didn't tell me to ask you about that. I was going to ask you if I could have a Dodge Charger for my birthday."

Debra fell back against the chair. "Oh, good Lord!"

Stephanie stared slack-jawed at Colt, stricken with the knowledge of what she had done.

Colt hurried with the rest of his explanation. "Mo said she got some money and that I could have a car for my birthday. But I had to ask you about the Charger, because she said you might not want me to have such a powerful car to start with."

"Why didn't you stop me?" Stephanie asked.

"I didn't know what you were going to say and once you got going, I didn't know *how* to stop you."

Debra leaned forward again. "Exactly what did you tell him, Stephanie?"

Colt flashed with anger. "She told me Mo cheated on her and she threw her out." He turned back to Stephanie. "Why didn't you tell me the truth when I was carrying those bags to the curb? That *was* Mo's stuff you had hauled away."

Stephanie almost laughed. It was a nervous reaction she sometimes had to serious circumstances. "No, I did not throw Mo's things away. Go look. Her stuff is still here."

Stephanie found herself on the defensive. Colt was angry with her. She hadn't seen that coming. She assumed he would be mad at Mo for ruining their family. Somehow, he was more upset with Stephanie for throwing Mo out.

"Is she coming back?" Colt asked, the tears welling in his eyes.

Stephanie tried to soothe him. "Yes, honey. She's coming back today."

"Here, she's coming home? Why didn't she tell me that this morning?"

"She's staying in a hotel, but yes, Mo will be in Durham sometime today or tonight. I'm not sure what time. She didn't say. I assume she didn't tell you, because she wanted to see me before she talked to you."

Colt stood up quickly. "And you're going out with Randy, instead of talking to her. That says it all, doesn't it?"

Stephanie rose to face him. "I made these plans before Mo said she was coming home. I'm going to talk to her, Colt. Just on my terms, not hers."

Colt glared at her. "The new hair, the sexy dress, it all makes sense now. Are you already looking for a replacement?"

Debra joined the standing pair. She stepped between them, facing Colt. Her voice was soft, but stern. "That's enough, Colt. I know you're hurting, but your mother is hurting as well. Stop now, before either of you say something you can't take back."

Before It Stains

Colt huffed and left the room. Stephanie heard him running up the stairs to his room and then his door slammed.

She turned to her mother. "Why is he so mad at me? Mo did this, not me."

"No one loves the messenger who brings bad news," Debra quoted, adding, "You're here, Mo's not. Simple as that."

"I thought that's what he wanted to know." Stephanie fell back on the couch. "I sure screwed that up."

Debra sat down beside Stephanie. "Yep. You stepped in it, but good. Now what are you going to do?"

"I guess I have to tell Mo he knows."

"What hotel is she staying in?" Debra asked.

Stephanie shrugged. "I don't know. I just told her to get a room. She's not staying here."

"Made up your mind then?"

Stephanie faced her mother. "I think so."

Debra patted Stephanie's knee. "You better know so." She stood up. "I'm going to take the irate teenager off your hands for the time being. Have some fun tonight and deal with Mo in the morning. We'll see you at the game tomorrow night."

Stephanie rose from the couch. "I have to make sure he has everything he needs packed in his bag." She went toward the stairs and hesitated.

Debra volunteered, "I'll go get him. He's not mad at me."

Stephanie was relieved. She didn't want to face another explosion from Colt right now. "I'll get his uniform out of the dryer."

Before It Stains

When she came out of the kitchen, Stephanie caught a glimpse of Colt disappearing into the foyer, and then heard the front door open and close.

Her mother shrugged. "He's hormonal. What are you going to do?"

Stephanie handed over the gym bag, the contents all freshly laundered and folded.

"And yet, he expected his uniform cleaned and handed to him," Stephanie said.

"He's just like another teenager I knew once. Too mad to speak a civil word, but still eating the food I put on the table."

Stephanie couldn't help but laugh. She knew she gave her parents hell for a while.

"Guess it's karma," Stephanie replied. "Tell him I love him, if he ever calms down."

Her mother leaned in for a hug. "He'll be all right. It's the parents that barely survive the teenage years."

Stephanie hugged her mother tightly. "I love you, Mom."

Debra released Stephanie from the embrace. "I love you too, honey."

She turned toward the door, Stephanie following. Just before Debra's hand found the handle she turned back to her daughter.

"Listen to what she has to say, Stephanie. You be sure, before you tell that boy it's over."

"I'm very conscious of how my decision will impact Colt, but I have to do what's right for me too. Do you think he'll ever understand that?"

Debra's smile softened. "In time." She paused a moment, and then issued a gentle warning. "Don't set your

Before It Stains

feet in concrete, until you are sure you can live with your decision. The rest of your life is a long time to be sorry."

Stephanie sounded more resolute than she actually was, when she replied, "If I end this marriage and regret it, I'll have to learn to live with it, but I think I've earned the right to make that mistake."

Debra opened the door and stepped out on the porch. She turned back, imparting one last pearl of wisdom, "Don't let your pride write a check your heart can't pay for."

#

Stephanie paced in the foyer. Occasionally, she would stop and check herself in the long mirror by the door. The soft, black, crepe-jersey fabric of the Narciso Rodriguez tank dress clung tightly to every curve of her body. The scooped-neck, cut out back, and long exposed zipper down to the hem, left more skin visible than Stephanie was usually comfortable with, but she had to admit it really was sexy. The extremely high heels of the new signature red soled Christian Louboutin, black platform pumps were taking some getting used to. She wore lacy black bikini panties, found in the back of her drawer during the cleaning frenzy a few nights ago. The tags were still there from when Mo gave them to her for Valentine's Day, last year. Stephanie was proud to have managed styling her hair just as it was when she left the salon. She took extra pains with her makeup. She was wearing over two thousand of dollars worth of clothes and shoddy makeup would not do.

Stephanie never spent that kind of money on herself, ever. It felt freeing to frivolously blow a chunk of Michaela's daddy's money on a dress and shoes. The Dior perfume was just icing on the cake. She looked wonderful, smelled delicious, and she knew it. That wasn't what was driving her anxiety. Stephanie did not want to have a scene with Mo, not now. Maybe tomorrow, but tonight she just wanted to feel good about herself and forget about her troubles. She checked the time on her cellphone. It was 6:58. Stephanie turned the phone off and slid it into a small black clutch purse, taking one last look in the mirror. She was wearing the teardrop diamond earrings and matching necklace Mo and Colt gave her for Christmas, a few years ago. The only other jewelry she wore was her wedding rings. She looked at the rings, twisting the solitaire diamond around with her thumb, a habit of late.

Stephanie heard a car pull up in the driveway. Through the glass in the door she saw a black town car come to a stop. The driver got out and opened the door for Randy, who stepped out of the car and headed up the walk. He was gorgeous in his Armani tuxedo. Much prettier than she was, Stephanie thought. She looked down at the wedding rings, slid them off, and left them on the table in the foyer. She opened the door, just as Randy was about to ring the bell.

"Oh my God, girl. You are astonishing," Randy said, stepping back. "Stand there and let me take your picture."

Stephanie smiled. "You look pretty good yourself, handsome."

Randy fished his phone out of his pocket. Stephanie posed and managed a smile, but her eyes were on the driveway, praying they could leave before Mo showed up. Picture taken, Randy extended his arm for her to take and helped her down the steps.

Stephanie cautioned, "I'd rather you not send that to Mo."

"Oh, but it would be such a good way to begin the negotiations," Randy countered. "It's a look what you had and lost kind of thing. Focuses the opposition right from the start."

"Don't do it, Randy, please," Stephanie pleaded. "I'd rather not antagonize her."

"Okay," Randy acquiesced, "but I'm sending it to your Mom and PJ."

"All right, if you simply must share," Stephanie said. Then wanting to move on, she added, "The town car is a nice touch."

Randy chuckled. "I had a hunch we'd be needing a ride home. This feels like a night to remember in the making."

"I could use a good time. I slipped up and told Colt what Mo did. He hates me," Stephanie said, sliding across the back seat of the car.

"Have you told Mo?" Randy asked, sitting down beside her, while the driver closed the door.

"No. I really don't want to talk to her, yet. Please, let's have a great evening and not talk about my problems," Stephanie pleaded. "This might be the last good time I have for a while."

The driver interrupted, "Sir, there's a car waiting to turn into the driveway. Should I wait?"

Stephanie looked out the rear window. Mo's Jeep Cherokee sat with its turn signal on. The town car was in the middle of the driveway, blocking both sides. Randy looked too. He turned to face Stephanie and raised his eyebrows, waiting for her to make the call. Stephanie was sure Mo could not see her behind the tinted glass. Her heart beating hard against the wall of her chest, she hesitated for only a second.

"I'm not wasting this dress on her. Let's go."

Randy leaned up and told the driver, "Take us downtown, Max."

Before It Stains

The big black car backed slowly out of the driveway and drove past Mo. Stephanie could see Mo in the shadows, peering into the dark glass of the town car. From somewhere deep in the recesses of the killing pain she held at bay, the anger rose quickly. Stephanie hit the window control button, lowering it just enough to get her hand out, and gave her wife of seventeen years the one finger salute that said it all.

"Fuck you!"

#

Downtown Durham watched the birth and the death of Big Tobacco. King tobacco built and ruled these streets for many years, and then abandoned the red brick warehouses and manufacturing buildings to blight and ruin. A revitalization of the area in recent years turned these old structures into commercial and residential properties. The bright-red brick iconic smokestack, emblazoned with "LUCKY STRIKE," looked down on the American Tobacco Historic District that only a few years ago was a derelict eyesore. Now, it was the centerpiece of Durham nightlife.

Stephanie loved coming downtown at night. She worked in the hustle and bustle of the day on these busy streets, but at night the mood changed. The amber glow of the streetlights cast shadows on the sidewalks and pavement. Smooth surfaces sparkled with the reflections of multicolored neon signs, just starting to come to life in the twilight. She had been quiet since leaving the house. Randy patted her leg, understanding what all this meant. Stephanie was stepping out, out of her old life, and symbolically out of her marriage.

Before It Stains

As they wound through the timeworn warehouses lining the streets, the air filled with change and possibility. She smiled over at Randy and took his hand.

"Thank you. Of all the things I have believed in my lifetime, knowing I can always count on you has been the one true thing."

Randy showed his perfect white teeth and dimple. "You know I would marry you, if you had a dick."

Stephanie did not miss a beat. "Well, you know we can buy one of those."

The driver stifled a laugh. Randy's head tilted to one side, as he sat back and examined his oldest friend.

He pursed his lips, studying her, and then said, "I think I like this Stephanie. A little sass goes well with the new look."

The car slowed to a crawl on a narrow street lined with parked vehicles on both sides. Near the entrance to one of the old warehouses, white-jacketed valets exchanged tickets with guests and then sped away to a nearby lot. Men and women in evening attire, ranging from classic black to artsy flamboyant, walked toward a large open garage door located in the side of the red brick building. Stopping at the entrance, the driver got out and opened the door for his passengers. Stephanie suddenly remembered the invitation she left on the foyer table, next to her rings.

"Randy, I forgot my invitation."

Randy stood up from the seat and extended his hand to Stephanie. He grinned at her. "Honey, wearing that dress, you don't need an invitation."

#

Stephanie stood alone looking up at a large painting suspended from the ceiling. Durham's art crowd milled

Before It Stains

about the vast warehouse, converted to gallery. Lauren Smith's paintings covered the walls and hung from wires throughout the room. The interior of the structure was left in its natural muted state, juxtaposing the fading paint, chipped bricks, and concrete floors against the colors from the art. The gallery was chic and simple at the same time. The crowd was rather large for a gallery opening, but then who could refuse an invitation from Martha Anne, or Lauren for that matter. The Smith women were alluring.

Randy left to retrieve drinks from one of the open bars situated around the room. Caterers buzzed about tables filled with hors d'oeuvres. A DJ played jazz and blues softly, but the giant speakers and wooden parquet dance floor portended there would be different music later. Stephanie could use a twirl or two, if she could manage it in these shoes. If she had to, she would go barefooted. It looked like it was going to be quite a party. Stephanie was crowd watching when the painting caught her eye. She moved over to stand under it.

Stephanie stared up at a ten-foot-tall naked woman, sleeping on her side. She was painted in different color blues, greens, and coppers, marbled together. The glossy finish made the paint appear wet, as it swirled around the woman's body, a liquid storm of emotions filling her soul, seeming to drain to her toe and drip off the canvas. The woman was painted on what looked like a solid black background, but if Stephanie moved to the side she could see the word 'PROMISES,' repeated in the pigment.

"Only a woman who knew great pain could look at this painting with your expression."

Stephanie turned to see Martha Anne Smith standing beside her, admiring the painting.

Before It Stains

"It's quite moving, isn't it?" Stephanie said, looking back at the painting. "So much emotion, I can't imagine the hurt that inspired this."

"Oh, I think you have some idea." Martha Anne stepped back examining Stephanie. "My word, that's quite a transformation from the other day. If this isn't a crisis makeover, I'll give you my tee time at the club." She leaned in with a grin. "And I hold that as dear as my daughter."

To Stephanie's great relief, the artist appeared. Lauren Smith, five-foot-seven inches of curvaceous, golden haired, blue-eyed, sweet Carolina girl beauty, stepped up to her mother's side. Stephanie knew Lauren and her partner, Dr. Shelby West, from the academic circle social events she attended with Mo. Although Shelby taught at a different university, they were often at the same fundraisers.

Martha Anne slipped an arm around Lauren's waist. "Ah, and here she is. Lauren, you remember Stephanie Austin."

Lauren smiled and extended her hand. "Of course I do. I think the last time we saw each other was at the film school benefit, a few years ago. Is Mo here with you?"

Stephanie was going to have to get used to answering this question, but since Mo wasn't really aware that she was being divorced yet, she thought it best not to explain.

"No, she's flying back from LA tonight. I'll tell her you asked about her." Stephanie changed the subject. "Your artwork is amazing. This one drew me from across the room."

Lauren looked up at the painting. "That was a dark time." She chuckled. "Glad that's over."

Martha Anne touched both younger women on the arm, as she passed in front of them, saying, "I see someone I must talk to. You two can make arrangements to discuss which pieces will go in my buildings. I'll catch back up to you later, and Stephanie, I hope you have the evening that dress deserves." Martha Anne winked and strode away.

Lauren looked at Stephanie's dress. "It is stunning. I watched you turn every head in the room when you made your entrance. I'm sure Mo likes it."

"She hasn't seen it," Stephanie answered without thinking.

"Not sure I would let Harper out alone, dressed like that," Lauren said, winking.

"Harper?" Stephanie was confused.

Lauren saw the puzzlement and answered, "Oh, that's right. I was still with Shelby when we last spoke. Harper is the new love of my life and I think I got it right this time. That's her over there." Lauren pointed at a tall, athletically built blonde, almost as good-looking as Lauren herself. "We've been together a little over a year now and I've never been happier."

Stephanie couldn't cover her shock. "Wow. I thought you and Shelby were so perfect together."

"Appearances can be deceiving," Lauren answered. Her words were cold, whispering of a romance ending in one concise sentence.

"Tell me about it," slipped from Stephanie's lips.

The expression on Lauren's face said she comprehended more than Stephanie had meant to imply. Randy sauntered up with two flutes of champagne, saving Stephanie from having to expound on her meaning.

"Hello Lauren," he said, handing Stephanie a glass. He offered the other to Lauren. "The belle of the ball should have a champagne flute in her hand."

Lauren laughed easily. "No thank you, Randy. I need to stay relatively sober, at least until the dancing starts."

Before It Stains

"The gallery is fabulous." He looked up at the woman in the painting. "This one is very powerful."

Lauren flashed a smile. "I'm glad you like it. You'll be seeing a lot of it. Molly bought it. She should be here tonight."

"How do you part with that much of your soul?" Stephanie asked, and then all of what Lauren said processed in her brain. "Wait, Molly is coming tonight?"

"Yes, she should be here any..." Lauren looked past Stephanie toward the door. "Well, speak of the devil."

Stephanie turned around to see Molly Kincaid coming toward her. She was dressed in a black, high collar, tailored jacket and matching slacks, with a white silk pleated blouse. Molly looked like the expensive lawyer she was, as she confidently strolled toward Stephanie's group, her eyes settling on each one in turn. When her gaze fell on Stephanie, she stopped in her tracks. Stephanie saw the recognition hit Molly and then her smile broaden into a beam, before she continued toward them. This was not lost on Lauren and Randy. Stephanie caught them exchanging looks out of the corner of her eye.

Molly arrived and accepted a hug from Lauren.

"Molly, I was just telling Randy and Stephanie you should be here soon and here you are. They were admiring your new acquisition."

Molly pulled out of Lauren's embrace. "Well then, I arrived right on cue. The gallery looks magnificent and you look as beautiful as ever." She turned to Randy. "You know I only hired you because you look good in a tux."

Randy laughed. "I thought you were still in Texas."

"I came back this afternoon. I couldn't miss Lauren's big opening."

Before It Stains

Lauren kissed Molly on the cheek. "You are very sweet."

Just as Stephanie was beginning to wonder if Molly was going to speak to her, Molly faced her. She could see the desire in those steel-blue eyes and Stephanie heard it in Molly's voice when she spoke.

"And you Ms. Austin, I see you've made some changes since I saw you last. I love the hair and that dress is, well, that dress should be illegal, at least on you."

More looks passed between Lauren and Randy. Stephanie felt the rush of the blush and knew she could not hide it. There was more exposed skin than not, and she was sure she would begin to glow any second. For the first time in seventeen years and to cover her reaction to Molly's loaded compliment, Stephanie flirted shamelessly with a woman other than her wife.

"If I decide to commit a crime tonight, you'll be the first person I call." She paused, lowering her voice for effect, adding, "I have your number."

Stephanie heard Randy comment, "Girl, I know she does."

She could see in her peripheral vision that Randy and Lauren were now leaning shoulder to shoulder, watching her exchange with Molly. Randy's statement was loud enough to draw Molly's attention, as well. Her eyes darted to him, with a "don't go there" look that warmed into a smile. Even Molly could not resist the smartass grin on Randy's face.

While this was going on, Stephanie was going into panic mode because she didn't know what to say next, or what old doors she'd just cracked open. She hadn't meant for her voice to sound so seductive, or had she? Molly was obviously still attracted to her, and Stephanie had been wildly in love with her once, a very long time ago, but then she met Mo and all that changed. Dare Stephanie play around with old embers? Molly was most definitely hazardous ground and extremely hot in her tailored designer suit.

To Stephanie's relief, Lauren started speaking. "Molly, let us find you some champagne. I have to rescue Harper anyway. She doesn't much care for the artsy crowd and appears to be surrounded and in some distress."

Molly winked at Lauren. "She liked you well enough."

Lauren beamed with pride. "Yes, she did, didn't she?" What Stephanie thought was a rescue was really a ploy to leave her alone with Molly. Lauren tucked her arm in Randy's. "Come on handsome, help me liberate my scientist from her torment."

Randy slid up close to Stephanie on his way by and whispered, "Don't make the same mistake twice."

Stephanie watched him walk away, stunned by his comment. Once again, it was clear that Molly heard what Randy said. If her facial expression wasn't enough, her comment was.

"Sometimes I'd like to wring his pretty neck, but he amuses me, so I keep him around."

Stephanie chuckled. "I feel the same way."

Stephanie was overcome with the bashful shyness of a first date. The sensation puzzled her and, truth be told, excited some long lost young woman inside. The evening had been filled with looks of desire from both women and men alike. People stopped talking when she walked by on Randy's arm. The open-mouthed expression on some faces had actually made the two of them giggle. He enjoyed their entrance as much as Stephanie did. Several times, Stephanie was sure the elbow jabs and whispers were about her handsome companion, but the look in Molly's eyes was just for her.

Molly seemed a bit shy herself, looking away from Stephanie to the painting. "I can't believe I bought that. I mean I love it, but it's going to take the right room. Look at it, it's gigantic."

Stephanie chuckled. "You probably should have thought about that before you purchased it."

Molly grinned at Stephanie. "Impulse buy."

"Hell of an impulse."

"I saw it," Molly explained, "and when Lauren said the proceeds from the sale were going to her inner city art foundation, I bought it."

"So it wasn't the subject matter that grabbed you, just your philanthropic heart strings," Stephanie teased.

Molly faced Stephanie, her usual air of impenetrable confidence waned. "No, I know a thing or two about promises broken. That's what drew you to it, wasn't it, the palatable pain of betrayal?"

Here it was, the unfinished business. Things were left unsaid in the past. Stephanie knew she broke Molly's heart, but she was so infatuated with Mo, she walked away without looking back. One quick conversation, a few tears, and Stephanie went out the door. Apparently, old hurts did not go away, but could she ask for forgiveness? A week ago, it would have been automatic, but now that Stephanie understood the weight of that question, it took courage to ask.

"I'm sorry, Molly, I truly am. Can you forgive me?"

"I forgave you years ago, Stephanie, although that was partly because I could see how happy you were. I'd see the pictures in Randy's office of you and Mo with Colt and

Before It Stains

think I made the right decision not to fight for you. Now, I'm wondering if that wasn't a mistake."

A waiter interrupted them with a tray of champagne. Molly took two glasses and Stephanie put her half-empty one on the tray. The waiter left. Stephanie raised her glass with Molly following suit. Stephanie made a toast.

"To no more mistakes."

They sipped from the glasses. The awkward silence returned, causing both of them to speak at once to end it.

Molly started, "Randy sent me a memo-"

Stephanie's words overlapped Molly's. "I need to thank you-"

They laughed together. Molly held her hand out indicating Stephanie should continue.

"I need to thank you. Randy tells me that Mo is out of her contract with a healthy confidentiality settlement."

"You're welcome. You shouldn't have any more problems with Michaela, in that regard anyway."

The corners of Stephanie's mouth turned up in a wicked grin. "Exactly how much did Randy tell you?"

Molly's dimple creased her cheek. "Enough for me to know Mo is a damn fool, but I've done my share of foolish things, so who am I to judge?"

Stephanie finished another swallow of champagne, this one larger than her previous sips. "I have a right to judge her and I have. Shall we just leave it at that and enjoy the evening? I didn't put on this dress for a pity party."

Molly clinked her glass against Stephanie's. "All right then." Molly looped her arm through Stephanie's elbow, her charming confidence returned. "How about we look at some art? You do still enjoy going to art museums, don't you?"

"This is my first in years," Stephanie answered with regret.

Before It Stains

"Then it will be my pleasure to escort you. Shall we?"

Stephanie relaxed against Molly's arm and said, "Lead the way."

#

Two hours later, the crowd had thinned, the lights were dimmed, and the dancing was in full swing. The DJ was pumping out the tunes, and what had been a gallery opening turned into a hell of a party. Stephanie danced with Randy, Molly, and a few other brave souls who ventured over to ask. The pumps were under the table now, kicked off an hour ago when she and Randy did the Carolina Shag to "I Love Beach Music," singing along at the top of their lungs. Stephanie hadn't had this much fun in a long while.

Mo wasn't a dancer. She would slow dance, but Stephanie was usually trapped at the table, tapping her toes. Mo didn't care if Stephanie danced with someone else, but it just wasn't the same as moving in rhythm with a real partner, someone you cared about and felt comfortable enough to let loose with. Molly, on the other hand, was as graceful on the parquet as she was in a courtroom.

Stephanie watched Molly on the local news several years ago, as she defended a woman for killing her abusive husband. Her charm and skill in front of a jury box caused one writer to refer to Molly as the female 'Matlock' of southern defense attorneys. She did not look her age, especially when she smiled and showed those endearing dimples. At thirty-eight, Molly never lost the athletic tone of her softball playing days at the University. Stephanie could feel the sculpted muscles in Molly's shoulder, as she was being waltzed around the floor, skillfully lead by Molly's hand in the small of her back.

Before It Stains

"I don't remember ever waltzing with you," Stephanie whispered into Molly's ear.

"Anne bought us lessons one year. I was forced to learn."

Anne had been Molly's girlfriend for a few years. Stephanie knew of her because Randy couldn't resist telling Stephanie about the new love in Molly's life. For a while there, they thought someone finally caught the elusive Molly Kincaid, but it ended. Randy never found out why. Stephanie didn't care at the moment. She was being swept off her feet, feeling lighter than air.

Stephanie let herself be pulled closer against Molly's body. "You learned well," she said, relaxing into Molly's arms.

The song ended and Molly led Stephanie to the edge of the dance floor, as the beat of the next song pounded through the speakers.

"Wait here. I'll get us something to drink," Molly said, moving away.

Stephanie looked around the room. Randy was dancing with Lauren's mother to the Black Eyed Peas. Surprisingly, Martha Anne was letting it all hang out. That woman had enough confidence for ten women. Stephanie admired her spirit. Her gaze left the dancing duo and circled the room. Stephanie's heart caught and rested a beat when she saw Mo Hunt on the other side of the dance floor, then it pounded so hard she was sure people could see it almost leap out of her chest. After all these years, the sight of Mo still took Stephanie's breath, although tonight the thrill was tinted with something else.

Stephanie heard a voice in her head whisper, "Promises."

Before It Stains

Mo was holding the invitation Stephanie left on the foyer table and searching the room. She was dressed up - for Mo - in the French cuffed, white silk blouse Stephanie bought for her. She wore black slacks and had spent time on her make-up and hair. Mo was one of those women who looked good without trying. When she did make the effort, Mo could be striking. She appeared to have come with one intention, to find her wife. Stephanie should have been impressed, but her mind was walking a tight rope between love and hate. She knew she still loved Mo, but at the moment the champagne and her resentment were in charge. Animosity ruled the day.

Mo scanned the room, her eyes settled on Randy and Martha Anne's wild gyrations. She chuckled visibly, and then refocused her search. Stephanie saw Mo's eyes move over her, continue a few feet before stopping, and then return to the familiar barefoot blonde in the black dress. Mo took a long look, exploring Stephanie from her bare feet to the top of her head. Her expression went from "That can't be her," to "Oh my God," in a fraction of a second. Mo liked what she saw. A look of intense desire was followed by a sly seductive smile. A smile that so often melted Stephanie's heart. It did not work. Stephanie stared back, locked on Mo's eyes, unmoved. She hoped the expression on her face projected what she was thinking.

"Was it worth losing me?"

Mo, undeterred by the cool reception, took a step toward Stephanie. In an instant, before her next step, Mo's demeanor changed. She froze in place, the color draining from her face, and her smile falling into gape-mouthed recognition.

Before It Stains

Stephanie felt a hand touch her elbow. "Here you go," Molly said, handing her another champagne flute, adding to the many Stephanie had already consumed.

Stephanie accepted the glass from Molly, took a sip, and then looked back to Mo. Time braked to a crawl, like the slow motion of an accident about to happen. The sounds turned to a white noise kind of hissing and tunnel vision took over. Stephanie's mind was warring over what to do next, when the answer was given to her. Mo closed her mouth, shot Stephanie a look of complete disdain, and turned on her heels to leave, but not before she got in one good glare at Molly. Stephanie stood still, watching Mo walk away.

Molly saw Mo's exit, too. She asked, "Do you need to go after her?"

Stephanie faced Molly. "No, I don't," she answered, and then downed half the contents of her glass in one swallow. She put the glass on a nearby table, took Molly's hand, and pulled her toward the dance floor. "I love this song."

Molly put her glass down and followed Stephanie. The first beats of Joss Stone's "Put Your Hands On Me" thumped in the air. Whether it was the copious amounts of champagne or her desire to forget Dr. Maureen Hunt, Stephanie slid up close to Molly.

Molly laughed and pulled Stephanie tight against her body, gliding into the grinding rhythm with her. She shouted over the music, "Enjoy yourself, Scarlet. Tomorrow is another day."

Stephanie had no idea what tomorrow held for her and tonight she just didn't care.

CHAPTER ELEVEN

An hour and a half more of hors d'oeuvres, champagne, and dancing was finally catching up with Stephanie. She leaned against Molly's chest, panting, after one more heart racing round on the dance floor. Randy took the town car and some hunk to hit the gay bars an hour ago. He half-heartedly asked Stephanie to go. Stephanie was sure Randy was hoping she would go home with Molly. She assured him she could get a taxi and sent him on with her blessing. Now, Stephanie was drunk and she knew it. She wasn't so inebriated that she didn't know what she was doing, but the alcohol made her next words easier to say.

"Take me home."

Molly pulled Stephanie away from her chest. "I don't think it's a good idea for me to take you to your house. That would just be taunting Mo, and I don't want to get in the middle of this."

A part of Stephanie couldn't believe what she was about to say, but the other part was cheering her on. Her judgment clouded by alcohol and Mo's betrayal, Stephanie peered

Before It Stains

into Molly's eyes and said, "I didn't ask you to take me to my house."

Molly scrutinized Stephanie's face, searching for something. Stephanie could tell Molly was weighing the cost of such a move. Stephanie had weighed it too. She measured the pain and rage against the feelings she'd been bathed in all night. Molly wanted her, desired her, and it was what Stephanie needed. Molly knew it and played the role of adoring lover to a tee, but she'd done the job too well. Stephanie was now willing to see how far she could push Mo out of her mind, and she was prepared to use Molly to do it. Sober, she would have listened to that voice calling her intentions selfish, but in Stephanie's current state, Molly's emotional wellbeing did not come in to play. Molly would be better than the wild monkey sex with a stranger that Randy recommended. Molly already knew her body, as Stephanie recalled, she knew it very well.

Stephanie wanted Molly to take the pain away, if only for one night. She wanted fingertips on her skin. She wanted steamy, hot sex with the sexy lawyer standing in front of her. She needed to shake Mo loose and this was the best way she'd come up with so far. It made perfect sense to her at the moment, quid pro quo. Mo was going to get a taste of her own medicine. Stephanie made up her mind to take what she needed and crossed the line of fair play. Sliding her hands to Molly's waist, Stephanie pressed in close. She moved her hips just enough to cause Molly to inhale sharply.

Their lips were just inches apart, when Stephanie whispered, "Don't tell me you haven't been thinking about unzipping this dress all night."

#

Before It Stains

Stephanie rode quietly in the backseat of the chauffeur driven car. Molly, Stephanie knew from the pipeline that was Randy, never drove anywhere after more than one drink. She couldn't afford to let the DA's office get a shot at her, not to mention the cops whose cases she had dismantled. Randy said one assistant DA had a dartboard with Molly's picture on it. She had a lot to lose and Stephanie was now seeing how much. Molly was as docile as Stephanie, spending most of the ride to her home staring out the window. She would smile over at Stephanie occasionally and she was holding her hand, but Molly was wrestling with doubts. Stephanie sat nervously next to her, praying the alcohol would hold out long enough to get through this.

The car pulled up to a guardhouse in the exclusive Rosemont Hill neighborhood. The driver's window went down.

An armed guard leaned in and smiled. "Good evening, Ms. Kincaid. Welcome home."

Molly waved. "Good evening, Jack."

The driver pulled ahead, winding the long vehicle through the streets, passing gated driveways leading to mansions that Stephanie could only dream of living in. The car slowed, turning into Molly's drive. They waited for the gate to swing open and drove through. A country French style, rock-walled manor rose into view. She knew Molly Kincaid was living large, but Stephanie now realized she had no idea just how huge her former lover's fortune must be. Despite the expensive dress she was wearing, Stephanie felt like an interloper in the world of the rich and the famous.

Before It Stains

The driver opened the door, but Molly didn't move. She turned to Stephanie. "Larry can take you home, if you've changed your mind."

"I assure you, home is the last place I want to go."

They exited the vehicle and Molly dismissed the driver. Using a keypad to disable an electronic lock on the front door, Molly explained, "I was always losing my key."

Stephanie knew, once again from foghorn Randy, that Molly had extra security installed at her home and office, after a particularly difficult murder trial involving the son of a drug lord from South America. She was able to get the son off, but implicated the drug lord's other son in the process, and seized his jet when he refused to pay her. He was not a happy camper, but Molly now traveled in a private jet, and most of time carried a gun. Stephanie was sure the driver was armed tonight. Randy was a fountain of knowledge, but he knew next to nothing about the women in Molly's life. She played that part of her life very close to the vest.

Stephanie followed Molly into the expansive foyer. On both sides were pocket doors, open to reveal a dining room on the right and a formal living room on the left. The arch at the end of the foyer opened onto a great room. Stephanie carried her shoes in from the car and left them under a small table, probably a French antique, where she placed her purse. She gazed around in awe at the crystal chandeliers and Italian marble tile. Stephanie thought, "This floor cost more than my car," but she remained silent. Molly closed the front door and armed the alarm. She took Stephanie by the hand and led her through the house. Stephanie caught a glimpse of the large fireplace and grandeur of it all. The place looked like a spread in Architectural Digest. Molly opened a set of French doors that led to an enclosed patio. Beyond the floor to ceiling windows, Stephanie could see a freeform pool, complete with waterfall, sparkling off the trees in the lusciously landscaped background.

"Molly, this is gorgeous. You've done very well for yourself."

"I took it off someone's hands when the market crashed," Molly said, going behind a bar at the end of the room. "I'd rather have a smaller place. It's way too much house for one person, but I can't afford to sell it, now."

Stephanie sat up on a barstool, while Molly poured them glasses of wine, no doubt from some expensive label.

"Why *are* you alone, Molly? I can't believe someone hasn't snatched you up by now."

Molly grinned. "I prefer to do the snatching."

"Ah, the lone wolf," Stephanie said, taking a glass from Molly's outstretched hand.

Molly stepped around the bar, carrying the bottle of wine and her glass. "Come on, let's sit by the pool."

Stephanie's lips curled in a grin. "The wolf is afraid to stay in the coop with the chicken."

Molly held the door open for Stephanie. "You could say that, or you could say the wolf is giving the chicken a chance to escape."

"It's good to know chivalry is not dead, but it isn't necessary," Stephanie said, pressing her body into Molly's as she passed her in the doorway, feeling the heat between them.

Stephanie skipped out in front of Molly, barefooted, and lightheaded from the sexual tension in the air. It was more intoxicating than the wine. Stephanie's mind was rationalizing what she was about to do. Hadn't she been released from her promises to Mo? Wasn't Mo's behavior enough to make the vows they took invalid? Having a sexual encounter with Molly may not mend her broken

Before It Stains

heart, but for the rest of the night, maybe, just maybe, she would not be able to feel its ever-present aching. She was desperate to have it gone, if only for a few minutes.

A sober space in Stephanie's mind tried to get her attention. The voice sounded like her mother's, whispering to her, "Sleeping with Molly is hardly the same as what Mo did. You know this will kill her."

Stephanie shook the voice away. She went to the edge of the pool, where steps led down into the clear blue water. Holding the handrail, Stephanie trailed one toe across the cool surface. She turned to see Molly put the wine bottle and her glass down on a nearby table. She silently watched, as Molly took off her jacket and carefully folded it over the back of a chair. She took out her cuff links and pulled the tails of her shirt out of her pants. If Molly was aware she was being observed, she made no indication. Desire started to grow in Stephanie, a sensation she'd felt only for Mo for so long it startled her. The shock didn't stop her from imagining sliding that shirt off Molly's shoulders, to see what lay underneath. A nude Molly would not be new to her, but some things got better with age, and Stephanie suspected that might be true in this case.

Stephanie was caught looking and she was sure Molly could tell what she was thinking. Her dimpled cheek said Molly at least had a good guess. She kept her eyes on Stephanie while she rolled up her sleeves and kicked off her low-heeled pumps. Stephanie's breathing changed, coming shallow and fast. The tide was turning and the chicken was looking increasingly like dinner for the wolf. The smoldering look Molly was giving her sent Stephanie's heart into panic rhythm. Her moral dilemma might be moot, if the desire in her depths got any stronger. Molly finally looked away. She picked up her wine glass and moved over to Stephanie.

Molly held up her glass. "And here we are, again." She tipped her glass at Stephanie and then took a sip.

Stephanie was suddenly shy. She sipped her wine without comment. Molly extended a hand for Stephanie to take.

"Come with me."

She led Stephanie to a cabana structure with overstuffed chairs and a love seat, under an awning. Molly grabbed the wine bottle on the way by the table.

Once they were seated on the loveseat, Molly began, "I see you've recently removed rings from your left hand. Is that just a jab at Mo, or are you seriously considering leaving her?"

Stephanie looked down at her hand and then up at Molly. "I'm here, aren't I?"

"As much as I'd like to believe you're here because you want to be, I'm not that naïve."

"I never thought you were," Stephanie countered.

"You're here to pay Mo back for what she did to you. I've had it done to me. You won't get the results you're hoping for, trust me."

Stephanie sipped the wine, peering over the rim of the glass at Molly. "And what results do you think I'm hoping for?"

"In my experience, it's either been the last 'fuck you' on the way out the door, or an attempt to make me feel something I don't. You see, I'm not without understanding for Mo. I've cheated and been caught. The difference being, I was never married or even really committed to any of these women. I wasn't trying that hard to hide it."

Before It Stains

"Women? You've done it more than once?" Stephanie asked, a bit taken aback by this admission. "I never would have pegged you for a player."

"Stephanie, I've been unfaithful to every woman I've ever been with in one way or another, physically or emotionally... except you."

"Well, thank you for that, I think."

Molly raised her glass in mock toast. "But then, you cheated on me, didn't you?"

Stephanie never told Molly that she slept with Mo before she ended their relationship. She didn't think anybody knew. She lowered her head and twirled the wine around in her glass.

"Yes, I did. I'm not proud of it," she finally said.

"I'm not looking for an apology. I just wanted to point out that you are capable of betraying trust. You're human and so is Mo."

"Oh my God, everybody is defending Mo, even you." Stephanie stood up and started walking away.

Molly put her glass down and followed, grabbing Stephanie by the elbow. "Hey, I'm not defending her. Steph, I've prayed for this day more often than I would care to admit. I've been in love with you all these years, but..."

"But what?"

"But not this way, not when you're just trying to get even with Mo. What better way to make her pay, than to sleep with the one person she would never forgive?"

Stephanie had enough talk. She didn't want to think. "Just shut up and kiss me."

She draped her arms around Molly's neck and pulled her lips to hers. Stephanie instantly remembered the soft lips pressed against her own. She kissed Molly until she gave into desire and pulled Stephanie into her arms.

Before It Stains

Stephanie's body remembered Molly, too. It woke up and began to yearn for Molly's touch. The kiss deepened, their bodies pressing into each other, picking up where they left off years ago.

Only it wasn't working. Mo's presence between them was unmistakable. Stephanie knew it was no use. The kiss that once melted her into Molly's arms was not Mo's kiss. It was not the kiss that grabbed her in the pit of her stomach and made her swoon each time Mo's lips brushed hers. She had hoped that she could feel that way from another's touch, but Stephanie gave into the knowledge that no one would ever move her the way Mo did, not even Molly. Stephanie was doomed to love Mo for the rest of her life. She was ruined for anyone else. The first tear hit her cheek, just before Molly pulled her lips away.

Molly held Stephanie's face in her hands and wiped the tears away with her thumbs. She smiled and spoke very softly.

"If one day, you really do leave Mo, I hope I'm still around, but you need to go home to your wife, Steph. I don't want you if I can't have all of you, and I know I can't. You belong to Mo. Do you understand?"

"I don't want to love her anymore," Stephanie cried.

She fell against Molly's chest, her tears falling freely now. Molly held her there and let her cry.

Molly spoke softly. "I know you don't want to love her right now, but you can't change the fact that you do, can you? She loves you, Steph. I never thought I'd hear myself say this, but you two belong together."

Still clinging to Molly, Stephanie said, "Then why did she cheat on me?"

"That really doesn't matter. If you love her, then fight for this relationship. Don't let her go because your pride is hurt. It will haunt you, if you don't at least try. Trust me, I've lived with that regret for seventeen years."

Stephanie's heart cracked again. A sharp pain gripped her chest, because she saw in Molly's face just how deep a wound she had inflicted, and Stephanie had done that with hardly a care for Molly's feelings.

"Oh God, Molly, I'm so sorry. I didn't realize how much I hurt you."

"You were my Mo, Steph. I just wasn't yours. It took me a while to figure that out, but every woman since you has paid a price for that betrayal," she smiled, "and for not being you."

"You must hate me. I can't believe you even speak to me." Stephanie searched Molly's face. "I know I asked you this before, but can you really forgive me? I never meant to hurt you."

"I'm sure Mo didn't mean to hurt you either. Can you forgive her?"

A nervous laugh escaped Stephanie's throat. "That wasn't an answer, counselor."

Molly leaned down and kissed Stephanie one last time, sweet and soft, a goodbye kiss. She pulled away, a little smile forming on her lips.

"I will always love you, and yes, I forgive you. I think it's time I get on with the rest of my life and you - you swallow your pride and go home. I very much want you to be happy and you'll only be happy with Mo."

Stephanie laughed, out of desperation. She knew what Molly was saying was true. She shook her head and said, "Molly Kincaid, you always were too smart for your own good. You just passed up a night of wild sex with a willing woman."

Molly grinned at her. "You may have been willing, but your heart wasn't."

Stephanie grinned back. "Randy is going to be very disappointed. I'm sure he was counting on this happening and then squeezing me for details."

Molly let go of Stephanie, taking her hand and leading her back to the seating area. "No, actually he took the time to warn me that you were in essence off limits. I think his words were, 'If you just want to fuck her, then go for it, but if you want her to love you, that ship has sailed. She'll go back to Mo. It's just a matter of how badly she wants Mo to suffer, before she does.'"

Stephanie sat down and picked up her wine glass. "You never intended to take me to bed, did you?"

Molly chuckled. "I'm not that noble. It did cross my mind, but no, I wouldn't take advantage of a drunk woman hell bent on revenge, well, at least not you."

"Why did you bring me here?"

"Because I thought one picture of you pressed up against me, your lips inches from mine, was enough for the lifestyle section of the paper."

Stephanie sat up quickly. "What picture? What are you talking about?"

"Well, that's the price you pay for hitting on a public figure while surrounded by local photographers. They'll use that picture just so they can print the words, 'well-known lesbian attorney.' It sells papers."

Stephanie was stricken. "You're kidding me, right?"

"Nope, I believe I heard the click of the camera right when you asked me if I had been thinking about unzipping that dress all night, which I had by the way. It'll probably be in the weekend section of tomorrow's evening addition."

Before It Stains

"Oh for the love of God," Stephanie pleaded. "Can my life get any worse? Mo is going to shit a brick over that."

Molly seemed to relax more, now that the hard part was over. She appeared to be enjoying Stephanie's plight just a bit. "Maybe she won't see it. She is somewhat distracted, trying to win you back. She looked good tonight. Always was a looker."

"You don't know how many people will make sure she sees that picture. They are clamoring in the wings, just waiting for me to cut her loose."

"Well, if you wanted to make her jealous, I think you accomplished that."

Stephanie chuckled. "Oh, you have no idea how badly she hates the mention of your name. She's always been scared you'd come back and take me away, especially after you became so successful. She actually said the other day that she didn't stand a chance if you got involved in this. I've never given her any reason to feel that way."

Molly threw her head back and laughed. "You have now."

"Did you see that look she gave me before she left tonight?"

"Yes, I did, but I was more concerned about the one she gave me. If looks could kill, I would be cold on a slab."

"You didn't seem concerned. You were cool as a cucumber," Stephanie said.

Molly showed her dimple, her eyes dancing with delight. "You're not the only one that has a score to settle with old Mo. I've been waiting for that little bit of payback for a long time. She stole my girl. At least I have the satisfaction of knowing she thinks I could steal you back." Molly toasted with her wine glass. "Thank you for that little victory."

Before It Stains

"Glad I could help," Stephanie said, laughing. She took a sip of wine and then asked, "So, what about this woman Randy says looks like Charlize Theron, a veterinarian, I think he said?"

Molly shook her head. "That's why I went to Texas. Had to cut the lovely Dr. Fox loose. She started expecting some sort of exclusive rights and that was never my intention."

"Just a piece of ass, eh?" Stephanie asked, grinning over her wine glass.

"Something like that," Molly answered.

A ringtone sounded from Molly's jacket by the table. Molly furrowed her brow. It was now nearly one-thirty in the morning. Stephanie wondered who could be calling Molly at this hour.

Molly stood up. "I'm sorry, I have to answer that particular tone. It's my service and they would only call with an emergency. Excuse me."

Molly crossed to her jacket and pulled out the phone. She hit a few buttons and said into the receiver, "This is Molly Kincaid." She listened to someone on the other end and answered, "Yes, I understand. You did the right thing. Please send the car to my residence. I'll alert the guard." Stephanie watched Molly end the call and then press more buttons. She put the receiver to her ear and spoke into the phone, "Jack, my car will be coming through in a few minutes... Yes, thank you."

Molly hung up and came back to where Stephanie was sitting. Her brow pinched with concern. She sat down and put her hand on Stephanie's knee.

"Stephanie, that message was from Randy. He's been trying to reach you for hours."

Before It Stains

Stephanie could tell by the tone of Molly's voice that this wasn't going to be good news. She sat up, placing her wine glass on the slate tile by the chair.

The fear was evident in her voice when she asked, "What? What's happened?"

Molly continued, "His message said not to panic, but Colt is at the emergency room."

Telling Stephanie not to panic was useless. She shot out of her chair. "Oh my God! What happened? Is he hurt?"

Molly tried to calm her. "His message said it wasn't life threatening, but you need to go to the hospital. A driver is coming. It usually takes them about fifteen minutes to get here. Come on, I'll make some coffee."

Stephanie charged toward the house. "You do own a car, don't you? I need to borrow it. I have to get there now."

Molly, grabbing her jacket and shoes, tried to keep up. "You need to listen to me, Steph. Let's get some food and coffee in you, before we go. You don't want the alcohol to hit you while you're trying to deal with your son."

Stephanie knew Molly was right. She'd had too much to drink to be driving, even if Molly would lend her a car. She was desperate to get to Colt. The frustration caused her to shout, "Where the fuck is Mo?"

Molly caught up and opened the patio door. Her honesty cut when she said, "She's probably wondering the same thing about you."

#

Stephanie gobbled down some bread, cheese, and two cups of coffee in Molly's gourmet kitchen. She tried to get her mother, Randy, and even Mo on the phone, but only reached voice mail. She knew from Colt's frequent sports related trips to the hospital that phones had to be turned off inside the emergency room. Still, she continued to try to reach someone, even as she and Molly zoomed down the highway toward the hospital. Molly came along, saying she'd feel better if she knew Stephanie and Colt were taken care of. Stephanie actually appreciated Molly's protectiveness. She wanted an ally, in case she ran into a hornet's nest of accusations when she arrived at the hospital.

Yes, Stephanie had turned off her phone. Yes, she had too much to drink. Yes, she went home with Molly, but she had done nothing wrong. She just hoped Mo would see it that way. Stephanie doubted it. If her own shame for being unreachable when her son needed her was any indication, Mo was going to be mad as hell, not to mention how Colt would feel. She squeezed the phone in her hand, until her knuckles turned white. Molly reached for Stephanie's hands, removed the phone, and slipped it back into Stephanie's clutch purse.

"He's going to be fine. Just hang on."

"I've always been there when he needed me," Stephanie said, guilt ridden.

"He's not alone, Steph."

"Yes, but he's a momma's boy."

Molly patted Stephanie's hand. "Good thing he has two of them."

The driver pulled the car up close to the emergency room entrance. Molly helped Stephanie, who was back in her heels, out of the car. Although Stephanie was happy to have Molly there to back her up should things go awry, she could also see just a shadow of a dimple, where Stephanie was sure Molly was concealing a tad of "Hey Mo, I brought your wife back" self-satisfaction. Stephanie couldn't fault Molly for toying with Mo; in fact, she was glad Molly was getting a little revenge. Molly and Stephanie were in agreement that Mo needed to be taken down a peg or two.

Stephanie noticed heads turning when she walked through the whooshing sound of the automatic doors. She surmised, from the reaction, that not many people dressed like her strolled into the emergency room at this hour of the morning. The nurses' stares proved her point. Those scrub-clad veterans saw everything imaginable and never batted an eye, but a tall blonde in a designer dress, now that was a novel occurrence. Molly remained at Stephanie's elbow, steadying her on the recently waxed lobby floor. If Stephanie wasn't careful, she was going to end up in a bed next to Colt, after busting her ass on the slick linoleum. She was just about to stop and take the shoes off, when Mo pushed her way through the double doors coming out of the treatment area.

Stephanie stopped in her tracks. Mo did the same. If this was a movie, the soundtrack would have held a high violin note, vibrating with tension, as the two spouses prepared to draw swords. Mo took the first lunge.

"I see you finally remembered you have a son," Mo said, scowling at Stephanie. She turned her glare on Molly, taking in her loose cuffs and shirttails. "She won't be long. I just need her to sign our son out of the hospital so I can take him home. Then you two can get back to wherever you left off. Just like old times."

Relieved that whatever happened was minor enough for Colt to be released, Stephanie ignored Mo's outburst. "What happened? Is he okay?"

Mo pulled her glowering eyes away from Molly. She focused on Stephanie, barely able to control her rage. Very few things could make Mo this mad. Stephanie with Molly was at the top of that list.

Before It Stains

"Your mother said he was too wound up to sleep and went to shoot hoops in the driveway. He landed wrong and twisted his ankle. They think it's a severe sprain. We won't know how severe until he sees the specialist. He's done with ball for the fall season and he'll be walking with crutches for a while."

"Oh, no! I know he's crushed. Where is he? I want to see him."

"They're getting him ready to go, putting a cast on until he sees the orthopedist."

Stephanie thought about it and asked, "Why couldn't you sign him out?"

"It's the insurance. I couldn't find my paperwork for him or his cards. Somebody dumped the entire contents of my desk in the floor of the office."

Since Mo was not Colt's natural mother, Randy drew up papers making Mo his guardian in Stephanie's absence. The law was still unclear on same sex and second parent adoptions in North Carolina. These legal papers gave Mo custody of Colt, should Stephanie not be able to act. All of these rights were automatic in heterosexual families. Not being able to handle the situation on her own had frustrated Mo, not to mention her wife was standing there with her ex-lover. Stephanie could see she was in a no win situation until Mo calmed down. That probably wasn't going to happen anytime soon.

Stephanie didn't help matters with her sarcasm. "I was looking for something."

Molly swallowed a chuckle, but not fast enough to keep Mo from noticing. She flashed Molly another smirk, but stayed focused on Stephanie.

"What were you looking for, material for your divorce lawyer here? Oh wait, can a lawyer actually fuck the client they're representing? It's a question of how ethical the lawyer is, I guess."

This was the moment Molly was waiting for. She had remained silent, except for the giggle, and now Mo had invited her into the conversation. She introduced it in direct questioning, a concept any good defense lawyer understood well. Mo opened the door and Molly strode straight in. Randy and Debra Austin came out of the double doors, immediately saw the standoff, and took observation posts just to the left of Mo. Stephanie held her breath when Molly took a step closer to Mo. She could see the fire in both women's eyes. This, ladies and gentlemen, had been a long time coming.

Molly's voice was low and not meant to be heard by anyone but Mo, but the hard surfaces bounced the sound enough for everyone within ten feet of them to hear clearly what attorney Molly Kincaid had to say in defense of her client.

"Maureen Hunt," she began.

Stephanie covered her mouth to hide her grin. Mo hated being called by her real name.

Molly continued, "I doubt seriously you want to get into a discussion about ethics with me."

Randy's mouth fell open. He mouthed, "Oh shit!" to Stephanie.

Mo did not back down, which in this particular case was not a smart thing to do. She bowed up her chest and spat out, "Mind your own business, Molly."

"You made this my business seventeen years ago, when you slept with my girlfriend, or have you forgotten? You made it my business again, when you let some little Hollywood fame-whore get in your pants. If you were half the woman Stephanie thinks you are, you might deserve her, but right now you are pathetic, angry, and insulting your wife in a public place. If you knew her at all, you would know Stephanie would never betray you, no matter what you've done. She has more character than either of us."

Molly took a breath and stared at Mo, daring her to make a challenge. Stephanie knew it wasn't over, as the two women in front of her remained locked in a chest-heaving standoff.

Molly had one more thing to say. "Wise up, Dr. Hunt. Fix your mess. A woman like that won't stay lonely, too long." She leaned in close and whispered. Stephanie strained to hear Molly say, "If you fuck up again, she'll be done with you. Don't give me another chance, you'll lose."

With those words said, Molly turned around to face Stephanie. "I enjoyed dancing with you, again. If you need me, you know how to find me. I assume you can get a ride home from here."

"Yes, I'm sure I can. Thank you, Molly," Stephanie said, tears welling. She hugged Molly, saying softly in her ear, "I do love you. Now, go find someone who deserves you."

Molly squeezed Stephanie tightly, whispering low, "Save your family, Steph, for both of us."

Stephanie watched as Molly Kincaid walked out of her life, again. This time the parting was bittersweet for both of them. Stephanie couldn't help but think about the road not taken. What would her life have been like had she been able to love Molly enough? Stephanie gave her heart to someone else, but the sexy lawyer strolling confidently out the door would always have a special place there, saved just for her.

The moment passed, Stephanie turned her attention back to Mo. Molly's scolding left its mark on Mo's expression. Some of the wind had been knocked out of her sails. She couldn't make eye contact with Stephanie. The other lobby occupants, who had been eavesdropping on the confrontation, returned to their previous pursuits. Debra and Randy looked on, anticipating the next segment of the drama. Stephanie was tired. Her head was beginning to throb and her stomach to sour. She'd had enough excitement for one evening.

"Mo, I'm going to fill out this paperwork. Then I want to see our son and take him home. I don't much care what you do, at the moment."

"Well, I do."

Stephanie was startled by Colt's voice. A nurse was pushing his wheelchair through the double doors, his right leg in a cast to his knee. Stephanie rushed to him, well as fast as she could, slipping and sliding on the too tall heels. After two steps, Randy grabbed her elbow and helped her the rest of the way. She held on to the arm of the wheelchair and squatted down in front of Colt, which wasn't easy in that dress, not to mention the shoes.

"Oh, honey, I'm so sorry they couldn't reach me. Are you okay?"

"I'm fine," Colt barked, "or I will be after physical therapy." He wasn't finished. "I'm not going home with you. I'm going with Grandma. I'm not coming home until you and Mo get your shit together."

Mo stepped in. "Hey, watch your mouth."

Colt must have been on painkillers. Stephanie was sure of it when he spat back at Mo, "Hey, don't cheat on my mother!"

Randy took charge. "Okay, big man, let's get you in the car."

He rounded the back of the wheelchair, relieving the stupefied nurse of her charge, and wheeled Colt away from his equally stunned parents. Stephanie's mother patted her on the shoulder.

"He'll be all right." Debra turned to Mo. "I've never been involved in your relationship with my daughter other than to approve. I love you as if you were my own, but you've made a mess here and I think it's high time you clean it up." She kissed them both on the cheek and followed Randy out the door.

After a moment of dazed silence, Stephanie dug in her small clutch for her ID and cell. She stored all their information on her phone, including scans of important things like Colt's insurance cards. For once, she was glad she was so organized and prepared for the worst. Mo leaned against the wall, while Stephanie gave the intake people Colt's information, signed some papers, and forked over a credit card number for the deductible. As she prepared to leave, the bureaucratic nonsense or the coming hangover got the best of her. Stephanie removed her shoes before standing up from the little cubicle chair. She was sure she was going to want to make this exit one to remember.

"Just so you know," she began to the woman behind the Plexiglas, "that's my wife over there, Colton's other parent. She was here the day he was born in this very hospital. She cut the cord that separated him from me. She has raised him for almost sixteen years. She could have very easily taken care of all of this, hours ago, but this backward-ass-society-take on who is and isn't legally a parent, prevents her from doing that without a handful of documents. Pedophiles who abuse their own children have more parental rights than she does. I don't think that's fair, do you?"

The surprised clerk stuttered out, "No ma'am, I don't."

Before It Stains

Stephanie had drawn a crowd of clerks and nurses with her outburst. She looked at their astonished faces. Her reply was simple, direct, and aimed at all of them.

"Good. Then think about that the next time you're asked to vote away our civil rights."

There was sporadic clapping from some of the onlookers. She even heard a "You go, girl," from the drunk hooker in the corner. Stephanie passed the grinning Mo on the way out of the emergency room. Mo may have thought things were looking up in her battle to win Stephanie's forgiveness. Stephanie thought the one thing had nothing to do with the other. She charged out of the emergency room ahead of Mo, but stopped halfway across the ambulance bay.

She mumbled to herself, "When you're trying to make a dramatic exit, Steph, you should at least know where the car is parked."

#

The drive home was more than silent. The air was so heavy Stephanie rolled her window down a few inches, trying to clear her head. She could not look at Mo. Stephanie didn't have the energy left to deal with any more drama this evening. She wanted out of these clothes and into her bed, alone. Mo's sleeping arrangements had not been discussed. They barely said two sentences to each other in the parking lot and after the doors closed on the car, not a word had been spoken. Stephanie thought she'd made it quite clear, Mo was not welcome at home, but she had already been there. Stephanie didn't know if Mo had a hotel room. What she did know was Mo was not sleeping in her bed.

Before It Stains

Stephanie entered the house through the kitchen door, leaving Mo in the garage. She closed the door behind her, not wanting to leave an implied invitation to enter. It was of no concern to Stephanie if Mo followed her or not. She stopped to take one of Colt's sports drinks from the refrigerator, in an effort to stave off the hangover she knew was coming. The back door opened and closed without Stephanie turning to see Mo enter. Striding out of the kitchen, shoes, purse, and drink in hand, Stephanie crossed the dining room and was halfway up the stairs when Mo called out to her.

"Stephanie, you're going to have to speak to me eventually."

Her foot poised to take the next step, Stephanie stopped. She didn't turn around. Her bedroom door was less than ten feet away. If she could just get there and lay her tired body down, she could forget about all this for a few hours.

Stephanie kept her eyes on the door and calmly said into the air, "I'll talk to you tomorrow. Right now, I'm going to go to bed and pray for a few hours of feeling nothing. I've had enough of this roller coaster today."

She didn't wait to hear Mo's response, if there was one. Stephanie shut and locked her bedroom door, just for peace of mind. She threw the shoes toward the closet door, set the drink on the bedside table, and then slipped out of the dress. The old Stephanie would have taken care to hang it up. The new Steph let it hit the floor, just before she turned out the lights and climbed into bed. Tomorrow things would be said and feelings would be hurt, but now she closed her eyes and dreamed of dancing. Tomorrow was another day.

CHAPTER TWELVE

It's common knowledge that if you want sleeping people to rise, all one needs do is cook bacon. The aroma filled Stephanie's nostrils, pulling her up from the depths of a deep sleep. She woke in the same position, where her head hit the pillow less than seven hours ago. She'd been allowed to sleep until almost nine o'clock, but whoever was in the kitchen had deemed it necessary to wake her. Stephanie assumed her mother was downstairs making sure the combatants had a good meal before the fight began.

Seventeen years of memories tried to crowd into Stephanie's brain, while she showered. Each snippet of their lives together wanted to weigh in on the matter at hand. There was so much going on in her head it became a jumble of noise while she brushed her teeth. She crossed to the bedside table, gulping down the warm remainder of the sports drink from last night. Between the dehydration and the low blood sugar from the alcohol, Stephanie needed the boost just to put on her clothes. Dressed in her favorite old pair of jeans and a tee shirt, she took her phone from the clutch purse on the dresser, and started down the stairs. She was hoping to encounter her mother and a cup of coffee, before she had to face the wife.

Two steps from the bottom, Stephanie's cellphone rang. She looked at the screen and saw her mother's face.

She answered, "I can't believe you called me from the kitchen. I'm almost there."

"I'm not in the kitchen, I'm in the den," her mother answered.

Stephanie chuckled. "Well, don't burn the bacon."

"What on earth are you talking about?"

Stephanie stopped in the dining room. The table was set for two, orange juice poured, toast in a basket. She heard noises from the kitchen.

"Mom, you're not at my house, are you?"

"No, honey, why would I be at your house?"

"Someone's cooking breakfast. I thought it was you."

Debra Austin laughed heartily. "Oh Lord, Mo is cooking? She must be desperate."

It was well known that Mo was not a cook. She subsisted off fast food, macaroni and cheese, and Ramen noodles before she met Stephanie. She could manage a sandwich in a pinch, or soup from a can, and microwaved things were her specialty, but Mo did not cook. She would wash the dishes and help serve the meals, even chop vegetables on occasion, but culinary arts eluded her. If she was attempting to cook breakfast, Mo *was* desperate. At least the toast was not burned.

Stephanie headed for the den, not wanting to see Mo just yet. She whispered into the receiver, "Hang on a sec." Once out of earshot, she asked, "How's Colt?"

Before It Stains

"I fed him a big breakfast about an hour ago. He's knocked out on painkillers in the den. Do I need to take him to the orthopedist later?"

"I just woke up. I haven't called them yet."

"Well, Mo called this morning and said he had an appointment at one o'clock, but she didn't say if you were coming to get him or if I should take him."

Mo had been busy. She already made an appointment for Colt and, Stephanie realized as she looked around the room, cleaned up the den. The pile of books by Mo's easy chair, her customary nesting place, had been removed. Only the newest magazines were in the rack by the couch. Stephanie asked repeatedly that the random objects she kept finding on the bookshelves be given permanent homes elsewhere. Those items were now absent. Everything was in its place and dusted to a sparkling shine.

Stephanie said to no one, "My Lord, how long has she been up?"

"What honey?"

"Nothing," Stephanie answered. "I'll pick him up at twelve-thirty."

"Okay, I'll feed him first so maybe he'll be civil."

Stephanie wrinkled her brow. "Just remind him, I am his mother and I can ground him for the rest of high school."

Debra laughed. "You tell him that. I'm the grandmother. I'm the only one he likes right now."

"Thanks for your support," Stephanie said, sarcastically.

"Go eat your breakfast. I'll see you this afternoon."

"Thanks, Mom, for everything."

"You're welcome. Good luck."

Her mother hung up. Stephanie glanced around the room once more. Mo was definitely desperate. She was cleaning house and cooking. What next? Stephanie was curious to find out. She took a deep breath and let it out slowly. It was time, no putting it off any longer. The balance of their lives together depended on what transpired over the next few days. Stephanie headed for the dining room, silently praying that she wouldn't find out this was all just wasted time.

She whispered under her breath, "No more mistakes."

When Stephanie rounded the corner, Mo was already seated at the table. She stood up as soon as she saw Stephanie, greeting her with a fragile smile.

"I know you like grits. I tried to make some, but I wound up with grit soup."

Stephanie couldn't help but laugh. "That's okay. This looks great. Thank you."

And it did look good. Mo had managed scrambled eggs and bacon without burning anything. She remained standing, pouring Stephanie coffee from a carafe they never used. Cream and sugar bowls that usually stayed in the china cabinet were filled and waiting by Stephanie's cup. Mo drank her coffee black. Orange slices and strawberries dressed Stephanie's plate. Mo had gone shopping sometime in the wee hours of the morning. She was trying very hard to please Stephanie. It tugged at Stephanie's heartstrings, but they weren't playing a tune yet.

"Sit. Eat," Stephanie offered.

Mo sat down, but only stared at the food on her plate. She could tell Mo had lost weight over the last week. Once again, Stephanie was going to have to force her to eat.

"You have to eat, Mo." Stephanie took a bite of her eggs. She chewed and swallowed. "See, it's okay. Actually, it's good."

Mo smiled. "That was my second batch. I kind of browned the first ones."

Before It Stains

Stephanie snapped off a piece of bacon. "And the bacon is crisp."

"I cooked the whole package. These were the pieces I could salvage."

"Did it take a whole loaf of bread to get four pieces of toast?" Stephanie teased.

Mo visibly relaxed. Stephanie was being civil for the first time in days.

Mo leaned up and reached for her fork, answering, "It only took two tries with the toast."

They ate in silence for a few minutes, before Mo said, "I called and made an appointment with Colt's orthopedist. It's at one o'clock."

"I know. I just talked to Mom. I told her I would pick him up at twelve-thirty."

Mo wiped her mouth with her napkin and sat back. "Would you mind if I took him? I need to talk to him and apparently he has a few things he'd like to say to me."

Stephanie put her fork down on the plate. She always took care of the doctor visits, kept up with Colt's records, and scheduled his appointments. These activities, like cooking, were not Mo's forte, not since the first time she slid down the wall when she took six-month-old Colt for his shots. Stephanie had the flu and couldn't go. The doctor's office called and asked Stephanie to pick up her wife and child. The nurses wouldn't let Mo drive. There was no danger of needles today, so Stephanie thought it was a good idea. Their son was livid with Mo. She had a lot of explaining to do.

"That would be fine," Stephanie said. "I'll find your insurance cards after breakfast. I'm sorry I didn't clean up the office."

"I found them. I cleaned up in there this morning."

Before It Stains

Stephanie sipped her coffee, peering at Mo over the rim of her cup. "Did you sleep at all? I noticed you cleaned the den, too."

"I slept some. I think it's the jet lag. My body is confused." Mo played with the food on her plate, before saying, "I need to know what you told him, Steph."

The polite chat was over. Stephanie sat back from the table. "I'm sorry, Mo. It was a misunderstanding. I thought you told him to ask me about it. He was really asking about a car."

Mo looked up from her plate. "That doesn't matter, it's done. I just need to know what he knows."

"Why, so you can lie to him?"

Stephanie was surprised by her own words. She saw them hit Mo and hurt. Okay, so Stephanie's mind was going to take over and her heart was not to be involved. New Steph was not about to sugarcoat her words or hide what she was thinking. All right, Stephanie could let her instincts take over for a while.

Mo swallowed hard, before answering, "Come on, Steph, he's fifteen. He doesn't need all the details. I have no intention of lying to him, but we need to agree on just how much we tell him. One day, when he's a grown man, if he wants to know, I'll lay it all out."

"I told him you had an affair, not with whom or when. That's it," Stephanie answered.

"I'll take responsibility. I won't make excuses, if that's what you're worried about."

"There's no excuse for what you did, Mo."

Mo seemed resigned to her fate. "I know, Stephanie. I won't make excuses to you either. All I can do is ask for forgiveness and pray, at this point." Mo stood and took her plate from the table. She looked down at Stephanie. "I know

Before It Stains

I fucked up. It'll be a miracle if I haven't lost you already. I was sure I had when I saw you with Molly."

The food fortified Stephanie's anger. It was rising back to the surface. "Would that account for your asinine behavior at the hospital?"

Mo raised her voice slightly. "Yes, seeing her with you – my heart actually stopped. I felt it."

"Good," Stephanie said, her volume topping Mo's. "Then you know how it feels every time I close my eyes and see you with that woman. How do you think I'm ever going to be able to get that image out of my head?"

Stephanie stood up abruptly, snatching her plate off the table. Mo reached a hand out and grasped the plate. Stephanie pulled the plate, but Mo would not let go.

"What are you doing?" Stephanie said, pulling harder. "I don't need you to take my plate to the kitchen."

"I thought you were going to throw it at me," Mo said, seriously.

Stephanie yanked hard, pulling the plate away. "I'm not breaking any more dishes over you."

The opening salvos had been fired. The battle moved into the kitchen. Stephanie banged around, cleaning her plate, putting it in the dishwasher, continuing to bring her blood to a boil. The anger itself was like a drug, taking control of her body. She had never wanted to physically hurt Mo, but in her current mood, Stephanie wanted to grab and shake her, screaming, "What were you thinking?" She didn't. She took herself out of the room and escaped to the den.

Stephanie was alone only for a moment, when she heard Mo's voice behind her. "Did you find anything?"

Stephanie turned to face her. "What?"

Before It Stains

Mo moved closer. "When you were tearing through the office and the files on my computer, did you find anything that indicated I had ever been unfaithful to you, until now?"

"No, but once is enough, don't you think?"

"Yes, I do," Mo answered. "And it will never happen again."

"I'm just supposed to trust you after this. Are you nuts?"

Mo grinned. It should have made Stephanie angrier, but it had the opposite effect. Mo's charm was a much stronger elixir than the anger.

"Don't grin at me," Stephanie said, but it was half hearted. "I'm mad as hell at you."

Still grinning, Mo said, "I know you are. I've never seen you this mad. Between the hot new look and the attitude, it's quite distracting."

The line was hardly original or appropriate, and despite her best efforts, it was drawing Stephanie in. She didn't know how badly she longed for Mo, until that moment. The grin, those hazel eyes, and the fact that Stephanie could now touch Mo – things she had been able to avoid the past few days – outweighed her indignation. Stephanie tried valiantly to resist the growing desire.

"Don't you think for one minute that throwing me into bed is going to fix this."

Mo must have sensed an opening. She stepped even closer. "It couldn't hurt."

Stephanie became acutely aware of how much sexual tension was in the air. She'd seen this kind of thing in movies, where two people were so mad at each other they just had to have sex.

A single chuckle left Stephanie's chest. "Yeah, right. Like I'm going to stop being pissed for the moment, have hot angry sex with you, and then we'll get back to fighting."

Before It Stains

Mo tilted her head to one side and raised an eyebrow, her grin seductive. "Hot angry sex?"

Stephanie was on her, before Mo knew what happened. There was no melting into arms or slow, long, tongue dancing kisses. It was all frantic and fast. Mo was a little taken aback by Stephanie's aggression, but she got into the action fairly quickly. They tore at each other's clothes, casting them aside, as they banged into the furniture, knocking over a side table, before Stephanie pushed Mo onto the couch. Frenzied, passionate, "have your way with me" sex ensued. Stephanie was finally getting the wild monkey sex she abruptly realized she so desperately needed. She had a sneaking suspicion it was better with Mo than it would have been with a stranger, because there was absolutely no guilt, no walls, no places Mo didn't know how to take her. They "had at it" with the wild abandon of their youth, when their love was new and intoxicating.

For a few minutes, Stephanie was able to forget. It was a sweet release.

#

Stephanie caught her breath, her chin resting in the beads of sweat between Mo's breasts. Mo ran her fingers along the back of Stephanie's neck.

"Did I tell you I like your hair?"

Looking up into Mo's smiling face, Stephanie said, "Don't think you're off the hook. That was simply necessary."

Mo's smile widened. "Working out a little frustration, huh? I'll be around if that becomes necessary again."

Stephanie started disentangling herself from the naked Mo. "You'll be around in the guest bedroom until I say

Before It Stains

otherwise. You haven't earned your way back into my bed, yet. That is if you're planning on staying here."

Mo reached for Stephanie, pulling her back down into her arms. "Just give me a chance. That's all I'm asking."

Stephanie peered deep into Mo's eyes. She hovered, hunting for the right words, finally settling on these, "I'll give you that chance because I have loved you so long, I don't know how not to. You broke my heart, Mo. It's going to take a lot more than an apology and wild sex to mend it."

Mo drew Stephanie into a kiss, this one deep and slow, the kind of kiss that stole Stephanie's heart all those years ago. It flooded Stephanie with warmth and tugged at the pit of her stomach. This was what she didn't feel with Molly. This is what she would only ever feel with Mo. Stephanie surrendered to the kiss, which elicited a moan from Mo's throat. Mo might not be coming back to her bed just yet, but she was well on her way back into Stephanie's heart. Stephanie pulled out of Mo's embrace and stood up. She held her hand out for Mo to take. Mo obeyed and followed Stephanie out of the den.

"I thought you said I couldn't come back to your bed."

Stephanie continued to lead Mo through the house. She looked over her shoulder at Mo. "I didn't say I was opposed to meeting you in the guest room, or the shower." She smiled mischievously. "Unless, of course, you'd rather I didn't."

Mo had been the chaser, the pursuer, throughout their relationship. She was a little off balance with the more assertive Stephanie. She stuttered out, "N-no, I'm okay with that."

#

Before It Stains

Mo left Stephanie sleeping, while she showered and changed clothes. She felt Mo leave the bed, but couldn't open her eyes. The late night and all the stress had taken its toll. She slept soundly and was awakened by Mo brushing her hair back from her forehead. Stephanie blinked open her eyes to find Mo sitting on the edge of the bed, already dressed.

"Hey," Mo said, softly. "I've got to go pick up Colt."

Stephanie roused, sitting up, covering her nakedness with the sheet. She wasn't quite ready to relax around Mo. She'd just spent the morning rolling around in the bed with her, but that was somehow different.

"What time is it?" Stephanie asked.

"It's quarter to twelve."

"Wow, I was knocked out there for a while. Are you sure you want to take him alone? I can be dressed in five minutes."

Mo stood up. "I really need to talk to him by myself, first. I'll take him somewhere after the doctor's appointment and let him have his say."

Stephanie climbed out of bed with the sheet still wrapped around her. "Take food," she said. "He's much easier to deal with on a full stomach."

Mo followed Stephanie to the base of the stairs. "He'll want to go to the game tonight, even if he can't play. So, I'll bring him back here and we can go together, if that's all right."

Stephanie stopped on the first step. "Yes, we can go together. I do have one request."

Mo smiled, saying, "Anything."

"You have to deal with the curious gawkers and gossips."

Mo's brow knitted. "What do you mean?"

Before It Stains

"Well, I'm not sure how much I told you already, but here's the story, so far. I threw a chair through a window and broke a bunch of china when I found out you were leaving me for a man in LA. There was blood on the walls that had to be painted over. That part was sort of true, since the prime rib did stain."

Mo started laughing, but not too much. She knew not to find it too amusing.

Stephanie held up one hand. "Wait, it gets better. Marlene has a secret crush on you and is waiting with baited breath for your return. Geri Lee would like me to join her for coffee and sex, and if we do get back together, we can both come over. Jordan's father volunteered to service me since he heard I was looking for a man."

Mo didn't like the part about Jordan's dad, but the rest she found entertaining.

"I also threw all your stuff out on the curb," Stephanie continued. "And evidently my haircut and the new clothes, which by the way you are paying for out of the settlement, are a sign of impending divorce. The sharks smell blood in the water and they're circling."

Mo lowered her head, her smile disappearing. She dug at the carpet with the toe of her shoe. "I suppose not having your wedding rings on had something to do with it."

Stephanie remembered the rings for the first time since Molly asked her about them last night. She looked at the white mark the absent rings left on her finger.

"No, I didn't take those off until just before I left last night."

Mo didn't look up. "Is that because you were going to meet Molly?"

Stephanie pulled the sheet tighter around her body. She felt vulnerable in her current state of dress, but she answered truthfully. It was time for honesty in their marriage, if nothing else.

"Molly being at the gallery was pure coincidence, but you should know I fully intended to sleep with her, just to get you out of my mind for a few hours."

Mo looked up from the floor. She asked, "What stopped you?"

"She did," Stephanie replied. "You owe my standing here now to Molly Kincaid's character, not mine."

"I really thought I'd lost you," Mo said, softly.

"You almost did."

Seconds ticked by, as they stood there, not speaking, searching each other's faces. Stephanie stepped down in front of Mo. She placed her hand over Mo's heart.

She spoke softly, "We need to talk Mo. Things are going to change around here. We'll sit down tonight after the game. I can't promise that everything is going to be all right, but I am trying to forgive you. That's all I have right now and you need to go deal with your son."

"I'm not giving up, Steph. I'll do whatever it takes. I want my family back."

Stephanie patted Mo's chest. "Well, start with your son." She climbed the stairs, calling over her shoulder. "I hope you are prepared for this. If you haven't noticed, he's a little put out with you and me."

Mo called up after her, "Yeah, I noticed. Hey, we'll be here around five, okay?"

Stephanie stopped at the top of the stairs, looking down at Mo. "The first thing that's going to change is you will be here when you say you will. I'll see you at five."

She opened the door to her bedroom, hearing Mo shout up to her, "Yes, ma'am."

Before It Stains

\#

Stephanie reclined in the bathtub, surrounded by lilac scented bubbles, and a wet cloth over her eyes. She was the most relaxed she'd felt since last Sunday, when the shit hit the fan. Sex, it seemed, was better than a massage for relieving stress. The house was quiet. The only sound was Stephanie's deep breathing against the cloth that was sliding down over her nose. The energy it would take to push the cloth back up was too high a price to pay. Stephanie slid a little further down into the warm water. More tension released from her body.

The explosion of the ringtone in the still air rocketed Stephanie into a sitting position. She brought the cellphone into the bathroom with her, in case Mo or Colt needed information for the doctor. Stephanie could see the phone from its perch on the table by the tub, Randy's gleaming teeth shined back at her. She dried her hands, slid a finger across the screen to answer, and pressed the speaker button.

"No, you are not getting the details," she said into the air.

Randy's voice filled the room from the little speaker in the phone. "Which ones? There are so many to choose from."

"You want to know what went on with Molly and I'm not telling."

"Did she take you to her house?" Randy was not to be dissuaded.

Despite her reluctance, Stephanie couldn't help herself. "Oh my God, I had no idea she was that fucking rich."

"And you passed that up to go back to your life in suburbia?"

Before It Stains

"Money can't buy what I have in suburbia." Stephanie said, defensively.

Randy kept digging. "Oh, so how is life back at the farm?"

"She cooked breakfast for me," Stephanie said, sliding back down into the water.

From his next comment, it appeared Randy thought it was his responsibility to keep Stephanie focused. "Well, that should make up for fucking around on you."

"She's trying, Randy."

"Oh shit, you've already slept with her, haven't you?"

Stephanie's laugh echoed around the room. "You're the one that said I needed wild monkey sex."

"Not with your wife. That's the whole point. I can't believe you didn't sleep with Molly. The way you were sliding up and down her body on the dance floor, I figured you for another notch on Ms. Kincaid's bed post."

Stephanie defended Molly. "Despite what you might think of her, Molly isn't really like that."

"She has quite the reputation as a heartbreaker and if the parade of women I've seen her with is any indication, she likes them tall and blond."

"Let's just say she's been looking for something. I admire her for not settling."

Randy sighed. "So, the old flame got put out last night, is that it?"

"I think she'll move on now. She had her say." Stephanie hoped Molly would find the love she deserved.

Randy laughed loudly. "That little scene at the hospital was priceless. Mo was way out of her league tangling with Miss Molly."

Stephanie chuckled too, remembering the stunned look on Mo's face. "Oh, I think Mo got the message."

Before It Stains

They were quiet after their laughter died down. Randy cleared his throat, serious now.

"Are you okay? Where's Mo?"

"She took Colt to the doctor. She wanted to talk to him alone."

Randy persisted. "You didn't answer my question. Are you okay?"

"We're going to the game and then we're going to sit down to talk. We got the sex out of the way this morning, so I think we're both a little calmer now. We still have a lot to work out."

"No more flying china?" Randy teased.

"No, no more broken dishes," Stephanie answered, chuckling. "I'm not as mad as I was, so that's progress."

"Yeah, sex will take the fight right out of you. I'm sure Mo knew that when she seduced you."

"For your information, Mr. Ransom, I initiated first contact."

"Hum, a girl that knows what she wants. I'll bet that blew Mo's mind."

Stephanie giggled. "I think it did."

"I knew you wouldn't leave her," Randy said. "Did you finally remember it takes two people to make a marriage and two people to let one fall apart?"

Stephanie waited a moment before she answered, "I know I love her and I wouldn't be happy without her. We just need to clear the air and start over, I think."

"I think that's wise, Steph. You and Mo have something most people only dream of. It's not always going to be perfect, but it's special none the less."

"Yeah, I know," Stephanie conceded.

"Okay, kiddo, I'll see you at the game."

"You know Colt isn't playing, right?" Stephanie asked.

Before It Stains

"I'm kind of invested in the team now and I sure don't want to miss the reaction in the stands to Mo being there. There will be multiple cases of whiplash."

"I'm glad we entertain you, Randy. See you tonight."

"Later."

The phone sounded the call lost signal and Stephanie slid down under the water, losing herself again in the warmth. She listened to her heartbeat in the water. It was still there, thumping strongly. It wasn't broken after all, just severely bruised. They could come back from this. It would take a lot of effort from both of them, but Stephanie had to believe they could clean up this spilled milk, as her mother had put it, before it stained.

CHAPTER THIRTEEN

The ball field was a blur of activity by the time Stephanie arrived with Colt and Mo. The two of them showed up at the house at four forty-five, acting as if everything went well. Stephanie didn't get a chance to ask Mo about the conversation with Colt. They wanted to go out to their favorite hamburger joint before the game and hustled Stephanie out the door. Colt informed Stephanie that his ankle would be well by his birthday, so driving shouldn't be an issue. Evidently, the subject of his car had come up in the conversation with Mo. Mo rolled her eyes at Stephanie, signaling their son was not above emotional blackmail. Just one more thing she and Mo had to talk about.

Five Guys Burgers was packed and by the time the food was consumed, they had to rush to the ballgame. Mo helped Colt stand on his crutches and stayed with him, as they walked toward the chairs Stephanie's mother and PJ already set up. Randy was right, heads were popping around and fingers were being pointed, as Stephanie and her family came into view. Stephanie veered off toward the concession stand to buy drinks. She saw Marlene stand up and head down the stands toward her.

"Great," Stephanie said under her breath.

She almost ran right into Geri Lee, coming back from the concession stand with drinks and popcorn balanced in front of her.

"Oh gosh, I'm sorry," Stephanie said, righting the tilting popcorn box on the top of Geri Lee's stack of snacks with her left hand.

Geri Lee recovered from almost dropping her purchases just as Marlene appeared. Geri Lee's eyes were on Stephanie's ring finger. Stephanie could actually see the wheels turning and the lights come on.

Geri Lee gasped. "So it is true. You and Mo are splitting up."

"No," Stephanie got out, before Geri Lee interrupted her.

"But you're not wearing your rings."

Stephanie saw Mo step up behind Geri Lee. Mo heard the last comment and came to Stephanie's rescue.

"Honey," she said, digging in her pocket, producing Stephanie's rings. "You left these in the bathroom. I meant to give them to you, but I forgot." Stephanie smiled and held out her hand for Mo to slip the rings back on her finger. Although the moment was significant, Mo continued as if it were any other day, "Well, hi Geri Lee, Marlene, thank you for keeping Stephanie company this week."

Marlene was still recovering from the shock of seeing Mo. She spoke, but her words had an empty sound, as if she was trying to process information while replying to Mo. "It was no trouble. Sorry to hear about Colt's ankle."

Before It Stains

Mo was charming, assuming control, and effectively discouraging any further rumors. "He'll be fine," she said to Marlene and then turned to Stephanie. "Come on, let's get those drinks." Mo touched Stephanie lightly on the elbow, steering her toward the line at the concession stand. Over her shoulder, Mo said to the two women who were now simply staring in disbelief, "Thanks again for taking care of her, I think I can handle it from here."

Stephanie whispered to Mo, "Thank you."

Mo winked. "The rings were a nice touch, don't you think?"

Stephanie felt herself giving up and letting go. She laughed and said, "You're just glad I put them back on so Marlene won't be chasing you."

Mo was distracted by something over Stephanie's shoulder. "Wait here in line, I'll be right back."

Stephanie looked on as Mo made a beeline for Jordan's father. She saw him smile at Mo's approach and then that smile disappeared, as Mo stood on her tiptoes and whispered something in his ear. He shook his head and said something to Mo. She smiled and walked back to Stephanie.

"What did you say to him?" Stephanie asked, when Mo was beside her again.

Mo leaned over so no one else could hear. "I told him if he hit on my wife again, I'd tell *his* wife about the college call-girl ring he supports at least twice a month."

Stephanie laughed. "How do you know that?"

"Always make friends with the housekeeping staff. They know everything."

Stephanie raised an eyebrow at Mo. "Maybe I should make friends with the ones in your building, or pay them to keep an eye on you."

"Save your money, Steph. I'm done keeping secrets."

Before It Stains

They reached the front of the line and the conversation ended. Stephanie made a mental note to bring the secret keeping up later. Mo bought water for everyone and a box of popcorn for her mother-in-law. Stephanie walked with Mo to the chairs occupied by their extended family. PJ stood to take the water from Stephanie and give her a hug.

She whispered into Stephanie's ear, "It's good to see you together."

"It's not a done deal," Stephanie said softly, "but we're working on it."

PJ released Stephanie from her grasp and smiled into her face. "You'll get it done. I have faith." PJ looked over Stephanie's shoulder, speaking loudly enough for Mo to hear this time. "Don't go too easy on her. I'm making her trade offices with me. Now, I'll have the better view. You make her pay."

Mo didn't just betray Stephanie. The whole extended family had been rocked by her behavior. PJ was collecting on the friendship faux pas, because best friends don't lie to each other, ever. A best friend was as close as the voice in your head, knew your true thoughts, and loved you anyway. Mo broke the code. Her corner office with the tall windows was the price. She would now be marking time in PJ's old dungeon in the basement, until someone retired and left an opening. PJ got her pound of flesh.

Stephanie chuckled and sat down, saying, "She's already several thousand in the hole on designer clothes and rumor has it, it's going to cost her a car."

PJ laughed. "I saw the dress. Randy sent a picture. You looked fantastic, by the way."

Mo asked, "That dress cost that much?"

"Don't forget the shoes," Stephanie teased.

Mo mumbled, "Too bad you won't be wearing it again."

Before It Stains

Stephanie pretended not to hear. She knew Mo would never want to see that dress again. It would always remind her of the night she almost lost Stephanie to Molly. Maybe Stephanie should just leave it hanging in the closet, as a reminder that she could put it back on again, anytime. Mo should be on her toes from now on. She would never again be allowed to take Stephanie for granted. That dress wasn't a threat; it was a promise.

Mo clapped loudly and yelled at the field, "Way to go, Trev!"

Stephanie had missed the beginning of the game, occupied with making note of the things she wanted to remember to say to Mo. Trevor was standing on second base, smiling back at the dugout. The first inning was going well. Mo was lost in the game, sitting up on the edge of her seat. It was probably killing Colt not to play, but Stephanie could hear him cheering loudly from inside the dugout. Everyone and everything around Stephanie was the same, as if this past week did not happen.

Randy strolled into view, his eyes on the field. He walked up beside Mo and placed a hand on her shoulder.

"Have I missed anything?" He asked, without looking down.

Randy's relationship with Mo was different from the one he had with Stephanie. He was Mo's buddy. The hand grasped strongly on Mo's shoulder was the buddy signal for, "You screwed up, but I'm glad you're back."

Mo did not look up at Randy, or acknowledge his presence, other than to say, "Two outs. Trevor hit a double. He's on second."

No reaction was part of the buddy code, as well. It meant, "Thanks, man."

Before It Stains

Mo was healing relationships all around her. It wasn't just Stephanie to whom she was answering. Mo's acceptance of guilt and obvious remorse were winning over those she had offended. Stephanie found herself admiring Mo for facing friends and family head on. The weakness Mo had shown was passing. She was regaining her confidence, as she mended her relationships.

"How's the ankle?" This question Randy directed at Stephanie.

"He'll be fine, just a bad sprain."

A second after the crack of the bat, a line drive slapped into the third baseman's glove. The top of the inning was over.

Randy patted Mo's back a few times and said, "Hey, let's take a walk."

This was to be the buddy talk. Down the fence line the buddies went, stopping once they were alone. Stephanie watched them. Mo stood with her fingers looped through the galvanized fence, looking up at Randy as he spoke. Stephanie's mother drew her attention away, leaning over PJ and poking Stephanie in the leg.

Debra said, "I know you slept with her, but did you talk to her?"

PJ burst out laughing. "You did not just say that. Woman, you are a trip. Stephanie, have I told you how much I love your mother?"

Stephanie was aghast. "How do you know I slept with her? Have you been talking to Randy? I'm going to kill him."

Debra's expression shifted to a knowing grin. "Honey, no one had to tell me. You don't go from as wound up as you two were to sedate and calm without sex being involved."

Before It Stains

PJ added, "Girl, y'all ain't foolin' nobody."

Stephanie felt the blush of heat from her embarrassment. She was close to her mother, but sex wasn't a topic they discussed often. Smiling at her the way they were, Stephanie was sure her mother and PJ knew it had been monumental stress sex, and they each had their own experiences in that regard.

Stephanie caved. "Okay, yes, I slept with her, but that doesn't mean anything was resolved. We're going to talk tonight."

"Do I need to keep Colt again?"

"It's okay, Mom. I'm not going to be throwing any more beef ribs at the walls. I think we're past the yelling part."

Relief washed over her mother's face. "Good," she said. "Now, you can get down to the heart of it. You're both smart and you love each other fiercely. You'll work this out and be stronger for it."

Stephanie sighed. "I hope so."

Randy and Mo returned, smiling, arms around each other, one more bridge repaired. Mo had only the last big one to cross, the one back to Stephanie.

#

The rest of the game, Stephanie actually paid attention. Colt's team came away with the tournament championship in a one to nothing victory. He wanted to celebrate with the team. She and Mo agreed to take him to Wyatt's house, but they stayed on, knowing the pain meds and the swelling inside his cast were going to take a toll on him soon. Stephanie and Mo were able to avoid the gossip by staying close together, but Stephanie observed Marlene and Geri Lee huddled together in the corner, obviously still not buying their act. Luckily, before they got the nerve to approach Stephanie, Colt was ready to go home and ice his ankle.

Mo got him situated on the couch in the den with ice bags and the remote, while Stephanie made him soup and a sandwich. Just once she'd like to feed him until he was full, but had yet to accomplish that. He needed to eat to take the pain pills anyway.

Mo came into the kitchen. "He's all set. Just hungry, as usual."

Stephanie was putting the mayonnaise on Colt's turkey sandwich. "Are you going to tell me what you said to him this afternoon?"

"Not with a knife in your hand," Mo said, almost seriously.

Finished with the knife, Stephanie put it down, closed the sandwich, and then turned around. She leaned on the counter, facing Mo, and said, "Okay, no weapons."

Mo leaned against the refrigerator door opposite her. "I told him I made some very bad choices, not just that night, but leading up to it. I also said I was taking responsibility for my actions and I'm very sorry for disappointing both of you."

Stephanie asked, eyebrows raised, "Did he buy it?"

"After he had his say."

Stephanie wanted to ask what Colt said, but a loud cry of "Mom!" from the den turned both of their heads. They bumped into each other running out of the kitchen, arriving panicked in the den to find Colt sitting up holding the newspaper.

"What?" Stephanie asked, breathless. "What was that blood curdling scream for?"

Colt held out the paper. "Look!"

Before It Stains

Stephanie took the Lifestyles section from her son's hand, knowing exactly what he had found. On the page opposite the movie listings, scattered among shots from Lauren's opening, was Stephanie seducing Molly in black and white. The caption read, "Well-known lesbian attorney, Molly Kincaid, and Durham businesswoman, Stephanie Austin, get cozy at gallery opening." Stephanie giggled. Molly had called that one.

Mo took the paper. Stephanie turned back to Colt, whose accusing stare made her giggle even more. It was nervous laughter, because they were both waiting for Mo's reaction. Mo folded the paper and handed it back to Colt.

"That's an old friend of your mother's and, as it turns out, a friend of mine, as well. Doesn't your mother look pretty?"

Colt was as surprised by Mo's demeanor as Stephanie. "Yeah, I guess," he answered, confused. "You're not mad?"

Mo walked over to him. "Why should I be mad? Your mom had a good time and she deserved that." She tussled his hair. "Don't believe everything you read in the papers."

Colt looked to his mother for confirmation. Stephanie wasn't going to start their new lives with half-truths.

Stephanie said, "That's Randy's boss. We were more than friends. I was dating her when I met Mo the first time."

Colt's face broke into a grin. "But you picked Mo over her, didn't you?" It was more of a statement, than a question.

Stephanie had to smile. "Yes, I did. Let me go warm up your soup." She turned to leave. "By the way, could you reserve the blood curdling screams for emergencies?"

"I thought it was an emergency," Colt said, and then continued, causing Stephanie to stop and listen. "I want to say something. You guys are always telling me that I have to be responsible for my actions and face the consequences of my decisions."

He was quoting Stephanie verbatim, which gave her hope that he did listen to them sometimes.

Colt went on, "But you also say that mistakes are okay, if you learn from them."

Stephanie nodded. "Yes, that's true." She could only guess where he was headed with this.

"So, when I screw up, you say I'm being punished so that I will learn not to do it again." He turned to face Mo. "I'm going to tell her what I told you."

Mo said, "Okay. Go ahead."

Colt was trying so hard to be mature, it was cute, but Stephanie didn't smile at him. She focused her eyes on his and gave him her attention.

"I told Mo that I forgave her for her mistake, but if she did it again then we were done with her. I think she learned her lesson, Mom. I don't want her to leave."

Stephanie let her lips curl into a smile. "It's okay, Colton." She only used his full name when it was serious. "Mo's not going anywhere. We just need to regroup, but everything is going to be fine. Don't worry." The two of them, beaming at her, caused Stephanie to laugh. She teased them, "But she's going to be on restriction for a while. Is that okay?"

Colt and Mo answered in unison, "Yes."

Stephanie shook her head. It was no use. They were a united front against her and she could not resist them. They were her family and she loved them both more than her pride. She winked at Mo.

"You promised him a car, didn't you?"

#

Before It Stains

Mo moved Colt's video game console down to the den. He was surrounded by pillows, snacks, and anything else he could possibly need. He hardly noticed when Stephanie told him they were going out on the back deck. She and Mo sat across from each other at the table, a bottle of water in front of each of them, like adversaries at a negotiation. Stephanie sat firmly against the back of her chair, arms crossed. She knew from the business world that body language was important. She had the advantage here and was projecting her position of power.

Stephanie began the conversation, "I want to make it very clear that if I thought for one minute you ever cared about Michaela, or that this was anything more than a drunken dalliance; we would not be having this conversation. You would be out of my life forever and I mean that."

"I know," Mo said.

Stephanie continued, "I'm not interested in any more apologies or groveling. You're sorry. I get that. What I do want to discuss are some observations I've made over the last week."

Mo sipped her water, but her throat was still dry, when she said, "Okay."

"I discovered the shoe boxes when I was cleaning the bathroom closet. While I found the idea endearing, it also brought to my attention that there is a whole side of you of which I have no knowledge."

Mo tilted her head, knitting her brow the way Colt did, the expression of a confused puppy.

Stephanie continued. "That CYA folder, I didn't know about half of the women in there."

Before It Stains

Mo knew the answer to this one. She perked up, bright eyed. "I didn't want to bother you with it. There was nothing for you to worry about."

"Why don't you let me decide what I'm going to worry about from now on? If you had talked to me about them, you would have found it easier to talk to me about Michaela."

Mo's shoulders fell. She had not given the right answer. She attempted a comeback, "But-"

Stephanie unfolded her arms and leaned forward on the table, cutting Mo off. "Women are attracted to you, I have always known that. Whether it's adoration from a student or pure lust, it must be exciting, at times, to know you're the object of someone's desire, other than mine. It's human nature to feel that way. I understand that, Mo, but if you told me about the little things, the big ones would be easier to deal with. I could have helped you with Michaela, before it got out of control. We're stronger together."

Mo asked, "So, if I tell you some woman is hitting on me, you're not going to be mad?"

This lead to another point Stephanie wanted to make. "You have to stop believing you know what I'm going to say, before you give me a chance to decide for myself. You think you're protecting me, but you're not."

"Okay, I'll tell you," Mo said, acquiescing.

"It's not just that," Stephanie said. "Randy told me you didn't want a child, that you gave up your dream to make mine come true. That wasn't fair, Mo."

The puppy dog returned. Mo was thoroughly confused now.

Stephanie filled in the details. "We based our whole lives on a decision you made alone, without consulting me.

What if I was scared? What if I only went through with it that soon, because you seemed so excited?"

"Did you?" Mo said, surprised.

"See, Mo, we both spend way too much time guessing what the other person is thinking, instead of actually asking. I'm as guilty as you are."

"I'm not sorry we had him when we did," Mo said, "but I see your point."

"I'm not sorry, either. He's the best of both of us."

Again, they became quiet, as they took in the moment of shared pride in their creation. Colt was all they had hoped for and more. Stephanie knew they were truly blessed.

"He sure is paying a lot closer attention than I thought," Mo said, finally. "He really nailed me on a couple of things."

Stephanie grinned. She'd had a taste of Colt's surliness. She was sure he let Mo have it.

"What did he say?" she asked.

"He reminded me that I always said people who use alcohol as an excuse for bad behavior are losers."

"Ooo, that must have hurt," Stephanie said, making a sympathetic face.

Mo chuckled. "Not as much as being told I was as bad as John Edwards."

"Oh my, he is paying attention." Stephanie laughed loudly, and then asked, "What did Randy say to you, at the ballpark?"

"He told me not to give up, that you would come back to me."

"Is that all?" Stephanie asked, knowing it wasn't.

Mo smiled sheepishly. "No. He told me if I screwed up again, he would personally dump you on Molly's doorstep."

Before It Stains

Stephanie laughed, which visibly relaxed Mo. The laughter settled into quiet and Mo took the lead in the conversation.

"What else? I know there's more than that."

"Yes, I have a few more items I'd like to discuss."

Mo winked. "I bet you do."

Stephanie relaxed back against the chair. "Be home when you're home. Organize your schedule better and stick to it. We need you too, Mo."

Mo answered quickly. "I wanted to talk to you about that. What if I just taught during the school year? I can turn much of what I do outside the classroom over to the grad students. They can supervise the undergraduate projects. That would eliminate hours viewing video at home. I'd only have to check on them a couple of times a semester and I won't take on any side projects."

"That would help," Stephanie said. "I know you have to do some of your grading and things here, and an occasional outside project isn't out of the question, but if you'll balance that with spending time with us, it would make me happy. You'll be gone this semester anyway."

Mo sat up taller in her chair. "That's another thing. I'm not going to be gone this semester or any semester, except possibly summer school. I made my own deal with the production company. We all agreed this particular project was not a good fit for me. They have some things coming up that will film in Wilmington or near there, next summer. It's only two and half hours away."

Stephanie leapt up, took the two steps around the table, and hugged her wife. "Thank you," was all she could manage at the moment.

Mo returned the hug and then slid the chair beside her out from the table. Stephanie sat down.

Before It Stains

Mo leaned over and took both of Stephanie's hands in hers. "I thought a lot about what you said, how we were in trouble long before I screwed up. Since you want me to be honest, I have a few requests."

Stephanie wanted to hear what Mo thought had caused this. "Please, tell me what I did wrong."

"You didn't do anything wrong. I'd just like to change some things, too."

"Okay," Stephanie replied. "Like what?"

Mo had a list and she started ticking things off. "Can we shut our bedroom door when we go to bed? I don't like getting up to shut it if we start fooling around, and then we have to open it again when we're done. He's not stupid, Steph, and I don't know, it just makes me feel weird."

That was easy enough to fix. Stephanie answered, "I don't have a problem with that. He's old enough to handle most everything himself," she laughed, "but you know that won't fix his bad timing."

Mo chuckled. "Yeah, but it will keep him guessing."

Stephanie winked. "Good plan. And, what else?"

"You take time off from work so we can go away for more than a weekend, and when we go, you have to really be on vacation. None of this, I can't go with you for a walk, because I have to deal with this little thing at the office."

Stephanie sat up straighter, a little defensive. "That one can apply to both of us."

Mo nodded. "I know. I'll do my part. Don't worry. I am also asking for a date night. Colt's old enough now that we can go out and not just to the early movie and home."

It was Stephanie's turn to admit she was fallible. "I know I have always put Colt's needs before ours. I understand now that we're not just parents, we're adults in a relationship that needs as much attention as he gets."

Before It Stains

"Steph, Colt will always come first, but we have to live a little, too."

"I stopped believing we could have a life outside of the one we have with Colt. All I kept thinking was soon I would have you all to myself again," Stephanie explained. "I thought it was just part of being parents that we sacrificed some of our relationship until he was grown."

Mo agreed. "I thought that too, but we can make time for us. I will make time for us. Will you?"

Stephanie nodded. "Yes, I will." Mo smiled at her and Stephanie added, "Okay then, I want to have dinner parties and go to art museums again, like we used to. Can we do that?"

"Yeah, we can do that," Mo answered.

On a roll, Stephanie continued, "And I want to go dancing. I know you don't like to, but we can take Randy with us sometimes, just so I can shag once in a while."

Mo's face lit up. "Is that it? Is that all you want?"

Stephanie thought a moment. She remembered a few more things. "Be on time, but I already told you that. Oh, and no more than two drinks, unless PJ or I are present."

Mo stood up, releasing Stephanie's hands. This sudden move startled Stephanie.

"Where are you going?"

Mo grinned. "Well, so far you haven't asked for anything I'm not willing to do. Well, except for one thing."

Now, Stephanie wore the confused puppy expression. Her head tilted to one side. "And what would that be?"

Mo headed for the back door. "You wait right here. I'll be back in a minute. Then I'll answer that question."

Mo disappeared into the house. Stephanie drank her water and listened to the bugs sing in the August night air. The conversation she dreaded all week had been relatively painless. Had they had this conversation several years ago, they would not have needed to have it tonight. She and Mo made many assumptions about each other along the way, thinking they knew each other's thoughts. That had been their mistake. That was where it went wrong. They were two very different people, and no matter how blended they felt, they were individuals with wants and needs of their own. Stephanie invested her own emotions in Mo's words and actions, perceiving things through a filter for years. She saw Mo clearly now, and she liked what she saw. Lesson learned.

#

Mo came back out of the house, grabbed Stephanie's hand, and said, "Come on."

"Where are we going?" Stephanie asked, while being pulled through the door and into the kitchen.

"You'll see," Mo said over her shoulder, leading Stephanie into the garage.

Stephanie saw Colt sitting at the end of the workbench near the opened rolling garage door, smiling broadly, his crutches leaning nearby. His iPod dock station was in front of him, with Mo's iPod plugged into it. Stephanie knew it was Mo's because of the color. Wires ran from the docking station to speakers, sitting just outside the door and pointed down the driveway. Stephanie had no idea what these two were up to, but if she knew them at all, she knew it involved loud music.

Mo pulled Stephanie out into the driveway. She put her right arm around Stephanie's waist, presenting her other hand for Stephanie to take. It dawned on Stephanie that Mo was about to attempt to dance with her. This was right up there with cooking, no telling how it would turn out.

Before It Stains

Stephanie hoped her toes didn't suffer too much. She smiled over at Mo, who was grinning ear to ear.

"I planned to do this for your anniversary present this year, but you said no more secrets and I really don't want to take Randy on our dates. I've been taking lessons from him, but I'd rather dance with you."

Stephanie was floored. "You've been doing what?"

Mo winked. "Just follow my lead."

She nodded at Colt and the first notes of the Temptations hit, "The Way You Do the Things You Do," began to play. Mo's hand slid from Stephanie's waist. She stepped back, finding the four-four-swing rhythm, bending her knees slightly on the second and fourth beat. Dr. Mo Hunt began to do the Carolina Shag with her wife, right there in the driveway. Stephanie laid her head back and cackled. Then she started following Mo's lead around the driveway, nearly floating on air. Mo had paid attention to Randy's tutelage and, despite what Stephanie thought all these years, was a very good dancer. Evidently, what Mo lacked was the confidence to dance with Stephanie. Randy taught Mo the nuances of dancing with a woman and Stephanie was in heaven.

The music was loud and halfway through the song Stephanie noticed the neighbors across the street were out on their lawns watching. Soon more neighbors appeared, some coming up the driveway. Mo did not stop twirling Stephanie around. Colt was smiling from his perch. The older couple from two doors down walked to the edge of the grass. The old man was grinning and keeping the beat with a hand on his thigh. And just like that, Stephanie's private dance turned into an impromptu cul-de-sac shag party in their driveway. Couples danced in house coats and cotton pajamas, shorts and tee shirts, with and without shoes, but they all danced, because if you grew up with the Carolina Shag it was impossible to stand on the sidelines without joining in.

The song ended and the neighbors all clapped for them, as Mo took Stephanie into a deep dip. The cheering ended when the horns at the beginning of Curtis Mayfield's "It's All Right" blared out of the speakers. The well-known beach music anthem inspired the neighbors for another dance.

Stephanie pulled Mo to her and whispered in her ear. "Did I tell you I loved you today?"

"Yeah, but I didn't think you meant it." Mo answered back.

"Oh, I meant it and I have one more thing to say, if we can get rid of these people."

#

After the third song, Mo ended the night politely and thanked the neighbors for not being upset about the music. Stephanie helped Colt back inside, while Mo put away the speakers and closed up the garage. With Colt once again securely back in the den, Stephanie told Mo to wait downstairs, and she would be back in a few minutes. Mo raised one eyebrow, but remained in the den with their son.

Stephanie ran up the stairs. She hustled around the bedroom, throwing the shoes from last night in the closet, and picked up the dress from the chair in the corner. She'd tossed it there this afternoon, after picking it up from the floor where it lay all morning. She put the dress on a hanger, but didn't put it away. Instead, Stephanie left it displayed on the outside of the closet door. She made up the bed and went into the bathroom to freshen up. She discovered, after arriving home from her shopping trip with

Before It Stains

Randy, a little something extra he'd thrown in her bag. She thought it was another hint that she needed to go out and have some fun, but she wasn't sure this is what Randy had in mind. Or was it?

By the time Stephanie came back downstairs, wearing Mo's bathrobe because she'd thrown hers away, Colt was already snoring on the couch.

She walked over to him and ran her fingers through his curls. "He had a big day," she said, softly.

Mo, who was sitting on the edge of the easy chair, said, "Yeah, me too."

Stephanie moved over to Mo. "Are you ready to go to bed?"

Mo swallowed hard. Stephanie saw her eyes move over the bathrobe, before she said, nervously, "If you are."

"Turn off the lights then and come upstairs."

This was more than Mo could have hoped for. She was out of the chair in a flash, switching off lights, and making sure the doors were locked. Stephanie went back up to the bedroom to wait. Mo was only seconds behind her.

When Mo arrived, she stopped at the door, hesitating, waiting for an invitation. Stephanie stood by the bed. She pointed at the dress.

"I'm keeping that dress. If you so much as step a toe out of line, it's coming out of the closet, and you can watch it walk away with me in it."

Mo simply nodded in agreement.

That said, and bridges mended, Stephanie invited Mo to come on over that last one. She dropped the bathrobe, revealing a black bustier with matching lace panties. Mo's expression of surprise quickly turned to lust.

Stephanie gave Mo her best seductive smile and said, "Shut the door... and lock it."

Before It Stains

\#

A few hours later, Stephanie unwound herself from the sleeping Mo. She climbed out of the bed and stood over her, watching Mo's deep breathing. Stephanie could tell Mo was exhausted. She was probably sleeping deeply for the first time in a week. Stephanie leaned down, smoothing the hair from Mo's face, and kissed her on the forehead. It was done. The healing had begun. It would be better now that they knew how quickly it could all vanish. Stephanie's life with Mo was somehow more precious to her than before.

Stephanie put on Mo's robe and left the bedroom quietly. She needed to check on Colt. Stephanie found him, game controller in hand, and the TV screen gone to screensaver mode. He must have awakened at some point. She took the controller from his hands and turned off the TV. She took the now warm ice packs from around his cast and covered him with the blanket. Cleaning up his empty water bottles and dishes, Stephanie carried them and the ice packs to the kitchen. The browned eggs, burnt bacon, and toast from this morning were beginning to smell in the garbage. Stephanie opened the back door to put the bin on the deck. She saw the grill and was hit with inspiration.

Stephanie slipped into the office and pulled the lipstick stained napkin from the safe. She carried it to the deck by one corner, as if it was a soiled diaper. Stephanie opened the lid on the grill, turned on the gas, pushed the start button, and flames burst from the burner. Stephanie looked at the napkin, one more time. This little four by four square had nearly brought down her marriage. She tossed it onto the grate and watched the ends curl up, before the fire erased the stain of that lipstick from their lives forever. When it was no more than an ash, Stephanie closed the lid.

Before It Stains

Forgiveness wasn't the easy way out of the mess Stephanie found herself in last Sunday afternoon. It would have been simpler to heap the blame on Mo, feed the hurt and anger, until it was too late to salvage their marriage. With the help of her wise mother, to whom she would always be grateful, Stephanie saw the value of setting aside pride in order to save her family. She looked up at the stars and spoke to the universe.

"I guess Mo got her happy ending, after all. I just wanted to say, I am supremely thankful for the gift of forgiveness. I'm going to let this pain go now, but may I always remember I took so much for granted. I'll be paying closer attention from here on out, trust me. Thank you for reminding me how blessed we are." Stephanie started to turn away, but looked up one more time. "If you need to tell me anything else, I'd prefer a gentle nudge and not a major crisis."

The back door opened and Mo stepped on the deck, rubbing the sleep from her eyes, wearing only a tee shirt and underwear. "What are you doing out here? Have you been burning something?"

Stephanie went to Mo and wrapped her arms around her. "I was just getting rid of a bad memory."

Mo squinted at her, still half asleep. "Are we okay?"

Stephanie kissed Mo gently on the lips. "Yes, we're good."

"Can we go back to bed then?" Mo asked, yawning.

Stephanie smiled, "Wore you out, huh?"

Mo woke up a bit more at the mention of their recent activities. She grinned and said, "I'm never too tired for you."

"Good," Stephanie said, and took Mo's hand, leading her back into the house. She looked back over her shoulder

Before It Stains

and winked. "Did I mention that I didn't throw out the Dirty Santa box?"

About the author…

R. E. "Decky" Bradshaw, a native of North Carolina and a proud Tar Heel, now makes her home in Oklahoma with her wife of 24 years. Holding a Master of Performing Arts degree, Bradshaw worked in professional theatre and taught University and High School classes, until leaving both professions to write full-time in 2010. She continues to be one of the best selling lesbian fiction authors on Amazon.com.

Made in the USA
Lexington, KY
22 December 2011